The Inner Garden

The Inner Garden

Stories by Sam Eisenstein

Sun & Moon Press
Los Angeles

Cover: Katie Messborn; sculpture from the collection of Sam and Betty Eisenstein

Some of these stories were published previously in *Ante, Edge, Invisible City, New England Review, Penthouse, The Reconstructionist, Sun & Moon: A Journal of Literature & Art, Trace,* and *TransPacific.*

The author wishes to express his appreciation to The Writers Group, Albert Olenius, Douglas Messerli, Frank Wattron, Marguerite Johnson, John Espey, Isabelle Ziegler, James Boyer May, William Alex, and Sonya Marjasch for their encouragement and support.

LIBRARY OF CONGRESS CATALOGING IN PUBLICATION DATA

Sam Eisenstein

The Inner Garden

ISBN: 0-940650-71-1
ISBN: 0-940650-75-4 (paper)

---

10 9 8 7 6 5 4 3 2 1

Sun & Moon Press
6363 Wilshire Boulevard, Suite 115
Los Angeles, California 90048
(213) 653-6711

For Bettyrae, who makes it possible

Table of Contents

A Place Of Refuge

G abriel Schwarz walked the night streets of an American city and thought: "Do I adopt this city or does it adopt me? Who is the orphan? Which of us has the most respectable antecedents?"

In the old city his mother sold fruit in a street casually antique. Sounds and smells lived at peace with each other. Sounds were the same as they had always been, and the smells were always just below the surface. The skin of France is like her grapes, juice just short of bursting, so little separating blood from outside world. Her blood spills quickly, gushes out like an eager child, is quenched by the flat of horny hands. Streets accept themselves. They owe nothing, they owe no one. Even the parks—when there is one—seemed to have grown from the body of the city, like a wart or like a breast.

Madame Schwarz had hands like the map of the Danube. Her veins branched and there were pulses in every one of them.

Gabriel walked and tried to explain to the street: "When I opened her hands to lay them flat over the covers, she was as stubborn and fierce as she was when she was alive. It was as though she hated showing what was inside her fist, or letting go what was there. Her hands were always crooked and hooked around something, a fruit, some money, my arm. She bruised whatever she held, but whatever she held was already bruised; she held on; she let nothing drop."

Gabriel remembered, the eyes would not close—she stared at the wall relentlessly. She would not let even the wall go. He saw the wall that she clutched, even dead. Every brick, crack, and stain in it seemed pulled toward the scrawny dead woman, only keeping itself back by means of a natural and equal magnetism that pulled it from the opposite direction. This dead woman, with her crooked finger nose, wanted to suck all that was with her there, into her death. Gabriel held on with toes that clawed the floor to splinters. Leaving his thin trail of blood, he groped around her and avoided only by fractions a disappearance into the track of her bloodied eyes.

The fat women who came in to wash her had no difficulty closing her eyes and unhooking her hands. They plodded and flapped from corner to corner of the grimy room, talking and clucking with the ill-concealed satisfaction all women feel at the death of someone who is of no kin. These women grew from the streets of Saint Paul; with their shoulders hunched against the piercing winds of winter they looked exactly like the tired buildings they passed. They and the blunt-nosed taxis flowed, and when they were balked, shrilled with the same noises. Their extremities had an affinity for the cobblestones. They were at home in their district.

But here, in the adopted city, Gabriel looked at the Swiss chalet in stucco, with its double garage, next to a home that was disguised as a Buddhist temple, with rocks and gravel, but also bird of paradise flowers on little mounds. Every house advertised its special virtue and convenience. Each house eagerly would, if the custom allowed, list its every possession, every uniqueness, on the door, like Luther's theses: "I do declare this splendid house to contain, as a miniscule of its complete wonders, two baths and a half (the half perhaps for the half-man?), a den (not for wolves, but for family and guests to crowd so as not to dirty the living room, which is found in another list, never for a man's retreat, to find his wall and corner and his right to snarl and snap at the family all together trying to enter his room), a kitchen with everything built in (in panic that they should squat right

10

down on the floor, all the cabinets and appliances tried with all their might, like small, square elephants trying to climb trees, to get up off the floor, to have no visible roots), and much more," all attesting the taste, the financial ability, the satisfaction with which the occupants of the chalet or the temple regarded themselves.

"Which one of these houses would be willing to adopt me?" asked Gabriel of the sidewalk.

All of the lawns were manicured. A pile of dung on one of them squirmed in solitary embarrassment. Waves of Orientals deployed there regularly, trimmed the lawns, shaped the bushes, and made symmetrical all that had negligently asserted its nature. Some bushes were emasculated and crucified on trellises, other flower beds were tombs for flowers that never wilted, never asked for attention, being polyethelene.

"This is my own, my adopted land," thought Gabriel.

On the street, approaching from the opposite direction, was another man; but, awkward at being caught out of his carapace, his car or house, he hurried by, suspicious and embarrassed, afraid of what Gabriel might do, but primarily of what he might think: perhaps it wasn't clear that the half-timbered English Tudor three doors down was his. But the man carried no proof of identification. So he cantered around Gabriel, in heavy armor, and the disturbed air closed again after him. Dogs reveal their identities with dignity, each under the other's tail, but to admit to a tail among humans was extreme poor taste. But how was Gabriel to prove himself worthy, with no tail, with no papers? If only it was allowed to have an identification tag under the anus; he would submit quietly to inspection from the police, even while the one officer held him by one leg while the other made notations in a green, official book. A record of Gabriel's movements would thus be put on every police blotter, giving him a kind of identity and sense of belonging, even if he were charted only as a dreaded weather front, an enemy missile, to be intercepted if possible, checked by available electronic means.

So dangerous to be on the streets. Sidewalks—like the few trees without the strangling concrete embrace of their place on the curb— were sometimes barely allowed anachronisms and sometimes disappeared altogether for long stretches. Who walks anyway but the homeless or the sub- or pervert? Either Gabriel would have to learn to enumerate his intentions and the possessions on his person, or be ejected by the city. He would never do as he was, as he did. His upper body, rendered sunken by an indiscreet explosion, suffered from its un-American past. His hair ripped out, burned away, would make him suspect without a homburg or a wig. So insistent was the clamor from every house on its individual pad, but adjoining that next to it like twin foetuses from the same placenta, his adopted city put up such a spotlight, turned on every deviation with such a polite rancor, was in such sour fear that its uniqueness be questioned, that Gabriel even suspected himself.

Gabriel imagined his mother with her square push-cart, the job of pushing which he had inherited when he was big enough to reach the handles. He saw her crying her fruits and vegetables down these same streets he now walked. Women would swish closed their wall-to-wall drapes and tap the windows for Madame Schwarz to leave their driveways.

In the summer, dark runnels of sweat streamed from his mother's armpits. The smell was acrid, like the scent of apples and peaches, and reached from wall to wall of their room. All people, young and old, smelled more or less like that, all with their similar differences. Some women were like apples, some like pears, some were sweet like cantaloupe or watermelon.

A girl who sat in front of Gabriel in school had long hair that smelled like fallen dead leaves, musty, musky in piles on the ground.

Gabriel leaned forward as close as he could to that hair and imagined lying in a bed of such crackling scent. He imagined twisting the hair in strands around his ears and eyes and nose.

So it was the connection that counted. Things that were too separated, too clean, lost their trails, lost themselves, were like the wax figures in Madame Tussaud's museum; but even there, with the tenacity of living things, even as wax, the figures struggled to free themselves from their masks and waft abroad their own identities. Gabriel would shut his eyes and know, for instance, where Hannibal was: there was the dry sharp odor of elephant about him; who was Napoleon: the snows of Russia burnt in Gabriel's nose; who was Marie Antoinette: when her heavy voluminous skirts sailed around, her legs exuded a white odor of milk, cow, and dung.

Gabriel used to stare at the mouths of those who talked to him and wonder, "What are they?" He decided when they came close to him; their breaths would tell. He divided all Paris into those whose breaths told him that they were alive, and those who secretly were dead, corpses, decomposing on their feet, whose fetid breaths gave the lie to their vivacity, their cruelty, or their kindly smiles. He shivered and ran away from those few people who had no breaths at all. Teachers were acid, rabbis were sweetish-sour, and Madame Schwarz, whose breath covered Gabriel with a fine spray, was always brackish, like the sodden reeds at the edge of the Seine, or in swamps.

In his adopted city Gabriel could not accustom himself to the disparity between a thing and its odor. A woman could smell like attar of roses when emerging from the toilet, where she had been sprayed automatically upon rising from the stool, or she could carry with her a synthesized cedar or eucalyptus. Armpits smelled of lilacs, hair of coral-reef, hands of cinnabar. Something that looked like wood, upon being touched, would confess its birth in a plastics factory and its aroma from a laboratory.

All weak and struggling things that insisted on their own odors were squashed. The pungent, greasy snap of grilled meat was smothered by a painted-on barbecue essence. A syringe-made color and odor assured him that the orange he ate was truly orange.

And a towering, thick desire descended upon Gabriel like ocean water and he longed to bury his head and nose in Myra's belly, kiss the thin wavering line of hair down the hemisphere of her belly to the wild luxury of the garden of her triangular mount. That was the world-place, the great trinity, the smooth foothills of the celestial Himalayas. Full, blushing flesh kissed thighs under the shimmer of Myra's walk. But that, that was a crucifixion, when the flesh, now no longer any different from any other, even from his mother's, lay together with all flesh, in the ground, thrown just anywhere, joined bone to bone, no longer Myra's. Now, from the present, could he say there had ever been any difference? Did it happen?

And did Gabriel ever slip into the room without making a sound, looking at a school book while he entered? Had he raised his eyes and seen Madame Schwarz, his mother, struggling into her girdle, her legs creased forward at the knees, belly thrust out, breasts slithering like caught snakes? She had fought with the girdle as with another serpent, covering herself only in pain and torture, afflicting herself with scourges. She gasped, seeing Gabriel cowering there, a witness, holding out the school book to be immolated, protecting his eyes. He tried to turn his head and step back from the room, but in a flash Madame Schwarz was across to him. Gabriel, paralyzed, watched her come, seeing her move like a series of jerky pictures in an old movie. Her fingers sank into his neck and he was spun, a block, into the wall. She shrieked, "Dirty scum! For this I am your mother, to have filth spy on me! What are you, pig, to look on your own mother."

Gabriel closed his eyes, he crawled out of her presence, into that other womb, the street.

And the casualness of them, the Paris prostitutes, crawlers in the great belly of Paris, laughing and scratching themselves, lifting one leg on a bench so that the men could see beneath their skirts, see the black tuft of glittering hair. Gabriel saw and averted his head, hackles rising on his neck, his breath coming and going as though it never intended returning.

Then, Myra, in the midst of the bombing, when Gabriel wept with fear and isolation and shame—his fault the walls danced and shivered and leaped from their places, that flying metal playfully snipped legs and heads and torsos so instantly that the parts continued to jig and twitch for minutes—Myra took his wet head onto her breast and pulled him in to her. When he struggled with wild red eyes fixed ahead of him, and pummeled her with fists, she pushed him deeper down into herself, a soft thing that encircled him, and her hands found his neck, entered his skin and closed tenderly around the grape of his skull, arresting all noise, all fear, and led him out of himself, concentrated his anguish in a towering column and directed the column to herself, pulled it into herself. He became a roaring torrent that poured into the great deepness of her, that muted all echoes and drew all pain after it.

When the raid was over, Gabriel looked at her for the first time. He was astonished. The world had not ended. They lay in a cellar. One wall still smoked; a brick crashed quietly into a rubble of plaster. The wan afternoon filtered through the dust. She was not as large and downy as a million geese, or miles of leaves piled crisp on top of each other. She was small, although rounded and dimpled. She was older than he, Gabriel had been sure, because of the way the light cut a shadow across her face. He would never know, because now the light cut through both face and bone, now, long away from that one afternoon.

His head lay on her lap. He raised himself to tremble on one elbow. His face grew closer to hers and then her eyes disappeared and he ducked toward her lips and touched them with his lips. She leaned to him. They kissed softly and chastely as across great distances. She looked down and smoothed out her skirt; he had no conception of who she was or how they had gotten to the cellar.

Gabriel walked pavements that had never splintered, new-laid in miles of precise tracks and measured in the tons of concrete. Houses reared like dry pods on brittle stems that cracked open to patter dryly on polished linoleum.

Gabriel followed Myra out of the cellar. She hushed his questions of "Where do you live, who are you, where can I find you."

She was sure, Gabriel thought. She was sure of what had been. She was a virgin, sure of herself, because that time was elemental, as though she were planet, he meteor, she the earth, he all edged and brittle, burning up in the air, until they met, like principles, to resolve all the horrid separation of all things. They had met, but not like people with names and addresses and plans. When would they touch again, as people?

"I'll meet you in the park tomorrow," Myra had said, when they had walked silently in the smoking sullen street for awhile. Gabriel protested, thinking she must mean Saint Paul, but she did not know Saint Paul, where he lived, where every inch was under the eyes of the mother. She meant the Tuileries. As soon as he had placed her, so, in time, Gabriel yearned to leave her, for the sooner he was gone, the sooner tomorrow would come that he would meet her, after he had spent the morning in bringing in the fruit, waiting on the few customers, delivering to the invalids who bought from Madame Schwarz, whose crazed, wavering, bony paws took from his shrinking hand those fuzzy globes that then disappeared awfully down sick gullets, chewed in fearful haste to forestall white Death.

"Myra, Myra," called Gabriel as her skirt fluttered away. "I love you." He cried out, not knowing what he meant.

She waved.

Gabriel turned into his street. There was no smoke, no sign of change, but people boiled around the shattered building where Madame Schwarz sold her fruits and ate and slept. They were clawing the bricks away from the low entrance door. When they had cleared a place to get in, Gabriel clawing with the rest, they scrambled into the dark room. There they found Madame Schwarz untouched, although dead, staring at the wall, drawing the brick and mortar to herself, looking beyond it, with fierce scorn, even dead attempting to suck the whole of the wall, the world, into her eyes, into her stiffened grip; Gabriel averted his eyes, turned once again into stone. A woman stepped forward to tug Madame Schwarz' skirt into a decent position around her flanks.

And from within the assembled circle of women, dead Madame Schwarz stared stonily at her son: "I knew you would never come to any good. Once in your life you were needed; where were you?"

Gabriel hung his head.

"You are like your father, to cut and run, to spy, to cry when you're hurt, to fall when there are no stones. Couldn't you have looked when I wanted you to look, stayed straight when the cart toppled and teetered?" In her death, she was enraged. "I would break your skull like eggs, you watery creature! You'd never get away!"

The eroded women began the traditional wail, put candles at Madame Schwarz' head and feet and left one of their number to sit up with the body.

Gabriel crept into his corner. Madame Schwarz reposed stiffly. The dusty fruits, vegetables and rubble lay together in confusion, unnerved at the absence of organization and tyrant. Gabriel had no desire, no power to bring order into the room. Tonight was a hovering mote of dust. Where would it settle?

Walking on the unyielding sidewalk of a dustless street, Gabriel thought: "I dreamed of Myra."

He fell asleep finally that night, breathing the breath of the candles, seeing his mother in wax, smelling the dense fruit and dreaming of Myra's lips and breasts.

Women talked to him, stroked his head and fed him things the morning following. They imagined him shocked and dazed with his grief, although the old woman had always, even in their sight, knocked and rattled the boy. But he was immobile with gushing joy. They did not realize, and counted out to him some sibilants of commiseration, for Madame Schwarz had been a fearful one, even among these women; they had cowered and cringed before her stiff index finger. She might still be able to bring bad luck, sterility, miscarriage. There was no use taking chances: be good to the son.

He was, maybe, good luck. Skinny, with a straight nose and long neck, he was perhaps a duckling swan, a changeling, a prince-charming stolen by chance by the ugly witch. They whispered these things now into his ear; they had so desired for years.

"Tell us, tell us, what your mother did at night, locked up here in this room with you? Be a good boy. Where did your father go? Was there ever a man here? How did he get out? Did she send him away? Did he come back at night, ever? Through the door? Did she whisper anything strange over the fruits? Tell us, but never tell anyone else, or we will stick you with pins and send our sons to handle you."

Gabriel shook and shook his head. He was proof of them. But there was no need for them to tell their sons to push and torment him; they always had, on their own, Jew and Gentile, for there was a freemasonry of both in the St. Paul district; general poverty made for camaraderie that hurdled religion. All the old women had strong roots in brewing charms, collecting cowrie shells, muttering at the foot of a hemlock tree, and curling hairs during the full of the moon.

He escaped them, escaped into the air from the room where his mother's veiled beak thrust and stabbed at the sheet. He ran through the streets dodging the piled-up brick and oddments of door jambs, pipes strangling in the air, out of their natural element, the walls; seeing cups and saucers set for tea on polished tables and stands, with no house, no walls around them, as though declaring a fragile last independence of their gross and clumsy owners.

Gabriel ran up to Myra, sitting with her knees pressed together on the park bench. "Hello. My mother's dead. Where can we go? I can go anywhere now. I can sell fruit. I can make money. I can do anything."

Myra smiled up into his face as though under the lid of a pot. "Gabriel," she said. "Gabriel. Do you know that there is a war? The Germans are going to come to Paris, to your house. And do you know that my family, my brothers, would kill you and burn me up if they knew that their sister had anything to do with a Jew? Gabriel."

The love in her voice and the meaning in her words, mixed all together, bewildered Gabriel. He wanted a talisman, as the old women had wanted to make him such a talisman, that would rip open the problem and spill its heart, as one gripped a fruit by its spheres and forced out the worm that gnawed within. Where was the answer? He should have felt crushed. But instead he grinned.

"How do you know I'm Jewish?"

Myra smiled her slow smile. "Nobody but a Jew could wail in such a melody when he thought he was going to die. Nobody but a Jew changes from despair to dancing in a minute. I knew Jews in Poland. My father used to pull the rabbi's beard. My brothers took the little Jewish boys and whispered things in their ears and when the boys would try to get away, my brothers took them and forced them to jump over fires. Did your mother give you money?"

19

"She died," said Gabriel: "She was suffocated when the bricks fell over the door, I think. I don't know. But she's gone."

"Your father, where's your father?" Myra asked, looking at him intently, breathless suddenly, as though she saw into a well of mercury.

Gabriel's breath caught, as though he had fallen against her. "My father went away, I think he died, too. Years ago, when I was little." And Gabriel remembered sorrow and loss, and was now desolated at the recognition of the end of the present little world, the store and his mother's bony fist and the nightly voyages into the wilderness of the fruit and vegetable markets, Les Halles, throught the caverns of Paris in search of bruised fruit for his mother to sell. Tears ran down Gabriel's cheeks. He realized it. "My father's dead. He's dead."

He slumped on the bench. Above, the faded spring sky was filled with budding chestnut branches that yearned out toward each other over the path. Myra stroked Gabriel's head and she looked up at the pink and white buds.

"You're just like a Polish girl," she laughed, pushing his head up from between her shoulders. "You cry so much."

"I can take care of you," he said. "I'm strong, we can escape the Germans. We'll find a place, I'll find work. We can be all right." He looked at her, knowing that it was all a mockery, hopeless because he knew he was too weak, too young, too new, to do what he said he would.

"Gabriel," Myra whispered. "If you want me, later, after the war is over, we'll be together. But if you are going to live," she explained carefully, "you are soon going to have to hide, because the Nazis are coming and they are going to kill you if they find you. They are doing it in Poland and everywhere else, except in America. Maybe we will go there together after the war is over." She turned her head onto which a few pink and white blossoms had floated, bobbing on a wispy sea.

"Do you have any money?" she said.

"I don't know."

"Go home, find out what your mother left, find out how much you can get together. I think I can help." She took his arm, got him off the bench, and put her arms around his neck. "It's spring, my Gabriel," she said.

Gabriel pulled her head and her hair to his mouth and kissed her face, her eyes; he breathed in her hair and blossoms and kissed her brow.

"Go home," she said. "I'll meet you here tomorrow," and she ran out of the park.

She would meet him in America, thought Gabriel. Here I am, and yet, could she be on this street, on this pavement, coming toward me through the shadow of a light pole. Could it be? Laughing and running here as well as she had in Paris, in the Tuileries?

"She could laugh at me," thought Gabriel.

And he wanted to drop to the ground, tear through the sedate grass and smear his face and chest with the somewhere-living dirt beneath. Pour the dirt over his death and rend his garments, and weep again.

Here, on the well-manicured lawns.

How she had taken his hand and led him to her reeking room, where her sullen, angry brothers stood together. She showed them the money Gabriel brought; they moved sullenly like ice shouldering the shore during the spring thaw. They took him through streets that even he, a Parisian, had never seen, and gave him into the charge of other people, strangers, sharp-eyed, vaguely formed people that Gabriel could never remember, in poor kitchens.

But the cellar remained in Gabriel's soul the earth's navel. It was the string on which he danced, played his fiddle and exploded sparks through his ears. Here, Myra's anvil forged Gabriel, hardened him and softened him in the process and made a new metal of him.

21

And one day Gabriel, Myra and the brothers were at the Gare Saint Lazare. The train for the north. Steam rose from every crack, from the trains, from the people, who steamed rivers of sweat from their faces. Gabriel had his instructions, he had the names of farmers who would hide him for the time of the war. Myra had managed all. Gabriel tried to hold her in the middle of the crowd. The brothers rose between, holding sacks of clothing and supplies. He could not reach her. The steam came between them.

Myra blurred before him, in his tears and behind the steam, behind the brothers. They wedged her and pushed him toward the steps into the train. Her head and neck arched and was clear down below.

Gabriel shouted, "I'll see you, I'll see you. I know you. I know you. Goodbye. Goodbye."

The impassive brothers blocked her way. They threw Gabriel's sacks into the train just as Gabriel rushed to the window to see her for the last time. He fell back under the sacks, the train jolted and thudded and crashed against itself. Then there was only a foamy white sea beneath the window, teeth and whites of eyes, but no Myra.

No Myra. No Myra. The ties of the railway said it, the belches of steam said it, he read it in his flowing reflection in the window. And the world said it with satisfaction, the brothers said, "No Myra for you!"

Welcome! Welcome to the shores of the adopted land, to the land of the cellophane fruit and the plastic tree.

"They would have put your love in polyethelene containers, Myra, to disinfect it. A cellar is no right place, no hygienic place, to love. In my new land, Myra, steam is sterilized and trains are silent."

Gabriel walked under a tree and the shadow hid him from the light post.

The Kassel Ballet

Dear Grace and Harry.

First of all, greetings of this time of year—and *alles gutes* for the coming year. Pity I am not in the States again this Xmas—as I certainly enjoyed my visit last year, and really need to get away from dreary Kassel for some weeks in the USA *kultur*—but work here and strained relations with family does not allow it.

I'm writing to inquire if you received the building blocks I sent over about two months ago—they may have been delayed via the shipping strike which ended just last week. As I wrote, I found them at a fleamarket in a town about 150 kilometers from here, and bargained them down.

By the bye, I finally met the Dutch/German couple, Friederich and Hilda Hofstaeder, you sent me the names of. Really lovely people if provincial, like Kassel itself. Like famous resistance-hero uncle, he is a Christian wrestling with the problem of Christian responsibility for the Holocaust. He looks very charming as he wrestles, sitting intently at a rickety table and straight chair. I'm sure Hilda would prefer some more ample accommodations, less spartan, since she's the typical *zoftik* Jewish girl, even after years of living in Germany under less than ideal circumstances.

We've all become quite friendly, though we wouldn't have known each other in the States—one of the bonuses of living abroad, a perpetual student traveler in attitude even if I am in reality *Herr Ober* Artistic Director-Choreographer of a German State

Theatre.

The work goes slowly and somewhat better than last year—I will lose many dancers again. One left me with the rather un-original epithet "dirty Jew" on his sneering lips. It was very satisfying that a thoroughly German *very* male dancer in the troupe leveled him with one punch. The sneerer's very pretty lips were bleeding profusely as he limped out of my life.

Germany is Germany. I feel tired after turning out so many creative works during the last three years—I suppose more because they've been seen by so few "important" people, and therefore I see no way out of these provincial situations I get myself into.

I've become quite a fleamarket addict. On Saturdays I consult the local "penny saver" for markets where one can buy just about anything so long as it's useless. Yes, you can have *Der Stürmer* (Goebbel's hate sheet), it's for sale quite shameless and un-apologetic. You can have Iron Crosses, but they are very dear, or complete SS uniforms including underwear. No portraits of *Der Führer* though, not yet. Lots of model airplane kits (made in Hong Kong, Japan, and good ol' USA) of Fokkewulfs, Junkers, Messerschmitts, with the legend, "Pride of Germany" splashed on the boxes.

Your Dutch friends live in a rather bare flat, what they can afford, I suppose, on his theological professor's salary. Friederich is usually scrunched over a rickety table writing or studying or asking me questions about Jewish life that I can't answer. Hilda darns or reads on a straight chair. While I was at a flea market I saw a very nice oak chair with a stuffed seat and back, needing only a little sewing to tuck back in the horsehair stuffing. I knew it would have to be too expensive a gift for me to consider, but I asked the price anyway. To my surprise, even the asking price wasn't bad, and after I bargained them down, it was even reasonable. Unlike most of the sellers, they were even helpful about tying it onto my Renault, and they stood

24

watching and waving in the road while I drove off.

I was pleased. I thought I was really getting onto how to comport myself among the natives. The very next weekend I called the good couple and told them I had a surprise for them. I tied the thing onto the car—not as well as the fleamarketeers, but enough to keep it from falling in the road.

You would think I'd brought the crown jewels of Bavaria or Queen Wilhelmina's commode. They took turns sitting in it, striking attitudes. I almost wanted to choreograph it: the chair on which a breakthrough in Christian rationalizing was begotten (I can't imagine their begetting anything else). After his death, smiling brave wife showing chair to pilgrims from everywhere, even Hannover, Kassel like a Chartres and my abode pointed out as the place where the donor of The Chair sat on his own stool.

The broke out the schnapps and we had a merry time. They politely asked after you two, and Hermann, but I usually leave him home when I go see the couple Hofstaeder. Despite their professed liberalism, I know they are uncomfortable with him, whether because he lives with me obviously in the nature of a conjugal relationship, or because he is the nephew of the famous Field Marshal Rommel. Hermann looks like a fox himself, an aristocratic one with his nose usually held somewhere around three o'clock, but only because he is myopic. You can imagine him whisking a riding crop, but about the only thing he whisks is his Honda—he is the gentlest and sweetest of men. Well, Hermann is a story for another time. He gives townspeople and critics something else to whisper about. One Hannover critic wrote that my work is "prurient," whatever that may mean in relation to my staging John the Baptist's head being brought in on a Volkswagen hubcap. I thought it was a neat touch, he obviously didn't. Wulfsburg is a holy place in the German mass mind. While the "economic miracle" isn't bragged about anymore, it's lived in *schlag,* puddings, red meat, sausage and gout. May they all die of it, in agonies. I'm sure he meant "decadent Jew," but he's not allowed to print that. Not yet.

When I went to see Hilda and Friederich the following week, they welcomed me with a certain nervous reserve I didn't understand. I wondered if I'd performed some *gaffe.* Glancing around for the soon-to-be-famous chair, I was astounded to see that it was in a corner, enshrouded in black crepe. I pretended not to see (a mistake, I ought to have asked instantly), they pretended not to see I saw.

They broke out the schnapps. I enquired as to whether we might take a walk. Hilda sniffed the air and nervously said, "It smells like rain," despite the fact that, for once, in that eternally gloomy city, there wasn't a cloud in the sky. Friederich added: "I have an appointment with the rector," put on his coat and hat as well as his muffler (it was at least 80 degrees Fahrenheit!), got on his bicycle and clattered off.

I really enjoy Hilda's company more than his, but when we had sat uncomfortably silent for a few minutes, I also made my excuses about rehearsals and made off.

Of course, I was miserable. Two of the only people I had some kind of human contact with in this city, and they appeared to be going out of my life.

A week or so later I drove to the same flea market where I had bought the chair, out of boredom. The couple that sold it to me were at their usual place. The wife saw me and waved her arms to get me to walk over. The man beamed, bowed, sweated. He directed my attention to an ottoman and made me an offer I couldn't resist, even without bargaining. So, onto the Renault it went and back into Kassel, straight over to the Hofstaeders. I knocked on the door, like Rapunzel, with the ottoman in hand.

Friederich opened and when he saw who it was turned pale, left the door open and went back inside without a word.

I'm American, Kids, and not a character in a turn-of-the-century novel. "Look here, Friederich," I yelled, "what's going on? Hilda, can I come in? I demand an explanation. When I get one I'll be glad to leave peacefully."

Hilda appeared and took my arm gently. She was crying and wiping her nose. Even her hand was damp.

Inside the flat sat five old men in black suits, black skull caps. Each had a long, white beard. One was reading from a prayer book. I was astonished. There isn't a Jewish community nearer than Hannover, three hundred kilometers to the north. And the Hofstaeders are a mixed couple, not religious as far as I knew.

Hilda spoke to the men in Yiddish, which I don't know, but my German is good enough for me to follow what she said. "The chair, the man who gave it to us, a Jew." Then I thought I heard the German word for pervert, but I'm not sure.

Hilda led me to a chair. The old men shifted a bit. It was just as though I was in court. After a few minutes the one who appeared to be the leader turned to me, speaking in English.

"Sir, we are sorry to inconvenience you," he said, as though I had been summoned. "It is the matter of the chair, and now also the ottoman. There was, of course, no way, no way, for you to realize what this chair is. You came by it at a fleamarket?"

I saw the chair had been moved. It was still covered with black cloth, but one corner was exposed, slit open, and more horse-hair stuffing was dribbling out.

The rabbi nodded. "You are seeing what we have done to your chair? That is not what you think, you think that is horse hair? No, it is not. In there is our people, our murdered brothers and especially sisters. Not the hair of horses, but the hair of murdered Jews with which the Germans were satisfied to stuff their furniture. This is the gift you have brought your friends."

(I thought of what the German word *Gift* means: poison.)

He continued. "And that is why we are here. A very difficult problem."

Hilda and Friederich were holding hands. He drummed on the table, she wept, "If I ever dreamed . . ." I began, but the rabbi continued after patting her shoulder and shaking his head.

"What to do with it?" he said to the other four men, who nodded their heads slowly. "It is written in the *Responsa* that the owner of one such piece of furniture asked permission to burn it. That was denied, as it is forbidden to burn the bodies of martyrs. May it be disposed of in the sea? No, for that would pollute the ocean. And if it is a gift, such as in the present case, may the gift be returned to the giver? That is also very complicated, as you, the giver, gave it in good faith, and you are, also, as we understand, a Jew, but a Jew not in good standing, because . . . . because . . ."

He paused to clear his throat and looked again for support to the other men. They shrugged. "You understand, no offense meant, because of your personal, ah, activities. Therefore, chair and ottoman may not be returned to you, because you are first a Jew, only second a sinner."

"Let me take it," I said, "and return it to the Germans who sold it to me."

"It is also forbidden to deliver the body of martyrs into the hands of, or to the successors of, those who performed this abomination. It is forbidden to buy the stolen goods of dead people, not to mention the very hair from their tortured bodies."

By now, all of us were weeping. The old men were praying and weeping, maybe thinking, "Is my mother's hair, my sister's, my wife's, my little girl's hair, is some part of them in that horror in the corner?" All the years I've spent trying to create something in Germany, to

28

make dance, choreography to be seen by the sort of people who sold me the chair and ottoman. But who am I? What am I? Not a real Jew, not an artist. To the German, a dirty Jew. To these Jews, only a pervert. Somehow, not only Hitler and his Germany but I also was being judged before this ecclesiastic court, and as much as I tried to think that it was only a superstitious throwback to the middle ages, I couldn't stand it. I wept and held my head. I needed for these old men to hold my head and tell me, "You are clean, you are not guilty."

They did not accuse me of anything, they were gentle, forbearing. For those few minutes, they were truly my people.

"What are you going to do?" I asked.

The five men stood at once. Friederich also struggled to his feet.

"We have a decision from the Chief Rabbi in Jerusalem. It is that the chair and now the ottoman be buried according to the Jewish faith and Kaddish is to be said over the grave. We have located hallowed ground near Kassel where formerly there was a Jewish cemetery. We will bury the remains there."

We tied the chair and ottoman onto the Renault. The rabbis, Hilda, and Friederich led in a Mercedes sedan. The cemetery was half an hour away. From a distance there was nothing standing to show it had ever been a cemetery. Only close by could one see bits and pieces of headstones.

Friederich took shovels out of the trunk of the Mercedes. Each of the men dug in the hot spring weather. But the old men were too feeble, so Friederich and I were principal diggers. One of the men put a skull cap on my head with his own hands. I dug violently, sweat getting into my eyes from unaccustomed exertion. I wondered how all this would look done as a ballet. But then where could such a ballet be performed? Not even in Israel, which is, frankly, even more provincial in its way than Kassel.

Friederich and I lowered the chair into the grave, with the ottoman on its lap, so to speak. The rabbis said the Kaddish while Friederich, Hilda and I stood mute with our heads bowed.

Then there was hand-shaking all around and the rabbis left for Hannover in their Mercedes sedan and we drove back in my Renault to Kassel.

The atmosphere in the car was as though we had buried a great weight. I treasured the feeling that I was part of a family for a little while.

The warm feelings gradually lifted until by the time we arrived at the Hofstaeder flat it was only another killingly dull day in Kassel. Then, schnapps and an invitation for Hermann and me for the following Sunday.

That's all the news and complaints for now. I hope you are all fine and the house is getting furnished and the termites are no longer. Had a few fine nights with you last summer, hopefully can again next summer as well.

Your friend,
Barry

From In Albania

I can leave Albania if I want to. All I need to do is want to leave
Albania. My village lies in sight of boats plying Greece to Italy.
The talus slope is to northwest of the villages. A zigzag road follows a
hill to Tirana and the radio station, which beams to Yugoslavia,
Greece, and several other places.

The smoke and the ship in the sea do not sink, the smoke is
disrupted only after an amount of air and distance interrupt the
source and the product. In Albania we do not count the amount of
smoke, and the smokestacks do what they have to do, although they
are rare. We have perhaps four ships. Our coast is greatly indented,
like the large intestine. But unlike that organ, it is the same on top as
it is on the bottom. Differences are frowned upon.

In point of shape, my analogy was not very apt. I am myself more
like the people on the boats that go by, I believe. I am separated from
myself. I can imagine myself standing on the edge of the deck, falling
off, or on the edge of the smokestack, falling in. People on deck
wouldn't turn an eye. They do not know me anyway, as I stand here.
Therefore, it is as though I had really fallen into the water or into the
stack. In this ridiculous way I have traveled widely, without leaving
Albania.

Now, I want to leave Albania, at last. The plan is as follows: I will
steal a fishing boat of medium size, because I am weak and cannot
row well. I will steal oars as well. Two—one for spare in case of
violence, if I become guilt-ridden and indecisive and fling one over

31

the side. I would not go overboard for it, since I don't want to lose any more face. And more backside, either. Mine is skinny, sometimes runny, and nobody can be bothered with it. Facesaving and backing into things both can lead to drowning.

The plan is as follows: steal a boat, with or without oars. I will in any case throw the oars away when I reach mid-Adriatic. Thousands of people pass my village each year in July and August, riding those great ships half a mile or so above the water. How many look toward my village? How many say to themselves, if they looked toward my village: "If I lived in Albania I would steal a boat and simply sail five miles into international waters and wave at a passing ship. Then they would lower a dinghy, I would ask for and receive political asylum."

So definite the western mind. That sort of thinking makes me want to set mines in the waters, rather than placing myself there. Those furry complacent fleas convinced of their rightness, as they attach themselves to the great bodies of the ships, and suck there. They think they do it voluntarily, but they are attracted as iron shavings to the magnet, they are without will.

If they lived in my village they would know what it is like to make a decision. In some moments, I have been able to see my way clear, to make a run for the boat. At the last minute the tide turns, my stomach runs over with bile, I have to lay down the oars, slide the boat back up on the beach. These days I am reckless; I don't attempt to hide my intentions. The fisherman-owner of the boat is calm. He believes I am eccentric, the way I slide his boat back and forth whenever he isn't using it. He doesn't care.

Nobody on the boat is requesting my attendance. Nobody considers the act of requesting political asylum, on the water, in the middle of the Adriatic. Still, even without the pull of someone's watching for my boat, I can go out there. I am an Albanian, not a flea! I can leave Albania if I want to. Every time I raise my eyes I see an underline of smoke on the waters. Italy is on the other side. To the north is Yugoslavia. To the south is Greece. To the east is Bulgaria. Everywhere boundaries. Maddening to be reminded every minute. Some people are never reminded. They do their duty, make their life within a village, never go to Tirana. They are wiser than I, perhaps, but this I cannot help. I hate them. They know it, but forgive me for an eccentric, who has known sorrow.

I am stuck as a harmless eccentric, though I originally planned it as a device to spin me off into the middle of the Adriatic. This pose takes time and care. As a mask it has grown into my skin. For me to get into the rowboat it requires a clear heart and an unblemished skin. Otherwise, I sink. Or even if I make it, only the shell of me will be hauled aboard. There I am, shaking hands with the fat pig of a captain, entirely without will, just waiting for them to do with me as they will.

I would rather remain here, as something, than be on board, nothing. I need only the clear, immediate necessity *to leave this place.*

Once I had a wife, two children. I told my wife, in the dark, my dream. If she had laughed I would have killed her, and that would have made an end also of the practical part of my scheme—prison or the firing squad. But she said nothing, a prudent wife, not knowing what to say. However, I needed her reaction, urgently. When it didn't come, I hated and despised her, I condemned her to the Security. Now the children are motherless, with relatives, far away. I remain alone.

Since beginning this, four ships have come and gone. I know all of them on sight. I know just how long they will remain in sight. Sailing from Greece to Italy, Italy to Greece. They *believe* they are free, that they have wills, but they do not, any more than maggots are free to leave garbage.

I will leave the bones of my ancestors behind me. We have always venerated our ancestors, a homegrown Confucianism having nothing to do with Albania's alliance with China. The Chinese don't really know what to do with an ally with only its backside showing, even on the open side, the side facing the water.

When I leave, my ancestors will fare for themselves. If it is an English ship, I will change my name to Jones or Smith. If Italian, Fratelli or Innocenti. Greek, Simos or Simonides. Most likely I will drift and die. If a big ship should see me, it could as easily ram me or swamp me, and I have no gunpowder to explode.

Here, in my village, I am a person, people know my name, whatever it is, whatever my father's name was. I have no need to even think of the next word, people furnish it to me, kindly. There is only one road, to the interior. And even it is unknown, although it goes to Tirana. To the sea the road is also unknown, though it is possible to take it. One needs the will and simplicity.

When I am simple enough I will dive in. I have decided to swim, as the harder, simpler way. By the time I am well in, I will be simplified of conflicting ideas. The apes aboard their floating tree will be unable to change or manipulate me in any way.

Once I am out, in another country, I can begin to plan my return to Albania. This is my home, my country, where my parents and grandparents are buried, as well as my wife, though the location of her grave is unknown to me.

I will return, whatever barriers are placed in my way.

Michali Among the Roses

H e pulls the long supple grasses with his right hand and then cradles them in the crook of his left, as he might a baby.

Before, the roses wore the grasses like summer coats. Now they are naked and Michali smiles his subtle way, knowledgeable, not quite the whoremaster, but not very brotherly either.

Who are the roses for? Why are they worked, weeded, fed, watered, transplanted? Michali gives bunches to the gas man, to the brick man, even to children.

The owner of our house pushes his glasses back over his high forehead and wipes his face, smiling too. The answer to funny questions is a smile.

"How does it feel to get direct commands from your ancestors dating to 1324?" "Can you do anything of your own?" Can anybody?

Michali holds the hose in his right hand. He is not like a Greek statue, though he also doesn't move. The trench around a rose fills, he moves to another. Hot afternoon, a wind stirs the heavy blossoms, my portable radio brings late news, the roses are in soil into which hands have dug or fallen for ten thousand years.

A Venetian aqueduct hauls its rock length across this valley; one side a vineyard, on the other a taverna featuring electrified bouzouki.

Ephigenia keeps the house clean. The fluids in her body keep reaching for the outside. She is an artesian well. When we moved in, she opened the house and dispossessed some of the native animals. They will have it again, and her too. An easy short term agreement

35

has been signed. We may not stay for long, for money. The rats are not hypocrites, they will not leave for the little time, they do not sign the agreement. Michali smiles and laughs shortly, his mustache curls a bit in fun. He will poison them.

In the night, poisoned rats leave the attic in their search for water. There is one tap for our village and the woman next door with four children will fight the rats for its use. Our little girl lies asleep. Directly above her five little rats swarm over the dugs of a poisoned mother. Probably Michali hasn't really poisoned them, and they are only crisscrossing the ceiling on their commuters' way to the evening meal.

Michali gave my daughter a cat, by its neck. Loved and mauled, she was with us for three days and disappeared on the fourth. Michali among the roses—fed another and laughed, raised a hand palm downward, half cupped, shrugged.

The roses arch under his hand like cats. He is subtle, or I do not understand his spoken language and so watch his motions, his harvesting arm doing the unnatural—plucking the grass and leaving the thorned flowers. But I think the grass will go to the goats.

Ephigenia leaves Agia Irini rarely, and then only to go to the hospital to have her arms lanced. I watch the labor on the hillsides that makes the olive trees and the grape arbors produce. Their roots must penetrate to the core of the island, because they receive no water all summer long.

Ephigenia and Michali, is your race older than mine? My origin is a land bridge a few hundred miles from here. My people scattered, one fleck clung to the San Joaquin Valley, hot and dry like Crete, where workers wear the wide straw hat and stoop to harvest. How long must you be vineyarded before you bear? and bear what? Tons of matter for a pound of produce. For money? To live? What are these things for?

Every day in the city a girl sprays a window with Azax to clear the souvlaki grease of the night before. I am impatient, the next place will be better. But each place stays where it is, forever, or so it appears, since it is only for a dozen years, for a hundred years, and then it is covered with a flat white wash and begun again. Every day Ephigenia cleans the same dust from the floors, puts out the rugs on the line, washes our clothes, rinses water over the dishes. The sun beats down. The weather changes a degree or two, the wind blows or it ceases to blow.

Ants carry a feathered burr to their nest, cooperating. Fluids rise and fall according to the moon and mortality. Distant tides dictate what part of a cucumber I may buy for my dollar. Tree frogs sing the eternal night through. Somewhere, a tiny cat corpse is plucked to (to me) invisible music. The earth everywhere throbs in new births and tomatoes ripen in waves for the market. Uncultivated fruit drops heavy to the ground, clouds rise and stand.

I hear a child's cry, my heart stops. When it is not my child, though the cry be desperate, I hear it no more. A moth beats against the window. Another day, Michali feeds the roses again, asking no questions. Everywhere tables are put out. I turn, the tables and chairs are occupied by different people, the ones before sunk into the earth like plump unpicked fruit. Everywhere sounds not heard, births unrecorded.

Three eternally bearded priests sit drinking coffee, completely obscuring the plastic table and bright chairs. They are gone like smoke. Millions of people have lived somewhere but I do not know them. In this corner of the world this house has swum to me, I climbed aboard. It is awash in roses. The Michali boatman clears a path of reeds and weeds. We sail through fields of roses, a miracle in the desert. What do I have to do with roses, a desert descendant? What underground river feeds my roots?

I read something more about this ancient island, equidistant from Egypt, Africa, Europe. Earthquakes roar like muffled bulls straining out of the earth. Civilizations crumble or fall in fire. Dust covers them, and a neon billboard erected by the colonels appears on every hillside. A village may be electrified for the only time in history because of the urgent need for an illuminated sign immortalizing 21 April 1967.

Under the asphalt pavement, the ancient roads; all lead through the passes, eternal even after earthquaking. From Iraklion to Knossos a mule can make it in two hours. I set out for Iraklion to buy ice to preserve yoghurt, a modern culture. Yoghurt is not more vulgar than labyrinths. Roses are more than double axes. Every man, also Michali, has two axes, but I do not know either of his faces. As water flows through the flexible black pipe it is impersonal and eternal, not Cretan. And roses are not Cretan either. They grow where there is sun and water.

My stock doesn't transplant so easily, so impersonally. I rage at the fate that has loosened me, allowing my spore to carry me where I make the winds to go. Minos on his throne does not speak to me. The sea does not speak. The mountains remain aloof. They are in no way my kingdom, sea or mountains. I rage at the petals of the rose. Michali smiles and waves when he sees me looking at him through the bedroom shutter.

An ancient sinister wet heat seeps out of Africa and drains across the two hundred miles to the rose garden. The flies go mad and crouch on my skin, biting to remind me we are existing on sufferance. The roses go a deeper violet and red against the low ceiling, enjoying a brazen intercourse with the wet wind. What can I do? They laugh at me. They do not care that I am here, they are aware, but only to laugh. This typewriter! At Agia Irini, occupied but looking blasted and long dead at midday, a donkey cries.

I wait for Michali to appear the next day. The supple green dancers are back as though he had never plucked them. Every day on the face of the earth the green beard sprouts. All things are for the first time. Michali is tilling the olive trees on the bluff overhead. The olives are a different race. Roses, he is paid to nurture. The olive trees own *him*. An older god for olive trees than for roses. But maybe at the end of days the rose will be growing and the olive consumed by locusts. Maybe when the trumpets sound I will still be standing, knee deep in the rank growth of my typewriter keys, still trying to make sense of these events.

Michali, as landowner and member of the middle class, do you hate the new foreigners from Athens who set up shop in your midst? I don't see any recent pictures on your walls, weddings and birth and grandfathers, but no kings, no colonels. In Agios Nicholaus, a gift store owner flipped off his radio and shouted: "Let the foreigners take their ambassadors back, what do we care?" Do Cretans regard him as a foreigner? "Let them, tourism is a sandpaper that smooths all differences." Michali, in the mountains, what are the men saying? "Trouble always starts with Crete!" Michali, are you planning trouble? Ephigenia goes to the hospital for treatments, her mother's teeth get fixed. There are no trains on Crete, though the buses run more or less on time. But what are they saying in the hills? In the little villages?

The European couple, smiling, move to their special table, special because they have sat at it now for two days consecutively. Nobody really wants a revolution; everybody feels good with tradition. Once something is there, it is there forever, and then it is gone or covered over. In my home town a Mexican produced large gypsum bulls. He was particularly proud of being able to get the horns out of the cast without breaking them and therefore needing to fake their length. He painted them himself and sold them door to door. I helped him, a small boy proud to be in commerce with a grownup. Now I see the same bulls on the walls of Knossos. This is no coincidence; it is also not a miracle.

While eating the acrid end of a packaged ice cream cone from a kiosk, I suddenly remember my mother's warning: "Never eat the end of the cone, a spider may be waiting down there." What tag-end of a folk memory was she repeating? Always leave a bit for elves and fairies? Never be so greedy or needy that you reveal to the world your desperation? Or don't, fat little boy, eat so many ice cream cones. I come, in middle age, to Crete, and I feel the spider crouching in the crotches of mountains—sudden floods following torrents of rain in winter wait to wash men and their works into the sea. A peeled cucumber sweats on my plate, what could be more fresh? But it loses its vital juices when it is opened, as we do when we love and open like flowers, then fall into seed and personal death. Dessicated is the one who sees only the spider down things and leaves the cone unplumbed from fear.

I wanted to take a picture of the threshing, the men made me stay to drink two glasses of wine. "Ohi Retsina—Crassi!" And then one of the men posed with a puppy while the bitch strained at her leash to tear at my leg. Do Michali and he speak the same language? Who are his foreigners, who treats me as a guest when I come to take pictures of his "picturesque" and primitive methods of agriculture. The rule is: the less you have, the more you are willing to share. My wife and child wait in the car, engine running, while I squat and drink, trying to avoid the teeth and the hill of ants.

Michali, if you or any of your countrymen complain that you do not understand what I am getting at, let me offer a parable of Crete: the coasts of Crete are washed by ancient waters, salted naturally and also by the tears of stranded seamen and widowed mothers. It is therefore very salt. Issuing from towering Ida and Lassithi, sluicing down their thighs, gush the wells and rivers of Crete. Where the two waters join there is confusion, like a lover's quarrel. Let me be as one of these waters, the river or the sea, and let this writing be the momentary obscurity. Each will accommodate the others, it has been so for more centuries than have so far been counted. We are both from ancient races and there is time enough.

When you see us in preparation to go to Amnisos beach you smile with some implement of digging in your hand and a broad-brimmed hat on your head. But your best irony is reserved for Cretans who are mad enough to go on the beach exposed to the sun, who bites deep enough into a man's arms and shoulders without invitation. When you are not working, you get under a roof of leaves, brick or timber. There is enough time to rot in the sun after dying.

I want to take something out of the ground of Crete too. I will buy a shovel in the market, dig in some spot of land where I will not be under observation by Irini, her four children, the goats, or Michali, Ephigenia, or Stelios, because I am afraid of appearing ridiculous. Where do I dig? Behind the kitchen, on the theory that kitchen middens are rich depositories of civilizations. Our level will reveal countless beer tops and plastic yoghurt containers among the squat cans of Gaz, some of which may yield a lingering petroleum bouquet to the unborn archaeologist. But if I actually find something, I will have to mount guard over it and worry continually until I can get it out of the country. This will spoil the rest of my time in Crete. There will be no "Odos" named for me in Agia Irini because I won't have time to go deeply enough into the kitchen burial ground, although I'm sure that this valley, this elegantly closing mouth that has chewed the plateau of Knossos to finest matter, has housed countless kitchens over the millennia. What a culture eats appears to tell more about it than how it behaves itself in the bedroom. Or at least the hardware of the kitchen endures better than the software of the

41

bedroom. Chances are that, through clumsiness or greed, my Iraklion spade will break the artifacts. And that would be the end of them.

Instead of digging, I take our ingenious can opener from Switzerland, a flashlight, and the spade one night under a half moon of great brilliance, bury the opener as deeply as I can, rearrange a rose bush over it, hoping that I have not killed it. In the days following I can see that I did not, and I can look Michali pleasantly in the face.

Among the oldest and most stationary trunks in the world, the olive and the grape appear the most dynamic. At dusk, the grape arbor seems to pour into the narrow valley under Agia Irini, while the olive trees march in strict discipline up the other side. Where have they been, and where are they going to spend the night? Don't worry about them, says Michali, they've been around for a while. They reassure the roses.

The Greek Smile

Hollow-sounding explosions began about 9:30, really 8:30 Greenwich Mean Time, but Greece is on a daylight saving scheme. The shutters are kept closed on our villa until 10, so we lay and didn't really listen or speculate until we were outside and drinking our morning coffee.

Ephigenia was already here, and to our questioning glances, she shrugged her shoulders, smiled, put her hands palms up, and went in to tidy up the bedroom. As we do not speak Greek, and she speaks no English, we are never sure what the sign of resignation or "I don't know" means. Because she usually smiles at us when we ask for or about anything, we have mainly given it up and simply move from one area to another when the time is appropriate.

If we had been looking for signs and alarms, there were considerable. Our kitten disappeared after my wife lost her temper when Ephigenia broke a crystal vase given to her years ago by her son. We searched for the kitty in a radius pitifully limited but all we could do. As I was standing above the rubbish hill I noticed something. I went away but was drawn back, despite the ever-present sweet stench of the area. I got a stick and pulled the wet messes this way and that. By the striations I could recognize that the steaming, streaming carcass was that of our cat.

We were careful to ask for nothing and avoided the maid's eyes after that. She relented, we believe, because two days ago a man with one arm brought us a sack. He smiled, made a kind of bow to

Ephigenia, motioned us into the villa, and dumped out the contents. Three streaks ran howling under bureaus and tables, screamed, ran some more while we cowered. Three wild cats, in return for our one sweet lovely one. My wife went into the bedroom, although it wasn't bedtime, to cry by herself. So we now share quarters with these creatures, which hiss and spit whenever we go to a drawer or closet or get near their always unpredictable hiding places.

Even after all this time, we still don't know what actions on our parts are likely to bring down on our heads this kind of indirect retaliation.

The big birds which live in the Venetian aqueduct began screeching overhead. The explosions could have been made by shotguns. Sharpshooters are stationed there day and night, and through our binoculars we sometimes see them killing birds. We imagined it was to protect the young grapes, but as the guns were equipped with long-range sights they might have been aimed just anywhere. One old man who couldn't be under eighty seems to be there for twenty-four hours at a time. He is always smiling.

The Greek smile is what primarily brought us to this island in the first place. We smile ourselves at how often we have been the objects of it since we arrived, ignorant and happy to be away from our home for our first extended holiday in years, and through a series of events, which we have discussed in the dark countless times but without understanding, found ourselves in this charming villa among the roses, grape arbors, and olive trees.

If I were a historian of the insignificant I would note how many pigeons the farmer across the ravine has cooped on his roof. When he lets them out and when he gathers them in. I could detail the progress of whitewashing on an old house standing semi-detached from the rest of the stone and stucco houses. I wait every day for the inevitable blue door to be painted on to stand out from the walls of the house. I watch the worker patiently weed one row of roses, and when he is through, how the weeds have overtaken him at the start of the row. This is a fertile place, and the air and earth are full of life. The sweet-smelling night is full of things eating each other.

The transformer atop the most distant visible hill just went up in a flash of light. I have heard this is possible under extremely humid conditions. And the wind has been coming from the south, from Africa, laden with wet, close, hot air. The flies cling desperately to one's skin, and no matter how many uncomfortable layers of clothing one puts on, they manage to bite through, leaving trails of tiny precise red welts. At night, very quietly, I smooth cream on my wife's back, while she bites her lip trying not to cry. I am afraid to ask Ephigenia for more cream, although I give her money good for three times what she used to bring.

The peasant who brought the cats waved to me atop his hill just as there was another explosion. Whether he fell or just normally disappeared I can't be sure. He certainly had been sent by Ephigenia, so why would he have been shot?

As she cleans, the maid keeps her transistor radio turned on loud. The valley is narrow, it echoes, so that the noise could have been a soap opera or a war story with explosions.

The sandpile we had had put in when we first arrived, anticipating the children of friends, disappeared. There is no way to ask about it. I use the binoculars, and I see a wall that was not there yesterday, facing the town, perhaps poured over sandbags. I don't know.

I slapped my wife across the mouth. It happened a short while ago. I don't know why I did it. I gritted my teeth and bit my lip until it bled and hit her as hard as I could. Afterwards, when she would let me, I held her like a baby in my arms. I was conscious of trickles of burning sweat forming between our bodies where they touched, but I was ashamed to take my arms away. We can take only two showers a day,

45

but it is usually enough, and not as though we have trudge to the village well for water to haul home in galvanized cans like the other villagers. We used to go to the caves for relief. It is always cool there, cool and dry, though acrid with bat droppings. Bats are the oldest residents; hanging upside down they endure everything.

My wife went to sleep, recklessly, even though I pleaded with her not to. She told me she was too tired to care. I stood guard hoping nobody would come and notice, although there was nothing I could do to prevent an inspection.

We were, I remember, discussing revolution. I don't remember whether I said I believed that the explosions had something to do with a new revolt or was certain that they did not, or that there were in reality no explosions at all. Whichever it was I suddenly flew into a red fury. That was when I hit her. We both saw clearly that I would have liked to do that to our smiling maid, and had to expend the hate and frustration on my wife instead, as in my mind remained the vision of both of us on the rubbish heap alongside our poor kitten, a feast for the small and large beasts of the valley.

We could end it all by burning ourselves up, but that, I laughingly say to my wife, would end our vacation as well.

The day oozes on and there are really explosions but of no identifiable origin. My wife decides to sew a slit into some walking shorts so as to leave the leg free for longer strides. She pricks herself but there are no bandages. I hold her finger, letting it drip blood into a washbasin so that it will not fester later. We wash it with luke-warm water (we have had no ice for some time now), and then put strips of relatively clean rags around it.

How can we indicate to the advancing men (if there is a front that is advancing) that we are on their side (if we are on their side) and have had nothing to do with the previous regime? We are living in this luxurious villa, served, it would seem, by servants. How could they be expected to know anything else about us except that we are damnable drones, lovingly cared for by a despised and loathed oppressor?

A jeep rumbles up through the pass between the olive grove and a long concrete shed that looks like a prison, coming to a stop before the village water tap. The driver puts out his head like a jack-in-the-box and backs up. Someone jumps or is hustled into the closed rear of the jeep. The driver has a large kerchief around his head; he looks like a traditional pirate. Wildly enough, the vehicle looks and sounds like the mail truck that comes to our real home, far away.

Should we put out white handkerchiefs on a flag pole? What would Ephigenia and her friends do to us then, if the tide turned in their favor? I have my double-edged hunting knife that I bought almost as a macho joke before we left for Greece. This is our only weapon, except for sticks. There is a way to convert kerosene into bombs, Molotov cocktails, but I don't know how. I am afraid to experiment for fear of maiming myself or throwing my hand away, in both senses.

There is absolutely no activity in the village to indicate anything out of the ordinary. I wish fervently that it were already night so that we could be put into the bedroom with door shut. Even as a grownup there is an absurd security about being tucked in for the night, even if the door is locked from the outside.

Curiously, I grow fatter, my wife leaner and more bony, with this tension. She doesn't move around as much as I do either. I allow myself to forget how we lie at night, listening to every sound outside, feeling for footsteps, clasping each other's hands when the rats begin their nightly forays with a rush from the northeast corner of the room where their nests must be, for the southwest corner, where they run down inside the walls to the garden and further. The explosions of tree frogs do not sound like footsteps.

A commercial jet plane, with the wind properly set, makes a noise like bombs or grenades. We are not sure that anything is going on. We do not know whether to hope or to fear. Perhaps foolishly, we have not attempted to leave this place.

The Sacrifice

S iegfried felt pulled by strings along the dusty inside road of the kibbutz.

"That's good," he thought and wiped his forehead. "It must mean they want me, they'll take me. Uphill, hot and steep, arriving without notice. But maybe someone will appear without a word and point the way, let me in, stay awhile, work."

He eased his knapsack off his fleshy back onto the baked dirt, flexed his hand. As he stooped, his body knit into a muscular back and legs. Relaxed again, the power disappeared into a heavy slackness.

From a cleft chin Siegfried's face pointed to his gross nose, once called "Jewish" by a spiteful neighbor. That incident had made him begin to ponder about Jewish noses, Jewish heads, about those others: the Jews.

At twenty-six he was already balding and gray at the temples. He pretended to even more years because of that grayness and the high forehead with deep furrows darkened now by the Israeli sun.

His past had for him the quality of glacial ice; love and feeling frozen in a limbo outside time. The years must be made to speak—of his father, a Party official, of his mother dead in an air raid, of the generation before, which should have spoken to him through its folk, his ancestors. But that generation spoke only of the present moment and pretended everyone had slept through the bad years.

He sought elders. But everyone old enough affected a false

contemporaneity and refused the gift of authority, fearful of mockery or accusations of complicity. The Fourth Reich dressed, acted, and spoke as though it had been born in 1945, when new western gods broke the old steins.

He came to see time as a dragon swallowing the world, and to feel that his education was only tattered scraps of paper accidentally passed up from some other century. His present: meaningless; the past—where according to history books Hitler and his Third Reich belonged, where he must have been as a child—was a desert of blank white pages. Some germ of power was buried in those years, but not in Germany, no, not in that dead land. Elsewhere, yes.

So he took to traveling and finally came to Israel to dig for a folk who might consent to take the place of lapsed parents and antique teachers.

Approaching, he had not noticed the tin shack. A man was framed in the window, utterly still. "How long has he been watching me?" Siegfried wondered.

"Ah . . . . Shalom," Siegfried called.

The man's lips pursed like those of proud, uneasy German duelists in nineteenth century portraits.

"Pardon, I am called Siegfried. Do you speak German or English?"

"I speak English and German. I am Shlomo ben Adam, like Shalom, but it derives from Solomon. Shalom on the other hand is peace. What do you want?"

"To work, sir. I want to work here in Israel. I come from Germany . . . . and Germany is dead, my parents are dead. There is no life there. I have heard there is life here still. Will you put me to work somewhere? I want to do something worthwhile in my life."

"Come inside."

The sudden heat in the shack struck Siegfried full in the face. A rifle leaning against the wall leaped sharp and crisp, but the corners were thick in shadows.

"You have found the proper person. I am chairman of work. This is the room where I coordinate all the work of this, our collective farm, which is called a kibbutz. But what do you think to find here?"

Siegfried tried to speak, but his thoughts were also hot shadows. "It's this land," he murmured, "so many dead, a debt to be paid, to be a comrade, to dance with the people . . . ."

"You have come here from Germany to dance? Speak up!"

Shreds of philosophy floated by. "The great dance, to love a brother, trace the cause of suffering, turn hate into love . . . ."

Shlomo stretched his neck. His eyes were jeering sparks. "Into love? What love? What do you know about love?"

"For you, for me," Siegfried said desperately, sure he had already alienated this little man. "Giving to . . . . Pardon, I'm dizzy, I'm not making sense. If we might go outside again?"

As Shlomo struggled out of his swivel chair, Siegfried noticed he wore a built-up shoe. Outside, Shlomo nodded toward a faucet. Siegfried ran to turn it on. He plunged his head into the stream of water.

When his head was soaked and clearer, he raised his dripping face. Through the dazzle of water, he saw a girl. She glittered. A gleaming halo of water outlined her hair. Close about her stood a group of children, all silent and curious, save one, dark and shriveled, who laughed with malicious glee, a sound that caught Siegfried's throat, a sound he wished he could produce. The boy was mocking him, rubbing his eyes and puffing out his cheeks.

Shlomo stepped clumsily in front of Siegfried. Did so few strangers come to the kibbutz? Or so few wet ones? Shlomo's words came through tight-drawn lips. "This is Zohar. She teaches the young children, when she's not gaping at Germans with their heads under a spigot!" Shlomo turned on the thickened heel, elaborately addressing the girl, very much the drill sergeant. "This, Zohar, is a German, Siegfried, an Aryan name, derived from the famous Teutonic myth. You might show him around, since he fascinates you so, and I can get back to my work. As for you, sir, you may stay tonight. In the morning I will call a meeting to decide what is to be done. You will sleep in my office. But you will not touch anything. And lock the windows, no matter how hot it should become. The dark is always dangerous here."

"Thank you, thank you," Siegfried said, blotting his face and arms with his handkerchief.

"What's your name?" Zohar asked softly. "I didn't understand Shlomo."

"Siegfried."

"Siegfried . . . . Mine is Zohar. That is Hebrew for light. Do you understand my English? All Germans speak English now, don't they? Is it American English or English English you speak? We speak English English here because we were occupied by England." She paused. "You were occupied by America, Russia, and England. This is something in common, isn't it?"

"Yes," he replied gratefully, "something in common. Except that here you are building a new country." Even now without water in his eyes, her hair shone brilliant black like a grackle's wing. She wore khaki and rough boots, and although she was friendly and lively, she looked tired and wilted.

"Oh, *I'm* not building it. Israel was old when I was born. Even the trees and houses here are older than I am."

Zohar looked down the path to some wire sheds at the bottom of the hill. Her troop of children had scattered among the buildings.

"Wait a minute," Shlomo called. "I have forgotten something." He jerked his head for them to follow him into his office. Shlomo's high narrow forehead shone in the gloom. The few sandy hairs that had survived years of burning sun ran like veins on his neck, his eyes burned too. He pushed a stack of papers to one side, elaborately positioned a blank piece before him. "Give me some facts, if you will, to present to the committee."

Heavy foot-steps, then a grunt, and a face with drooping handle-bar moustache peered through the window.

"Shlomo! *Ma shlom cha?* How are you? Are you in there?" a voice boomed from beneath the moustache.

"Shalom, Dov; yes I'm here. Why must you do that? Can't you knock at the door like everyone else?"

Dov spied Zohar, cried "Ha!", disappeared, ran in through the door, grabbed her in a bear hug. "So! An infiltrator. You're caught, one Arab less. Shlomo, your knife." He stabbed her in the rib with his thumb. "Feh! No blood!"

Zohar beat her fists against his chest. "Let me go, you idiot!" she cried, her voice muffled in his gigantic embrace. "Get away, you smell bad."

"I smell bad?" Dov's hairy eyebrows shot up. "From the good Jewish manure I feed the bananas I could smell bad?" He let her twist free.

"But you do," Zohar said, smoothing her hair.

Dov looked over to Shlomo, down to his foot. "The hot dry weather helps a little? It doesn't hurt so much?"

Shlomo's cheek twitched.

"What's the matter, Shlomo?"

"What's the matter with you? Don't you see someone else here? A German—Siegfried. This is Dov."

Siegfried caught the big man's flicker of observation.

"He says he wants to work here," Shlomo said. "He said he wants to make reparation for the crimes of his parents, isn't that it? A remarkable thing!"

Siegfried didn't recall having said he wished to "Make reparation."

Dov squinted elaborately at Siegfried, miles off. "They're very direct, these Germans," he remarked to Zohar, as though on the lecture platform. "It's a quality we share with them. Never take no for an answer, whether taming the desert or bombing the Poles. Maybe it's the climate. There are beautiful forests in Germany, Shlomo, just like your Canadian ones. Did you ever see Germany, Shlomo? Israel is green, but only where we force the water to go. In German forests, even people bleed green, in fairy tales. What does your brother-in-climate want, Shlomo, in this howling desert of ours?"

"Ask him yourself," Shlomo replied sullenly. "You make a joke of everything." His eyes began to shine again. "He wants to atone, if you want to know."

Siegfried opened his mouth to say something, but Shlomo went on.

"He wants to atone, he told me so. He's to be a symbol."

"Atone? For what? He was a baby."

"He wants to atone," Shlomo repeated. "For everyone there comes the time of atonement. For every injury, someone is chosen to heal the cripple, or take up his burden."

Dov's mouth turned down, but his eyes softened as he glanced again at the feverish Shlomo. "What's your name, fellow?"

"Siegfried." He wondered how many more times he would be required to repeat his name. It had begun to have a strange ring, not exactly his own name any more.

"Siegfried, is it? Well, Siegfried, did you tell us you were coming? No? So, he comes, Shlomo, states his case precisely, papers *alles in Ordnung. Alles?* Not a word wasted, right? Our Shlomo, starring as Prince of Peace, mates him to our very own Vestal Virgin. In your touching sentiment, Shlomo ben Adam, there is, please forgive me, something very Teutonic for a Canadian expatriate—a mistiness one finds in German romances. All the proper feelings, *in Ordnung,*

54

the proper degree of penance. You have catalogued the situation and into your office comes a worthy German penitent to fulfill the story . . . or even the prophecy, if you will."

"The only situation is that you will vote against letting him stay for a limited time, isn't that it? You've set yourself against this boy because you like making me appear weak and foolish, an emotional cripple."

"No, Shlomo, I did not mean that. Don't jump on my back, I'm the weak man here. You are too passionate, Shlomo, too hot. I didn't say to throw him out. Why, here he is! Possession is nine-tenths, et cetera, precision timing, Volkswagens, train schedules, Shlomo. I don't say anything. Why should I? Who am I? But, if I may be permitted to ask in passing, what does a Siegfried want? Does he know? What do you want, or Zohar—"

"Or Dov?" Shlomo shot back.

"—Or Dov, yes. What do we want? Do we hand him a rifle, send him to the towers to shoot infiltrators or be shot himself, that he might become a martyr of the Land of Israel? Well," Dov said waving his hand to include them all, "why not? Take the rifle now, in fact!" he said directly to Siegfried with a smile. "Since we don't know why we're here or for what purpose, you may be what Shlomo seems to think you are."

Shlomo opened his mouth to object, but Siegfried managed to interrupt. "I've just come to be here. I don't have any other motives. Really, if I am so much trouble, I will leave. I will leave you in peace."

"Oh, no, don't," Zohar cried. "First we should get out of this hot dark room, and I have to see after the savages, and he can come with me. You all talk too much."

Shlomo ignored her. "I will see to him, Dov."

"Of course," Dov smiled. "Zohar, what do you think of Germans and Canadians?" He pulled her kerchief over her nose.

"Stop that, you beast. I don't think anything. Leave me alone or I'll pour sand in your bed."

Shlomo stood in the door of his office and watched the three leave together. "Some day you will be forced to stop your sneering, Dov. Some time."

"It's not the end of the world yet," Dov snapped. "As for you, Siegfried," he stopped and laid a hand on the boy's shoulder, "I do have some work for you. Pick three bushels of oranges and shovel four cubic feet of dung for every Jew who was put in the ovens. That ought to do it."

Shlomo ducked his head in the shadow of the doorway. Zohar said, her voice trembling, 'I think that's cruel and unfair, Dov. He didn't have to come here."

Dov shrugged. He squeezed Zohar's arm and took Siegfried's hand and began to pull him away from the cabin.

Shlomo's voice came from the doorway like a coil reaching at Dov's ankles. "Some who left Israel when the War broke out are here now. They were forgiven when they came back after it was all over. When it was safe."

"That's just as unfair, Shlomo," Zohar cried. "Dov believes that Arabs have a right to the land just like us. He lost his brother in the war. Dov came back and fought three times as hard as any other man, and now he works like three men."

"Who compels him to do manual labor? He should be doing the work he was trained to do—not play with tractors."

"I do not tell you what work to do, Shlomo ben Adam."

"No," Shlomo said bitterly, "what else is there for me to do?"

"Stop it, both of you," cried Zohar. "What will the German think of us? Put your smelly old arm around me," she commanded Dov, "and stop being evil to Shlomo, and you stop reminding Dov of things that happened a long time ago, or I'll make you both wash diapers for a week."

"I have nothing against the boy's coming here," Dov said, "but a man always hates a benefactor. Everybody hates charity, yes, Shlomo? Siegfried makes his Rhine journey in strange company." He patted Zohar's hand and walked heavily away.

Shlomo glanced at Siegfried over whose head the storm had raged. "Well," he said to the wall, "well, the children are making a racket. It's her first day with them as their teacher," he explained to Siegfried. "They're not too much?"

"No."

"We had to choose among three applicants. One of them was a certified teacher before she left Egypt."

"Thank you, Shlomo, I know you put in a good word for me. I thank you for it."

Shlomo's red face turned copper. "You don't have to thank me. I wasn't fishing. The work committee chose you. The children need the warmth and attention you can give them. You are gay and young."

"Shlomo, I am no longer so young, and I am not so gay."

Shlomo turned to enter the cabin. He slipped, flung out his arm for support, but hit the wall instead. It clanged like an alarm. Zohar ran and held him by the shoulders. He shivered and leaned against her, but kept his face turned away. She helped him inside to the swivel chair. Siegfried followed helplessly.

"Some water?"

"No, never mind," he whispered. "Go, go back, go back, there's nothing the matter. Go back to the children, both of you. Goodbye. Shalom. Please get out."

The kibbutz buildings lay on rolling hills, commanding views of fields stitched by irrigation ditches and rows of green plants. On one side, a plantation of banana trees was a sudden splash of green spears. Lemon and orange groves colored another hill. The cultivated fields halted at a dry river bed that marked the border of Israel with Jordan. Guard towers rose every hundred feet, the area between them closed in by continuous barbed-wire fence.

As he followed Zohar, Siegfried marveled at her loose and careless stride, children circling her like tugboats. "Can this girl have a history too?" he wondered, "and if she does, where does she hide it?"

"Here's the hen-house," she shouted over a shattering din, and pushed him under a flimsy tin roof suspended by some shaky boards. The floor was covered with droppings so pungent that tears rose in his eyes.

Zohar's pupils roamed close by, but a wizened dark child followed the two adults. From the outside he wiggled his fingers at them through the wire. Why was this weird child following them? Did he know Siegfried was German? Had he listened to all that talk? But Zohar was also in the cage. Was she making fun of him by taking him first to a chicken-shed? For his pilgrimage in search of "unredeemed time," "truth," "authority"—how could he think in a stinking hen-house.

A chicken lurched across Siegfried's shoe, trailing ooze. He kicked and some clung to his stocking. He felt ill. The dark child laughed out loud, that penetrating and to Siegfried peculiarly moving sound. He silently appealed to him, but the dark child only waggled his fingers.

"Stop it, Isaac!" Zohar commanded. Her face was hard and vexed. "Poor thing," she said with no conviction. "He has a sad life. His parents were killed trying to come to Israel from Jordan. Isaac was found starving next to the bodies of the mother and father. No one knows whether Arabs or our guards killed them. The boy would never talk about it. He hardly ever speaks. He plays jokes that frighten or annoy the other children, he watches, he laughs. Go on, go with the others." The boy ran. "Would you believe that these foolish things try to die?" She frowned after seeing that Isaac, who had run a few feet, had stopped again and was watching them from the end of the shed. "Just when they are old enough to begin to produce, they get lice or rotten liver." She lunged, got one by the foot. The bird, flapping its wings upside down, fouled its belly. "See that sore place? They don't know any better than to scratch and peck until their insides fall out."

Siegfried nodded faintly. The heat was as dense as in the tin shack, and the ammonia smell was a thin knife in his nostrils. He knew he would die either of nausea or heat. He wondered if he could faint. Would she catch him, put cold water on his head?

"Come out," she said, tugging his hand. "Now let's go see the cow-shed."

Isaac mimicked the sound of the English words. The other children took it up.

"Lez see z'koshid!" Isaac shouted.

Zohar smiled automatically and tousled one child's hair. Isaac bumped against Siegfried.

"Z'koshid," he shouted in Siegfried's ear.

Zohar sighed. "They don't know what to make of him. I don't either. His accent is strange to them, he doesn't fight back when the others hit him, he laughs and runs away, but not because he is afraid of them."

Isaac circled just beyond Zohar's reach, like a wary animal. "Go play, Isaac, please."

"Koshid," he laughed, the sound of an old man coming from his mouth.

They walked on a path where the bushes lay obscured by gray dust, but here and there glinted a bone-white thorn. It seemed to

Siegfried that the cows were floating feet down in a sea of dung. He wondered they didn't sink and drown. Flies swarmed on their flanks and udders, long tongues flicked into nostrils, dung-coated tails swished at the flies.

"The kibbutz," Zohar said, "produces all its own milk and meat; we export the best dried milk to Germany. Maybe you drank some when you were at home."

The young man looked at the smiling girl and wondered again whether she was making fun of him, tried to think what these cows or people had to do with him, with a decision vaguely recalled. What would Zohar do, for example, if the children banded together with Isaac to throw him in the quicksand of dung? To change the direction of his thoughts, he asked, "What kind of work do you think I might really do?"

"Maybe they will put you here," she grinned. "You wash off the cows and put the milkers to them. Sometimes you clean stalls, and always there is hot milk. Would you like some now?"

"No. No, thank you very much. No." There was a roar. He jumped.

"It's Dov on the tractor," Zohar said, squinting into the sun. "He must be going to the banana plantation. Dov!" she waved.

Isaac ran to the big man, who jumped from the saddle of the tractor throwing at the same time his broad-brimmed Stetson at the boy. When Siegfried and Zohar came close enough to hear him, Dov took Isaac's arm and whispered loudly in English: "Tell me, how goes the atoning business?"

Isaac shrugged and grinned.

"Does it prosper?" Dov hissed theatrically. "Beware the Canadian dog that's friend to true love and brotherhood, he'll dig up a rotted ankle bone, bring it to you in his own mouth and ask you to love it." He pointed Isaac at Siegfried. His face close to Isaac's brown almost pointed ear, he asked seriously, "Is that a penitent messiah or is it not?

I am only a laborer, Isaac, I don't know the theory of loving my neighbor. The German comes to teach us how to love each other. Tell him, Isaac, how Shlomo loves me, with his crooked foot, how you loved your mother and father stinking dead in the ditch. Tell Zohar how to love Arabs of any color or creed." His voice trembled while he smiled and held on to the small boy. "Tell him!"

Isaac peered into Dov's face, looking for a clue to Dov's hushed choked words in the unfamiliar language. "Z'koshid!" he yelled. He ran and jumped on Siegfried's back, crammed the hat down on his head and jumped away before the German could move.

"Dov! Take him away," Zohar said. "No," she sighed, "leave him with me and take the German with you. It's time for the children to go back to the house."

"All right, we'll make a little tour before supper. Get on." He gunned the motor. The tractor trembled, plunged down a deeply rutted path. Afternoon sun chipped pieces of light into shadow under the trees, the dust closed solid behind them.

Siegfried felt like a rubber toy on a spring. Dov kept talking, gesturing to one side or another, but Siegfried could not hear more than fragments.

"There's no chance of . . . . when we were near the end . . . . never a second chance . . . ."

They stopped under green leaves so wide they blotted out the sky. The air itself dripped. In Siegfried's mind the puzzle began to fall together, buzzing with the flies and gnats around his ears.

Dov motioned Siegfried to jump off. He followed Dov down a narrow corridor between the bulging greasy-looking stalks. Ropy tendrils dangled between leaves that ended in flickering green clusters of bananas.

There was the snick of something metallic. Siegfried saw Dov pull a curved, long blade from a scabbard. The action consumed an infinite amount of time. Siegfried wondered if the metal had been tempered in a German steel plant. He saw minutely the pattern rust made on the metal. In his bones he felt the weight of the blade. Time stood and waited politely, as it had done all of his life. Would it move now? Siegfried felt almost relieved that something of permanence and importance would now be decided, even if it meant the end of his travels.

The blade swung, a stem of bananas fell on Siegfried's feet.

"The trick is to aim," Dov laughed. "Did you taste any Jewish bananas yet? Pick one, that's all right, just get out from under, they're sweet, even the green ones. Was I going to kill you? Wishful thinking! For that you need a friend! Is that what you came for?" He thrust a banana into Siegfried's hand.

Siegfried peeled it automatically, dropped the skin, then felt he should put it somewhere. He stooped and then felt too weak to get up again, empty as the banana skin. "But Dov's hands are empty too," he thought, surprised. "That was a child's trick to play on me, no better than what Isaac does, maybe for the same reason!" He looked quickly up at Dov, who was cleaning the blade of his long machete. "Empty! Even with his tractor, his jokes, he offers bitter bananas, tricks." He could get up.

Insects and water resumed their humming and dripping. Dov sighed, perhaps reacting to the young man's standing suddenly straighter and taller than he had seen him before. "Shlomo may be able to help you. Where is he putting you up for the night?"

"He's letting me sleep in his office."

"Good. We'll go back now. I'll get you soap and towel."

Dov drove slackly. The sun printed vague bands of pink and white clouds in the dusty air. Siegfried held one streamer of cloud in his eye, stretched it over him, and tried to connect it to the lights of the kibbutz. As the tractor approached the buildings, Siegfried grieved to feel the onset of another kind of dissection, this one also familiar. He gripped the tractor seat hard to avoid the sensation of being ejected like his banana skin, half to the sky, half to the earth. It was the agony of being torn in pieces by the desire to live by ideas or to dance naked and thoughtless before the unknowable. He remembered a real girl whose river of hair had fallen across breasts. He had tried to speak to her of love, philosophy, truth, but he trembled with the desire to rip off all their clothes and dance together naked and then lie down and join their bodies.

A dissection was essential. But what would have to go? And having chosen, would he be a fool?

Dov stopped the tractor. Siegfried's flesh knitted again. "I'll get you a towel." They walked again past cow-shed and chicken-shed, up the hill by Shlomo's empty window.

Siegfried stumbled, barely able to sense the heavier obscurity in front of him that was Dov.

A faint light from naked bulbs strung on poles came on slowly, dimmed, steadied, slithered around tree trunks and threw shadows from one side of the path to the other.

"Come in," Dov called, approaching a detached wooden hut. He switched on the light, threw his rifle on the bed. Siegfried leaned against a wall.

The room was bare except for the bed, a cupboard and table covered with books, a portable short-wave radio on the floor, and a print of a Roman or Greek temple tacked to one wall.

"Come on. Shlomo will be there waiting for you."

Siegfried was on the point of asking, "Does everybody bathe together, even women? Do you scrub each other's backs?" He was afraid that in the shower he would feel more alien, since he imagined that for the rest of them nakedness was probably as anonymous as fur. "Let me wait here for you," he said out loud. "I don't need a shower."

"Oh, yes you do," Dov smiled. "These are Israeli showers, with real water. You don't meddle in cow-sheds and what all without bathing. We all baptise ourselves every evening. Don't worry, in this communion service, nobody will pay any attention to you."

Siegfried didn't move. "You are our guest," Dov said, "now that you are here, that is, and this is part of being a guest." He threw Siegfried a piece of soap, shouldered the rifle, and called briskly, "Let's go."

They were instantly swallowed by darkness that was filled with the thin voices of thousands of small living things that went silent as they passed by. The two men were moving islands of temporary silence.

Siegfried shuddered. "If I stop," he thought, "I'll be attacked; they will bite my feet, crawl up my pants, suck my blood." He hurried to stay close to Dov.

Up the path a brilliant light appeared, the two bathhouses. Underfoot swarmed more thousands of insects. Other insects crept out of the shadows, collected the dead, and disappeared again.

Groups of loud-talking men smelling of the earth stood around the entrance to the shower. Dov smiled or nodded a response to men who greeted him but made no move to introduce Siegfried. The men looked at Siegfried without curiosity.

They entered a bamboo-screened enclosure. Siegfried tried to pull his shirt over his head with the top button closed. For a moment he was trapped inside his shirt, surrounded by the acrid smell of his fear. He tore the button off with the shirt. Dov hadn't noticed; he was removing his trousers. Siegfried threw all his clothes in a basket and stood naked. His head was empty.

"Naked came I into the world . . . . from Job," Dov said, pushing Siegfried ahead of him into another room, with basins and mirrors on the walls and stalls of showers.

Siegfried was surprised to feel hot water on his skin. He avoided looking at Dov opposite him.

Dov waved a soapy hand. "Hello, Shlomo ben Adam. You're late. Here's your protege. I didn't eat him up. He was cleansed in the green blood of the banana plantation."

Shlomo nodded his shy grimace, limping to one of the stalls. Siegfried saw the reason for his pain: his foot and ankle were fused.

By the time the three men were finished dressing night was a dense mold, stars could have been tiny holes in an iron sieve.

"Now we eat together." Dov made the announcement as though conducting dull officials through an asylum.

"Don't expect to see Zohar," Shlomo said, "she eats with the children."

"Yes, I thought so, thank you."

"We eat," Dov continued, "in a common dining hall, except for the feeble, children, and the very religious. For differing breeds, we provide exceptional accommodations, even unto work chairmen."

"Who's a different breed?"

Dov was silent.

"Why must you continue this campaign?" Shlomo persisted. "So it's not easy to live together. We try to consider everyone's feelings and needs and so some eat separated from others. Where should I go to eat, Dov? Or the German, where do you want him to eat?"

"He should break bread with every group, since you haven't arranged for him to bathe with all of them—"

Siegfried's face flamed in the dark.

"—even with purest love in your heart. And why not? Everything in the kibbutz is community property. Has Shlomo mentioned that aspect to you. We share everything here."

"That's not true!" Shlomo cried. "You distort everything."

"Yes, naturally you are in the right, Shlomo ben Adam, I should not have put it quite that way. Everything is available, but first you must earn your right to it. It's something like the Christian purgatory. You can lay claim to property rights, when you have been initiated."

"Who gives the initiation, you?" Shlomo asked.

"When time comes for initiation," Dov said softly, "someone appropriate sees to it, and that one may even be the least likely candidate."

Siegfried felt trapped between these two raw nerves, sharing their single sheath. He was enclosed in their common prison.

Dov pushed back his tray and tipped his chair. "Shlomo, is the concert in Tel Aviv being broadcast tonight?"

"You know it is."

"What are they playing?" Siegfried said, glad to be able to ask a question.

"The main piece is Schoenberg's *Verklaerte Nacht.*"

"Schoenberg!" Dov exclaimed, "another German transplant, transfigured by love. Have you read Thomas Mann, Siegfried? He wrote about Isaac and Joseph and sacrifice while he lived comfortably in exile on one of the magic mountains of California. In your company we will especially enjoy Schoenberg, since even after a day with us you must still learn a little more about love."

"Us!" Shlomo retorted. "The authority on music, love, and everything else—an intellectual!"

Dov smiled distantly. "Well, Siegfried, do you come to my house to listen? Are you coming?" he asked Shlomo.

"I'm coming."

"Shlomo has a radio of his own, but Zohar comes too. I don't think she listens very closely to the music, but she knits and she beats time, and she is good to have there. I will ask her to come and get you. In an hour." He took their trays and left the table.

"Come with me," Shlomo said. In his office a camp cot lay on the floor. "Someone will bring up bedding. I can't guarantee you more than a few days. I haven't talked to anyone on the work committee yet."

"Thank you." Siegfried felt that the little man was thirsty for his thanks, now that they were alone. "I will appreciate whatever you can do for me."

"You can assemble the cot. Zohar will come."

"But I can find Dov's house by myself. She doesn't have to bother about me."

"She will come for you," Shlomo answered abruptly.

Siegfried listened to the sound of Shlomo's uneven footsteps until insect noises swallowed them. He looked out the door into the night, a pool of black water. As he began to fit together the pegs of the camp bed, a shadow fell over the room. A moth beat in erratic spirals against the bulb. Siegfried drew taut the canvas of the cot and lay down without removing his shoes, meaning only to rest for a moment while he waited for Zohar. Instead, he slept.

The sound and shadow of the moth grew in Siegfried's sleep; its hairy body and dusty wings brushed against his throat, flew up, and flung itself into his mouth. He choked, his throat worked but could not move, he would die if he couldn't get it out.

He rushed to the cabin door, struggling to throw off the dream. He heard noises while fumbling with the lock. A cone of light from the cabin crystalized Zohar with terrible clarity. She was shrinking from a figure in Arab head-dress and robe. As the light struck him, he leaped toward Zohar with a wild cry.

Mouth and eyes filled by ash of moth, Siegfried remembered "Someone will initiate you." He found and caught up a stone, and for an eternity the wild glittering while at the same time soft, baffled eyes of the Arab looked up through his own, asking Siegfried's own question, before the stone smashed into his face and closed his eyes.

"Siegfried!"

"Zohar!"

"He—" Siegfried began.

"What did—"

"He didn't hurt you?" Siegfried asked, teeth chattering, feeling he must fall, pulled down by his heavy hands.

"Siegfried," repeated Zohar, "what have you done?"

"What?"

"Siegfried, what did you see?"

He looked down at the huddled body. The white robes fell apart and were sheets; the Arab head-dress was a pillow case. Siegfried was at the end of a tunnel spinning chunks of Zohar's voice at him.

"Siegfried, what did you think?"

"I thought," he whispered, "I saw—"

"Wait," Zohar whispered, "don't talk now, wait inside. I'll run for Dov and Shlomo. Inside."

Siegfried faced the blank door. The body lay outside, lapped in the thick fluids of the night.

The body lay on the canvas cot, covered by the same sheet the boy had worn. Dov sat on the table, Shlomo at his chair. Zohar sat on a stool across from Siegfried, who leaned again on the wall.

"So it's Isaac again," Dov said.

"I sent him," Zohar said. "I couldn't bear for him to sit another minute in the story-circle tonight. I sent him here with sheets for the cot."

"He was like an Arab," Dov said. "It was easy for the German to make the mistake."

"He always, always pounded on the wall of my office to annoy me," Shlomo said.

"He never let me get near him," Zohar said, "he made everybody nervous, his accent was different, he never would tell us anything."

"Never has it been healthy for children to make jokes like that here," Dov said. "Children should play tricks on other children." He looked at Siegfried. "Why don't you sit down? You killed him, one of ours. Sit down anyway. You thought he was an Arab, and Zohar had to be protected, didn't she?"

Siegfried nodded.

Shlomo turned a bitter face at Dov's mocking tone. "He was willing, wasn't he? What do you do?"

"Shlomo, Shlomo, not now," murmured Zohar.

"Didn't he talk about duty? And treasures books and mocks real people? You don't exactly kill me with kindness. For what do I work here? Is it so much better than a Jew-hating Canadian town? I die either way. We all die, not just Isaac. Dov doesn't try, but I still bleed, I try. Do you care about that? You educated Europeans!" he yelled. "What do you know about a cripple in the Promised Land!" Shlomo's cheek twitched; he turned his face to the wall. "He came to atone, to put a ray of light in your hearts. To him you could give, or to Dov, Zohar."

"Did you want me to love you, Shlomo ben Adam?"

"No! I . . . ." Shlomo gasped, raised his fists and lunged at Dov. Dov reached and caught hold of his fists and held them until the little man sagged. Then, as gently as Zohar, he took Shlomo's shoulders and lifted him to his chair.

"Shlomo," Zohar said, "you know how much I care for you. You have been so good to me, coming for me after school when my mother and father were killed, bringing me things, pretending that it didn't hurt you to walk with me, because I was afraid to be alone. I love you, Shlomo, very much."

Shlomo shook his head.

"I love you more than I could have loved my own brother."

"That isn't what he wanted," Dov said.

"I know," she said. "I know it."

"Stop this!" Shlomo cried.

"You see, Siegfried, how much it costs to love?" Dov said. "Maybe it would have been better not to try to save Zohar?"

"Did you ever try to save me, Dov?"

"Did he need to kill Arabs for us?" Dov asked. "We kill each other enough. He came looking for a virgin to rescue from the dragon. A sentimental journey to release his soul. But even make-believe dragons pour blood and die, like Isaac. When you run after one bug you step on another. Here's the conclusion: don't throw stones, even to save your soul. Don't excite poor Shlomo with 'unselfish' love." He stopped and examined the back of Shlomo's head. "And leave the cripples alone!" He looked in turn into the other silent faces, turned and tapped Shlomo's shoulder. "So? What are the work orders, Shlomo?"

"What will happen now?" Zohar asked. "What will they do to him, Shlomo?"

Shlomo did not turn his head from the wall. The others stared at Siegfried, who stood quite still by the window's black hole.

Dov said, "What did Jesus say? 'Let him who is without guilt cast the first stone.' Yes? All right!" He flung the door open. "I will not pick up that stone."

Siegfried stared at him without comprehension.

Dov stood at the open door and waved. "Go on. Go. We will say you escaped. You can be over the border in a few minutes, even without knowing the country. The Arabs will welcome you; they like Germans. Tell them the truth, that you killed an Israeli. They'll hold you for a day or so, find out that it's true, and let you go. You can go on ,traveling."

"No, don't send him out. They'll kill him, like Isaac's mother and father."

Siegfried did not move. He looked at the open door. The night was solid, massed behind it, like troops.

"Shlomo," Dov pleaded, "you tell him. You tell him to go. It's no good here."

"Do what he says," Shlomo whispered to the wall. "You tried. It didn't work. It wasn't your fault. Go."

"It wasn't for you to rescue me." Zohar said. "I sent Isaac away, I did that."

Siegfried sighed. The room, which had been spinning since his hand dropped the stone and Isaac's head fell from his hand to the earth, slowly came to a stop while the people spoke. The walls were steady around him now, more solid than the night.

The spark, in the eye of the dead boy, asking him—no, telling him—something, even as it faded, fell back. The eyes had spoken, before they disappeared, before the body dropped the masquerade. That was now, time sped, not time entombed. Isaac's eyes burning away the ice. Isaac, all eyes in a face that jeered at some huge joke, not afraid to be the fool. With his life spilt, his laughter burned into Siegfried. The eyes said that it was good to play, to masquerade in sheets, and laugh. It said, the play is not nearly over when fool and lover are only disguised as executioner.

Siegfried stroked Isaac's ankle and bare dusty foot, and the darkness was for a moment perfumed.

They all sat, in the warm cabin, like a family that sits together to spend an evening.

The Inner Garden

There was an illegally high walled garden, which, along with other qualifications, probably attracted the unicorn in the first place.

It was obvious that he had investigated pretty thoroughly: there were two children, Shawn and Tina; two dogs, Baldor and Hillary, big dogs, with a family resemblance to the unicorn, probably awakening memories of a less complicated time, when he was related to many things. Two cats, with lively instincts, many instruments for the making of music, stringed, unstrung, and percussive.

Most important, everyone in the household moved around deliberately and nobody made sudden moves, the mother of the household was not able to move much at all, being confined to her bed. She was dependent on her children and husband and animals and instruments for reports of what was going on in the garden, and less important, in the figment of reality, like the supermarket, outside the garden.

The unicorn had been gone for quite a long time before he came to their garden.

Tina, when asked: "He just looks sad."

"Aww," said Shawn, "he's all right. He doesn't want to answer any stupid questions. From you."

The unicorn asked for some plaster for the garden walls, which were in pretty bad shape, and Shawn picked up the dog dirt without being asked. Tina got a paint brush and tied it to the unicorn's horn.

They all painted the walls some color that nobody around there had ever seen before.

Then the unicorn scraped some pictures into the wet plaster.

Tina got a letter from an ice cream establishment wishing her a happy birthday and the unicorn opened the letter.

It was a happy birthday, but the unicorn didn't eat a thing.

"He looks sad, Mother," said Tina.

"Aww, he's too busy to fool around," said Shawn.

The dogs were, at first, on their extreme dignity in the presence of the unicorn, who received them sitting down. They sniffed at the horn and lay down with the unicorn in the corner he had decorated.

The cats arched their backs, but did not bristle, and they hummed.

The unicorn took the strings from one of the stringed instruments and played music between the thighs of the female dog. He seemed to be thinking of other tunes when he did this. The female dog, Hillary, did not mind. Her large reddish nose curved over her head and she listened to the music.

Baldor laid one large paw over the unicorn's hinder leg.

"We have to be careful not to touch the horn," Tina reported to her mother. "It's very sharp. When he puts his head in my lap he is awfully careful to put the horn on the left hand side."

"I'm not afraid of his horn," said Shawn.

"He won't say how old he is," said Tina.

"Older than the hills," said Shawn.

The unicorn pawed and paced in front of the wall and looked up sometimes at the rubber tree that curled like his horn.

Tina decorated his head with rubber-tree leaves and pomegranate blossoms.

"She makes a mess, Mom," complained Shawn.

"You put on too much and it all falls off," retorted Tina.

Grass grew very thick in the garden and ropy shrubbery began to grow, and it was very private and invisible from the street.

Sometimes the unicorn was visible in the dark.

Sometimes all the animals and instruments were visible too.

Even Tina and Shawn began to glow in the dark. But basically, it was what was usually inside that showed outside in the dark. The unicorn was always like this: his veins and bones stood out and pulled and pushed the way things do inside the body; only with him, all the activity was visible.

"I asked him, did you ever get married?" reported Tina.

"Boy, was that a dumb thing to ask him," said Shawn.

Tina was growing up.

The dogs were uneasy, and the cats, because the unicorn avoided Tina. Tina was hurt and Shawn taunted her because the unicorn moved aside and pretended to be busy with some project or other when she bounced into the garden after school.

Her veins were not showing so much, because she was becoming plump and womanly. Her form was filling out, although she skipped rope and starved herself, so that the mother had to be firm, on the advice of her doctor.

Tina came in to her mother with a white face. "Wouldn't it be awful," she said in a hushed voice, "to live forever?"

Shawn was outside riding on the unicorn's back. The unicorn seemed to listen for Tina's voice in her mother's room.

The unicorn's horn appeared sharper as he pawed, and it thrust like a shining blade in the air. Shawn threw him a pomegranate and the horn sliced it so cleanly that the whole fruit fell down in one piece and opened on the ground, spilling the bright red seeds in a little cascade.

On the unicorn's horn hung little drops of red nectar that trickled down his neck and mane. The cats crept up and lapped it with their

74

little tongues that looked like pomegranate seeds.

The flanks of the unicorn heaved as though the air were buzzing with heat.

Tina hesitated. She tried to speak to Shawn. "Wouldn't you like to live with the unicorn forever?"

"Sure," said Shawn.

"I mean," she said, "if we were all married."

"Aww," scoffed Shawn, "the unicorn's a boy. You'd have to marry him, and he wouldn't want to marry you!"

Tina dipped her foot and pointed it at the floor. She was growing up and everything that had been on the surface was now buried and deep very far inside her.

In the night Tina tiptoed to the unicorn's corner.

The figures on the walls glowed and cascaded and leaped over each other. The horn glowed like a bonfire of pearls.

The unicorn snorted and reared to his feet.

Tina calmly advanced on him.

The veins and sinew of him were bright flashes colliding in the heavens.

The unicorn trembled, but Tina was still, deep down inside herself.

The horn dipped, Tina held her breath and closed her eyes.

From all silence to the noise and sudden movement, not anybody could have foretold. Shawn reared up in bed, and it was like fireworks outside.

"Mom?" he cried.

He thought he had heard his mother's voice outside, but that was impossible. He jumped out of bed and ran to her room; the bed was empty. He ran outside and Tina was crouched, holding her eyes.

And his mother lay strange and still in the middle of the garden. The unicorn was gone.

Doll's House

She wants to commission a doll's house for our little girl and I approve of the project, so long as certain criteria are met: there must be room enough for expansion of the family, but not enough room so that the neighbors will make fun of us for being ostentatious, or so that taxes rise to a point of no return.

For now, the builder will have to work through me before he sees my wife. I sit in my study and wait for the doorbell to ring. All other projects must hang fire because of the doll's house, but I hold my annoyance in abeyance.

My daughter is too young to play with the house. It will be my wife's plaything. She will live in it, so to speak. There will be hours of joy for her through this wooden contraption, which I will insist should be completely collapsible in case we have to move.

The furniture is also collapsible—tables, chairs, ironing board, refrigerator. Everything in this large house can fit into one room, 14x16, if necessary. Storage costs, moving costs, repair—I have taken them all into consideration. My desk alone does not collapse, although the chair does.

She has already studied books on decoration in miniature. She has cut out pictures, pretend old ones, from the Sunday supplement. Curtains are a problem for her; she doesn't know whether to make real ones, or cut them from paper. I told her they have to be fire retardant. She is thoughtful.

I enjoy harpsichord and virginal, she likes piano. A piano is heavy and bulkier, except when it is upright. A harpsichord can be as small as a portative organ, but costs more and is harder to keep in tune. I told her I will learn to tune the virginal, but she tosses her head and mentions the grass. I will buy a gas-powered lawnmower as soon as one is available that allows one to use the motor for other purposes when not needed for cutting grass. I will not be moved on this point.

The designer and my wife have many conferences. I sit in my study at my desk. She comes out beaming with another idea—the animals will live upstairs, just as in a Swiss farmhouse, with a ramp leading from ground level to the second story. The cross-hatched effect can be achieved with black gummed paper. All well and good. The animals will provide warmth with only a small inconvenience of odor. What about vermin? How soon can it be done? It has taken an amazing amount of time already. What if we should need it in a hurry? The cost of materials has climbed almost 65% since the start of construction. I ask my wife to speak very straight to the designer and contractor. We don't have forever. I am not precisely a young man. How stupid it would be if my daughter grew up and married and moved to another country before her doll's house was completed.

Now that there is more than plans, there is the house growing on its foundations, they whisper even when they are alone. They are delaying completion on purpose. They do not allow my daughter to see the plans any more.

I begin to understand the scheme. I asked the builder where my study is to be. He scratched his head. He doesn't know. Maybe one of the upstairs rooms is the study? It doesn't look like it to me. There are no windows north-facing in a room of appropriate size. Nothing upstairs. Downstairs, all rooms have been spoken for.

There is no study in the house! I will not make my move too

hastily. There may be some explanation after all. Maybe she knows I would prefer one on the property, but not in the house proper, giving me more privacy in our growing family.

That's it. She has confirmed it. There will be a small study (I overlooked the place) in the house, but a larger one, free-standing, in the orchard. Where will the orchard be? I haven't bought the trees yet, she said. They're not in stock. What kind do you prefer? Oranges, I say, can they make the oranges in wood? In orange-wood, she laughed. She's very easy about it now.

The place I overlooked is obviously a pantry or large broom closet. There is no way it could possibly be a study. There is no room there for anything. She has deliberately cut the study out of her plans for the house. I don't see any free-standing structure going up. And even if it were, it wasn't included in the cost analysis, it wasn't in the original plans, it isn't anywhere. So here I sit, waiting for them to tell me what I already know.

I will wait a little while longer. My daughter is so thrilled with the charming thing that she will scarcely leave it for a minute. I need a time when she is away, when she takes her dolls out of the rooms to play with them. She is growing rapidly. She argues with my wife about furnishings and picture placing. My daughter favors Whistler.

I cannot wait any more. There is no place for me. I have been systematically removed from the new house. She only awaits a convenient moment to get rid of me. And so I will move first.

Post Coitus Tristus

I am 54 years old, conductor of a semi-professional symphony orchestra in a large American city, married. I still speak in a charming Viennese accent after 20 years. So late in my life I am in love with one of my own sex, a young man.

When he first made suggestions to me, I was furious. I nearly threw him out of my sight. He saw something in me, saw that I was suffering, but I did not recognize the nature of the pain until it was too late for me. He offered me an unselfish hand, a gift I had never before had offered to me.

I have kept many women in my life. I could never bear to be without one. But the novelty and the pursuit were always the most enchanting parts. Once, like fish, safely landed, women lose their glitter and begin to smell. They demand, they protest, they whine, they cry—there is nothing that can remain unexplained and unspoken. If I could have retained the silent communion with other males I had as a boy and young man! But guilts and repressions crept in. After all, it was the age of Freud. I had to prove myself.

Innocence is lost when one takes up with women. As boys, we walked arm and arm, we touched freely. Boys slept together until an advanced age. We engaged in every kind of activity together, bathed naked in rivers, wrestled naked on the banks, and thought nothing of it.

Did I experience any extraordinary thrill from these contacts? I don't think so.

My hair was not cut until I was six years old and ready to go to school. It was the custom. I look at pictures of me, girlish, cute, with long eyelashes. What about Oedipus? Did I hate my father and want to sleep with my mother? But I did sleep with my mother, every night my father was away on business. Even, I put my head on her bare breast when she was ill or sad to see if she was breathing.

The memory of her flesh arouses me even now. When I gave Laura perfume my mother used, the chemistry of her body reacted to it in the same way, and I was enormously excited; yet I did not hate my father. The sight of his heavy penis and testicles filled me with wonder, but they did not disgust or attract me. He did not handle or beat me. He was a kind man, a little fat, given to Turkish baths (which did not have a bad name in Europe), and wore a little moustache that he cultivated as carefully as my mother kept her long hair.

They were happy, I think. Why not? In well-ordered households, relationships were formal and we did not feel the depression after the Great War. We were envied and respected. I went to school and, when the time came, I masturbated together with my friends. We used French postcards. I believe I am not deluding myself when I call these activities normal.

When I was 16 we went to a whorehouse, a well-known establishment, furnished in red-flocked wallpaper and deep carpets, an altogether proper place, suitable for upper-middle-class boys. There I had my first experience, a willowy country girl who spoke German with the soft rural dialect superior people find charming.

I was not afraid. Rather, I felt like protecting the girl, and I knew what to do. Though I was excited and our contact was brief, I was prepared for that and felt no shame. Moreover the rest of the boys were long since waiting for me, because of the time I took to talk to the girl. She was so grateful that I had a fantasy of her becoming my mistress, but of course I had no money of my own and so it came to nothing. I never went back.

I wondered what happened to her during the war. Did she find someone and leave the house, or was she one of those sent near the front to service Hitler's troops as a field whore? I pictured myself in her place, spread out on a pallet, muddy, brutal soldiers trampling into my cubicle, falling on my body, not taking off anything but their boots, grinding into me with their massive organs. Was it horror or anticipation?

My orchestra is composed of doctors and lawyers, accountants, housewives even, but we have a very good reputation; we have been written up in national magazines, an indication of a "cultural renaissance" in America, a blend of "Old World and New." Very gratifying, like the consolation prize in a circus. I am second-rate, I knew it early. Laura knows it, but she never said anything when we listened to Toscanini, then the younger conductors like von Karajan, Boulez or others. My musicians are good, however, and they come to rehearsals sometimes at tremendous sacrifice, and when they call me "Maestro," I don't flinch.

Laura is like a large, sleek cat, pardon the hackneyed expression. She comes of very good family, we have an excellent relationship—only she is so healthy! Her abundant health is not quite an insult, yet sometimes I imagine she is dead, and I can weep openly, everyone sympathizing. She lies in a coffin, top part like a dutch door open and surrounded by the roses she spends so much time tending. I weep and weep. People take me by the shoulder to comfort me.

But then, what do I do the night of her death? A heroine in a novel of Thomas Hardy had a rendezvous for a ball and so she locked the door on her dead husband and went. Mostly I think I would seek one of the parties, orgies rather, to which I am now welcome, on account of my daughter. "My wife is dead," I might say. Someone would swivel his leg, hand me a drink, and announce: "I'm *so* sorry, darling. *Do* have a drink, it's the only thing." I would be drunk, pass out. A stranger might take me to bed out of kindness. Or maybe I would wake to find the clear face of my own young man, his arms cradling my head.

This is only fantasy; I have many. My life has stood in their way.

This is the way life has been: Laura sighs and snores a little. It's hot and we are covered by a single sheet. Her belly is convex. She has always been voluptuous, like a thick spring. When I was 25, playing in a good orchestra, a young musician on the way up, she came to hear me every night. I noticed her, thinking the situation very like stories one reads in the lives of musicians of great note. Later came nights in hotels—wonderful, wet, slippery nights of lovemaking. Then she was pregnant. I offered to marry her immediately but she refused and had an abortion entirely on her own, and told me only weeks later. I was horrified—but, now that I think about it, I was more excited by an image of a strange man, I don't know whether a doctor even, pulling Laura's legs apart, opening her up, inserting his hand and instruments into her. I shiver!

She had no ill effects. In her own good time, we married.

When we were about to leave for America, she was again pregnant. This time, I wanted her to have an abortion, because I was involved with one of the girls in the orchestra. Laura sat at home with the roses, giving piano lessons, and waiting, big and pregnant. When I came home she always had drinks prepared, then she would stretch her fleshy arms for me to kiss her, and I would have to fall into bed with her, sharing space with my unborn daughter. I liked bed, even Laura's body, but at that time I did not want to fall into bed with her.

My girl friend was Jewish, skinny compared to Laura, with exquisite nervous breasts. She was so hungry, so passionate, that she initiated almost every movement, she made love to *me*. But I was

82

young, I didn't mind, it posed no threat. But she was not able to achieve a climax. Sometimes, when I could hold no longer, she continued on, pushing and rubbing us both raw.

"I won't be any man's mistress," she told me. "What do you want of your life? Do you love Laura? Do you want to stay with her?"

"I don't love her."

"Then do you get pleasure from sleeping with her?"

I would squirm and have to answer, "Yes, I try to leave her alone, but when it starts, I enjoy it."

I thought, married to this girl, what would be my life? Now, it was exciting and illicit. She had so many questions I became evasive. I didn't want to think about complications, about love. But we clung to each other. She was definite about her future, *our* future together, with her intense black eyes, her hands always alive. She expected great things of me, especially if I left Laura; she saw that I was stagnant. She herself practised through the night on her piano after I left her to go home to Laura's arms and bed.

I'm sure Laura knew all about the affair. We continued to make love, and she had those deep climaxes along with a great muscular control that pulled me into her in such a wave I have not experienced with other women. It should have been delicious.

We left for the United States. The Jewish girl escaped to South America and became a famous soloist. We corresponded and met again, in New York, when she finally came to the U.S. during the war. She was still thin and nervous, dressed in a mannish suit with lapels. We made love awkwardly, almost as a duty to our past and to our impassioned letters. I had only dreamed of running away with her. My life was already hopelessly compromised and lackluster. We had lost our chance long before. Rather, I had.

I always fell back on my comfortably demanding Laura, never truly ever leaving the nest. I took what came easily. I never shook life by the shoulders. If I had been a hero, I would have broken with the past, but the affairs I have had with life have been just a long coitus interruptus. I have had good jobs, a beautiful wife, security, and then a lovely daughter. But my love affairs have ended ridiculous.

I was alone in our hotel room. Laura was out having her hair done. The hotel was not a very good one, and our bathroom had a common air vent with the bathroom in the next room. While I was there, I heard voices, so I got up on the rim of the tub and looked into the next room. I saw two men clasped in each other's arms, kissing. I had a vision of a Rodin statue and fragments of all the romantic music I had ever played.

I have always been a voyeur, hoping to see naked women at their windows. Now, stirred and ashamed, I watched—only, it was nakedness of a higher order. I was not ashamed or disturbed at this act of homosexuality. I was stirred because it looked like an act of *love*. The men were *in* love.

Before this I had sneered at young homosexuals walking hand in hand in the park. The young man I had turned away played in my orchestra. He used to wait for me to help to put away something, he wanted to talk, he seemed to want to make me his father confessor. I misunderstood. Even at 40 or 45, I meant to be young. I was piqued that the young man didn't want *me* as I am, instead of my counsel, like a desexed old woman. I didn't want to be his father confessor. Finally when he brought another young man to meet me, obviously involved with him, I let them know that I felt them to be abnormal, all the time imagining what they did together. I didn't know I was jealous, or rather, that I wanted him. I could have learned slowly what unselfish love can be.

I never had a *love* affair. I made love, enjoyed doing it, but it has been always like a mutual masturbation. Clearly this was how it was with the Jewish girl. With Laura I performed faithfully, not a virtuoso, but adequate. Now I am tired and afraid. The deception is that I *love* to do it. I believed that I loved the women with whom I have slept, but I have found no love; yet, Laura continues to bloom. Whereas I am not more than six, seven years older, I am mistaken for her father—thin, pot-bellied, with eyes sunken and cheeks hectic when they are not chalk-white. I walk with a quick, nervous step mistaken for boundless energy, but when I go home to be faced with Laura, my unhurried Laura, with her endless smile, her ample bosom and overflowing bloom, I begin to suffocate.

To avoid her everlasting amorous digestion, I more and more rehearse, hold conferences, guest conduct. I am more frantic, my music is always the same. My eye is out for a savior, someone or something to expel me from my dead alley. The truth is, I am more exasperated by lack of variety than intimidated by Laura's inexhaustibility. I am sure there exists in homosexuality infinitely more variety, more chance of connection and communion in the love that is between men.

But my young man left the orchestra and never returned. I have sat, his phone number on my pad, for hours, then torn it up into long, narrow strips.

My daughter, also a musician, plays in my orchestra when I need her, but she prefers coffee houses. She brings young poets home. I began to notice them and to sit with them in the living room. Many were homosexual. I went with my daughter and a young man to a coffee house where he gave a reading of a long poem that among many incomprehensible items celebrated the orgasm. There was no ambiguity in his poem concerning the partners between whom the most exalted orgasms occur.

We later sat at a table, the three of us, the boy in the middle, our knees all touching. In my solar plexus grew a nervous excitement to feel his thin, young knees on my legs and thighs. I was even experiencing the thrill, at second hand, of touching my daughter's legs. It is true among humans, even as with animals, that offspring arouse a parent as no mere stranger can do. My teeth chattered and my skinny shanks trembled all evening. Was I catching a cold? My daughter and her friend were solicitous, while she smiled her knowing smile.

I had occasion to travel to New York. Near Greenwich Village is an avant-garde movie house, which shows gay movies. The place was full of bearded young men, and what was worse, bearded older men. Nobody looked clean; everybody looked artistic. In my white shirt and tie I was as conspicuous as possible. And yet, am I not as artistic as most of them?

Next door was a Turkish bath. I had not been near one since my father took me as a child; yet I know their reputation in the United States. Weak and trembling, I walked away and turned into a coffee shop. I could hardly breathe. A slender long-haired girl, like an actress, took my order.

The Turkish bath sign flashed on and off in my mind. I had to go back. I finished my coffee, spilled change on the counter, climbed stairs, put money on another counter, and tried to ignore men who sat with legs spread, towels around their waists. I was shown to a locker and my "resting" room.

Certainly this was not a place where two true, male lovers would go? What was it but a whorehouse with men as inmates? The corridors were dim. I stepped into a steam room where I felt many eyes explore me, but I looked back at no one. I went out, showered, and walked upstairs. Men lay on cots in an open dormitory and also behind partly closed doors in little cubicles. Others prowled the corridors. Sometimes one man nodded to another and they both disappeared into a cubicle. There was no question in my mind about what they were doing. The only question was: did I want to do that too?

I turned a corner, and on a cot in view of several silent spectators was a couple locked to each other's organs. I was rooted to the floor. Then I turned, and with trembling fingers found my locker and threw my clothes on. I was sick with the desire to look on and then allow someone to draw me into one of those dark holes, to do whatever he pleased with me.

I got out, but I knew with sickening clarity that I would be back, if only to test the thing to its very end.

I remember with pain that once the young homosexual musician gave me a massage in my hotel room. We were on tour and my muscles were taut and painful. I was in shorts when he knocked softly on the door and apologetically told me he had noticed my twisting and turning my neck and shoulders. Could he give me a massage? His hands were tender and searching, as Laura's never were. Most good masseurs are men. But his hands also secretly caressed. This was before I turned him and his friend away, of course. He could have been one of the men in the bathroom. The massage never went beyond propriety. "Put your hands all over me," I should have said, to save my soul, to put unspoken desire in the open. I didn't have the courage to say it.

Before the war, I traveled through France with a friend. We stayed at youth hostels. In early spring there were not many other travelers, so we had a big room with many bunk beds all to ourselves. After an exhilarating day of mountain-climbing, drinking and eating, we lay after taking cold showers in the empty room. I knew he was still awake, and now I realize he was waiting for something. My teeth began to chatter, I didn't know why, or perhaps I did.

"Are you cold?" he asked me.

"Not so much. My teeth are clacking a little."

He didn't say anything more. I was in expectation that he would. Pine trees scraped at the windowpanes, the ground was wet with disappearing snow. This was all before I was married, and I had a hot-blooded girl waiting for me in Vienna. I suppose I was shivering with desire for the girl. But perhaps it was not her I wanted so much as wanting to be able to want her.

Young men are pliant, even more feminine than a woman like my wife, who is not much womanly as catlike, as I mentioned before. Young homosexual men are fine and delicate. I grow older but not impotent, only reluctant. I want all of me drawn into lovemaking, like a fugue. I want a fugue that is not predictable. I want the thrill of the unexpected, but I never burn bridges. Romanticism is what has made of me a second-rate musician and third-rate human being. I fear the unpredictable and crave it.

My friend was not a known homosexual, but could we not have lain sweetly in each other's arms all night without sin and without pain? It would have been the first and perhaps only time for us both. Instead, I turned him away with a bad joke and a pretended yawn, rolled over and shammed sleep. In the morning there was awkwardness. Before long, we invented excuses to terminate the trip early.

I am trying to write a confession, but it doesn't work. All is too reversible, too guarded, nothing is conclusive. I have not been found in "flagrante delicto," and some things I have not recorded out of shame. Here it is: I am 54 years old, cringe from my wife and cry in my heart for the pale, slender boy in whatever incarnation he may be hiding, and I fail, fail and fail again in my life and in my work, which does not interest me. The more desperate I am to know, to love, to *participate*, the more am I led into experimentation, and this is what destroys me, as I am immutably middle-class, bourgeois, and careful.

My daughter brought home another poet; I couldn't really tell about him. He invited all to a party, including Laura, in honor of the publication of his first book of poems. The usual type of crowd, Laura and I the only outsiders. I was introduced and some of the guests knew my name. I was feverishly aware of everyone around me. At once, here seemed a last chance, as though I might die if something conclusive were not to happen.

Laura soon pleaded headache, but urged me to stay on though I offered to accompany her home. I was drinking with some of the young men, who talked a private language, at which I smiled knowingly. I noticed that my daughter was looking at me, her eyes glowing, stimulated by the party or too much liquor.

I had to go to the toilet, knocked on the door, and hearing nothing, entered. There was a young man urinating. I mumbled an apology and began to back out, but he put out an arm. "Come on in, the water's fine. Don't mind me." My heart thumped, but I stood looking away while he shook himself. "Have a good one," he said, waiting for me to take mine out.

"Well," I said.

I tried, I couldn't. I couldn't take it out. In the dark, maybe. When I left the room, I was sober, my evening was over.

My daughter's young man brought over a lovely girl for me to meet. "This is Sally. She's attended your concerts for years. Say hello to Walter, Sally." He talked to her as though to a little girl. I was charmed. The top of her head came up only to my eyes, though I am not tall.

"I'm so glad to meet you," she said.

I made a ridiculously low bow. "I'm charmed to make your acquaintance."

We went out together several times, the poet, my daughter, Sally and me. One afternoon I called her and we had lunch alone in a small, charming place. We then visited a museum, outside which were exhibited straw huts reconstructed from prehistoric houses of the region. It began to rain. I scrambled up the plank into one of the houses. She was surprised but hobbled up after me when I put out my hand.

"Now we are living 2000 years ago," I explained, squatting and motioning over a fire. She was delighted. "Would you mind, would you find it very terrible," I said, "If I kissed you?" I put my arms around her shoulders and kissed her without waiting for an answer. Her lips were so yielding that tears came to my eyes. There was no hard demand, only response. We stood and kissed again.

Saying nothing at all, we climbed down from the hut and walked hand in hand in the light rain. I took her to a little hotel. She was so much smaller than my wife, almost a teenager! She was 30, 35 years younger!

"Don't," she said at first. "It's dangerous for me right now."

I asked her to wait, dressed, and went out to a drug store.

"Please, some prophylactics," I whispered. The clerk looked at me admiringly, or was I imagining? I hurried back to the hotel, but when the time came the lovely girl thrust the rubber appliance aside. We made *love*.

I cannot tell the long or the short of it. For this time, for the first time, it was unimportant. We lay and hugged each other and laughed and cried.

"I must call my wife. She will be wondering where I am."

"Shall I do it for you?" Sally laughed.

"Never mind," I said.

"Are you afraid of her?"

"I certainly am. Aren't most men afraid of their wives?"

"You're honest," she said, falling back and drawing me again on top of her. People have always thought that I am very honest.

At first, I was afraid that Sally would insist or demand or reject. I thought it might be better for me to court young men in a Turkish bath, where there is no fear of failure or disappointment. Sally lived with a room mate. It was difficult for us to arrange times when she would not be at home. Hotels are not satisfactory for long-term relationships. Even so, life! How it became fresh in my nostrils, and colors, like flavors, sharpened! My daughter smiled to see me bounce into a room. Now she introduced me to no new young men. And Laura, as long as she had her rations, was content.

But I began to feel that I must leave my wife, as it became harder and harder to part with Sally every time. But I was comfortable at home. To think of separating—piano, records, books, pictures, things Laura and I had accumulated. Everything upset. Who would own what? And I was afraid of Laura's rarely stirred anger.

Sally, feeling that we must know *all* about each other, revealed among other things that the car she drove was not hers but belonged to another boy friend. At my insistence, she offered him the keys, but he refused. I was intensely relieved. Would I have had to provide her with other transportation? She was determined to help me. She remembered a performance of one of my overtures, a highly imitative work: I would begin to write again. I would flower.

We went to all the romantic places Laura and I had worn out. Was I using Sally that the colors and flavors might be renewed? Did I love her, or was she again an instrument? But this question is vital to a man only when he is sure of the devotion of the other person.

"Do you always have to wear a tie?" she asked, a little irritated, masking it with a smiling shake of her pert head. We were dressing. I found it hard to be casually dressed.

But I wanted to take her to places where people her own age went. She frowned and made excuses; she found these places boring, the kids were too childish. Her homework, never before a problem, began to keep us apart.

"You have real elegance in your face and hands," she told me once. "But you've got to act your age."

I had not been rejected by a woman for many years, but I knew the signs. She still talked about my leaving Laura, but her encouragement had more the sound of my saving my soul *from* sloth than saving it *for* herself.

Secretly I was relieved—from the intensity, our honesty, her probing. I knew I would never be any better than I had come to be.

Sally wrote to let me know that her boyfriend, never really out of the picture, was now re-entered and clearly in focus, etc. It was better, etc. I didn't delude myself. I knew I had been a fool. Not love, but variety, that was what it had been about. All right then!

My daughter began again to take me to parties with her young men. It began to be accepted implicitly that we all slept together. The homosexuals greeted me like one of their own. After returning home from such a party I had sex with Laura in a kind of fury which she enjoyed quite as much as anything else. So she approved of my going to parties. She even invented situations so that young men could often be at the house. I was otherwise at loose ends.

I became an accomplice to other men's smallest physical acts. I suffered walking up stairs when someone's behind was on a level with my nose. I was in a sweat during rush hour when I was pressed together with the crowd. Where are my hands? Where are the hands of the person next to me? I noticed men hitching up their trousers. When I went to ballet, I noticed only the bulge of men's sexual organs. While I conducted I waited for the moment the french horn player emptied his saliva tube; I imagined being caught under the instrument. I began to look furtively at magazines that displayed muscular young men in shorts. In all this hysteria I hoped my young man would come back, bearing some sort of poultice that would end the fever and begin a cure.

Like a fool, I went to a tailor. I had always dressed conservatively, hoping to be "discovered" without calling attention to myself on account of my clothes. Now I saw it was because I had early given up competing. I had myself fitted in tight, thin pants and narrow jackets. My daughter admired me, Laura smiled and pinched my behind.

I had an impulse to expose myself in a crowd or faint. In a restaurant I saw a man dressed exactly like me, surrounded by smiling young men. His face sagged and his eyes were greedy. Like *Death in Venice*—finite, let the comedy end, I thought! I went, even in my new clothes, to confession—I had not gone since I was a child. The incense was like perfume, peaceful. The priest walked by to light candles. His robe swished as he bent to caress an altar boy. The sweet, sickish excitement was on me. I fled.

I recklessly drank too much at the party. Reeling and sick, I tottered into the garden. Let someone come to me now, I prayed. Let me be helped, let cool hands love me and bless me. Nausea rose and fell in my stomach. A young man was in front of me where I clutched a tree. He touched my hand.

"Anything I can do?"

"Get out of here," I yelled.

He went away, but came back with a cold towel and gently sponged my face. I nestled my face into his hand. He put his arm around me.

"That's all right now, isn't it?"

I felt he must kiss me, but I was repelled by my own sickness. He would get dirty. Would he be careful about personal hygiene? Yet, if he loved me, it would not matter. He half-carried me into one of the bedrooms where he fondled me as I lay in the dark. My daughter came to the door and stood whispering with someone.

I lay, cold and rigid. There was no love in me, nor echoes of love in any pore or inch of my soul or skin. I wept. The young man cradled me like a baby, and I wept. After a short, unconscious time, I put out my hand for him, but he was gone.

I staggered to the door. The guests had taken off most of their clothes, men were dancing with men. There were a few girls, in bras and panties. Where was my daughter?

In the bedroom, another couple had taken my place. I could make out little in the dark. I too lay down on the bed with them.

"Hey, get out of here. Can't you see we're busy?"—accompanied by a kick from one and a giggle from the other.

Were they making love? I stood and rearranged my clothes. I put on my tight fashionable jacket and closed the door behind me. As I stood in the light someone in only his shorts smiled at me.

"Why such a sad look, post coitus tristus? Try again."

Maybe my daughter will be coming home soon. There will be another party. She will bring someone home for me to meet.

The Contortionist

As this girl turned to me the wind came up again and blew her veil over her mouth. Her words seemed to come from a cave covered by a waterfall. I think I heard 'Irene' as she pointed to herself. I saw the words but I couldn't hear them.

My son was polishing a headlight chrome rim with steady strokes and paid no attention whether I stayed or went. He noticed the girl and probably knew her, or how else would he have known exactly where to take me—to this entrance, this parking lot, this school? I surely knew nothing of the place. There are thousands of such schools in the city, some of them disguised from the outside as office buildings, gasoline stations, restaurants—as with the famous nunneries in Mexico, hidden in the bowels of simple-looking structures.

"Don't you care where I'm going?" I querulously asked the son. "Why don't you look so that you can come after me when it's time? I'll be taken away as usual and god knows where I'll be put."

I addressed the boy to gain time. The woman's veil puffed in and out of her mouth like the tide between Scylla and Charybdis, although she seemed harmless enough on the whole, probably only suffering from asthma brought on by the wind, which must have had considerable dust in it, taking into consideration the state of the campus: deplorable. Holes everywhere, like a bombardment, with skeletons of new buildings and the skins of old buildings just torn down. Rather too close an analogy between my unconcerned son, his headlight, and me being led away by just anybody who happened

95

to be handy.

Temporary signs in a language I couldn't understand sloped everywhere, pointing it seemed contradictorily. One after another they leaned dangerously and fell with crackling noises into the wet muddy clay soil. I even slipped and slid as I stood, trying to muster my voice over the wind. I don't think the boy heard me, or he purposely continued his work anyway. I picked up a piece of mud, hurled it at him, and lost my balance at the same time. He was instantly at my side and steadied me just before my head could hit a rock jutting out nakedly from the soil. It seemed to be the cornerstone of some ancient edifice. I was ashamed and mumbled my apologies, but he was already back carefully flaking mud from the tire rim where I had accurately although accidentally thrown it. He waved at me, hopped over the door, threw the gears into reverse and spun the car back toward the automatic gate.

"Hey, wait," I cried. I ran forward a bit, but I felt the hand of the woman at my shoulder and heard her stentorian breathing through the veil.

"Come on," Irene said cheerfully, "it's not far." She threw the veil off her face and drew it in a brisk knot around her hair. "Thank god I can stop practicing for now. Have you ever tried to breathe through one nostril? With a cold? What stinking lousy weather for a reception. We had things so nice for you when all this came up." She waved her arm and crinkled her mouth. She was certainly a friendly open-looking creature.

"What place am I in?" I asked.

"You're in the lousiest parking lot of all, temporary unpaved B-11, where Administration used to be. It's over in North Campus now; nobody goes over there. The bungalows were moved from Metropolitan Campus. They were condemned, so they're at the junior high school now. Less weight on the floor. We keep the skinniest teachers for junior high. Nobody from home ec can teach there. That's how it became a university degree course—space and weight limitations. But that's history." She took me by the shoulder, guiding me like a horse.

"What will I do in this place?" I asked.

"O god, there's plenty of time for that. I'll just show you around if this goddamned wind doesn't blow us out to sea. As fat as you are, you're like a sail. I don't mean to be insulting. I like a well-fleshed man, he eats good. No offense meant."

I couldn't be offended by this cheerful, frank girl. Her face was as open as the sky, freckled, with a little cleft in her chin, a hint of one dimple on the left cheek, hair she kept pushing back into the veil, and a stiff slightly falling gait. The hand felt cold, because of the chilly wind, I supposed. I wanted to gallantly convey her hand to my own to warm it, but when I vaguely took my other hand (opposite the shoulder she gripped) and made to take hers, she waved it away.

"Then let's be off," I cried gaily, entering into the spirit of the thing. I had, after all, asked for this. It was an adventure, perhaps the only one that counted. I began to love the face of this girl, which was most like that of an intelligent baby carried on the back of its mother, observing the world through detached all-aware eyes, but with no memory to turn it into a miniature monster. I hoped that no ill-advised teacher would try to mold that head and mind into anything even vaguely retentive, spoiling and distorting it. Now it was healthy and wise in the way of the earth, picking its way around craters and the crumbling lips of excavations, standing sturdily against the increasingly violent gusts of wind.

"Through one nostril," Irene was saying, although I lost the half of her words. "That's the way it has to be done, with no time out, except for now, because I can't talk and breathe through one nostril, especially with a cold."

"Why," I shouted at her ear, "must you do that?"

"It's to train my organs," she shouted. "They're completely untrained. It's something like having inside legs and arms to make the organs do what you want them to do. It's spiritual."

Then I said something, but the wind completely carried the words away. She nodded sympathetically. I tottered under the worst buffet and began to slide into a ditch. She put out one arm as rigid as a stick and I grabbed it in sheer panic and began to climb it like a tree. She stood planted on the lip of the bank until I recovered my balance. I looked ruefully back on the black cavity and shuddered.

"Men working down that one. Don't worry. We'll get there."

But her words were doomed to inaccuracy. Before we knew it, even with the vision of friendly lighted windows in the new building ahead of me, I felt myself sliding without surcease, and the girl with me. 'Irene!' I cried, but it was no use. We tumbled head over heels, hard and soft, soft and hard, into the blackness.

And that was the last I knew for a while.

I came to myself in a half-dark haze, the dust settling; after a while I made out a candle, a blanket on which I was lying, and a blanket over me. I realized that I had no clothes on; they were draped steaming over some wooden members next to a fire. "Where are you, Irene?" I cried. "Are you all right?"

"Relax," I heard the girl say from somewhere. "Don't get excited."

Irene's voice was as calm as though we were still outside, but I couldn't see her. But then I could; she was so near me I was ashamed I had lost control and babbled for her. I cursed my female hysteria. She was sitting facing away from me, on the edge of the blanket, also without clothes. Hers too I noticed were steaming by the fire. I saw for the first time how a woman's back and buttocks are like a perfect full drop of water ready to fall on the earth, except here they were already against the earth, or at least the blanket.

"That was quite a fall," she said cheerfully.

"Yes," I said in a weak voice, the combination of circumstances rather overwhelming.

She made a peculiar jerking, jerking movement and turned to face me. At the same moment, I recognized the members the clothes were hanging on, the memory of the coldness of her hands and the strength of her legs came to me as I saw all of her. She was a smiling dimpled torso, smooth on all sides, rosy in the firelight, with red, or reflected red fiery pubic hair like a living pedestal on which she sat. My mind disappeared into the dark again.

"You can stop patting my face," I told her, "I'm perfectly all right."

"You really are," she said, admiring me. "Most times the shock takes days to wear off." She turned half around on her torso. She did it with little hopping movements, landing plump on her buttocks, which, as I stealthily snaked a hand around, I found to be hard as rocks.

She laughed. "I can make them any degree of give or take. Feel that one."

I touched it: like iron.

"I've taken care of those things; it's the interior organs that I breathe through the nostril for. Legs and arms you really don't need. It's true, you don't need them. Everything you need to do you can do sitting or lying, especially since I have those sticks—" and she jerked her head in scorn at the hands, arms, legs and feet holding up our steaming clothes— "to do the unimportant things."

It seemed to me that I had never seen so much flesh before. Irene was not a heavy girl, but where legs and arms join our bodies she had more flesh, more surface, more unobstructed area, all creamy and dimpled in the firelight. I realized that with our squirming twitching legs and arms, we must look like spiders to someone like this girl, who had been stripped to the most direct proportions. I reflected how legs must provide too much drainage for fluids to be really practical. I wondered if this girl would ever be able to find her ideal mate, a legless armless man. But how difficult! Hard enough to find someone of roughly the same economic, social, and intellectual background—but to add such very distinct and unique qualifications!

I hardly noticed at first shock, which took time to wear off—even though I was conscious—her breasts. I suspected that they must be more functional, taking over some duty from legs or arms, than at first appeared. "Can you do something special with your—your...?" How ridiculous to be squeamish, but it was my training.

"With this?" she cried cheerfully, nodding toward her glistening bush. "Certainly." She stooped, if you can stoop without legs, picked up an edge of the blanket, did a kind of skip and folded the edge neatly over the middle. "Throw that shoe at me," she ordered.

"I can't," I protested, "really," but I reached for the shoe and as gently as I could hefted it toward her. Into the air she went, caught it deftly with some incredible muscle she had there, and, in effect, leaning back, presented the shoe to me. I had the ridiculous feeling of being offered my slippers by a large woolly dog. I had only to pat it, saying, "Nice Fido," and take my slippers from its mouth to complete the picture. And it was obvious that she wanted, even needed, for me to pat it and stroke its head, now that she was near me.

"I meant the breasts."

"Later," she said. "Later."

You will call it fantasy, pornography. But the law says nothing against a man's exciting himself. What if he writes a book to perpetuate an excitement he felt once? Moreover, what if he writes

to begin an excitement he never had, creating in his mind a universe
of sense that cannot exist? And then, for less imaginative men,
locked in their undeveloped minds, what if he produces an outlet, a
fantastic dream world for their famished senses to feast on?

I have visions of men and women, boys and girls, reading this
account of my destruction, enjoying it, producing their own fantasies
spun from my substance, beginning to open the ducts of their
disused glands—the subtle glands that only a special doom can open,
perhaps even the wetness produced by watching a hanging or any
execution or love-making by mortally ill people.

It is all meant to be pornography, but it is highly moral. It points a
lesson. Jesus on the cross dripped with blood and semen; the people
caught it in buckets as it ran from him. Half the Middle East was
populated with the product of artificial insemination from Jesus; this
was the first miracle, the most ironic one. All that good stuff.
Barabbas was the one who carried it around in hollow bones.

You can believe that Irene would have had some rather unusual
muscles in her womb, considering the manifold uses she made of it
quite separate from its usual functions. I am not so impotent in the
conventional way as I might have indicated, and I am not proof
against unromantic rather-brisk junctures. The long and short of it
is—I took her in my arms, feeling a combination of revulsion and a
high degree of interest and ease; I had the uncanny feeling of being
delightfully manipulated around my organ. I looked down and the
activity in and around that area was amazing. Simultaneously I had
my answer about her breasts. My arms, armpits, and face were being
massaged with the most delicious erotic pseudopodia you can
imagine—imagine, as I said. I was enveloped, intoxicated as she
murmured to me: everywhere I was totally involved, except for my
cursed mind as she drew me, it seemed, ever further into her. How
far I went I can't say. I never knew I could penetrate so deeply, with

feeling extending so far down the line, so to speak, maintaining communication on every front.

I am overwhelmed by a spasm of disgust at myself. My intentions are clear: I have to tell everything. This is a pilgrimage to the end of a life, my own. The tale is moral, the details are hideous, complex, frightening. I have been deluded during the past few pages into telling something for its own sake. I am pandering to your salacious desires, hoping to trick you into following my story even when there are no such mouth-watering details to give. But I love the language, the grotesque for its own sake, a holdover from a time when I indulged myself in loving humanity for its weird freaks and turns, when I could look and see myself reflected in every perversion; every twisted tree-trunk or man was my brother. How much more so was this torso, a frank open-faced young girl at once unveiled, unfrocked, and dismasted.

Didn't Melville indulge himself with portraying a legless emasculated captain too engrossed with evil and pasteboard to save his life? And mine? Is it already lost. This is the last gasp. Why do I waste my time?

But if you have any perception, you have already moved beyond this sticky altogether-usual pastiche of sexual symbolism; you know that what I want to get across is that this gruesome wreck, as deft as she was, is the very personification of the toothed womb, the *dentata*; the hints I have dropped of Scylla and Charybdis were not for nothing. But I am either oversubtle or too crude. I'm sorry, but I wanted to delay again. You have rushed on ahead. This girl is naturally waiting for the man whom she can make her own. She is more than willing to rend his limbs from his body, encasing him all the while in the skein of a swooning sensuality. She will suck him until his senses leave him and then she will hack him lovingly until he is just like her.

That is her function, that is what she lives for. I was only a practice dummy, so to speak. And her function in that place from which she was sent to accompany me? If I escaped this encounter with only the loss of some dignity, some remnant of character, it is because there are obviously other plans in store for me. She cannot take me for her own because my wife has reserved another kind of doom for me, as custodian of my doom. I am condemned to be a special kind of sacrifice or pattern or example. For all I know, the girl had instructions to drop us both into this pit. Even now, with hardly a backward look, the girl propels herself toward her limbs and with uncanny dexterity attaches them, heaving in my direction clothes that smell of clay, like funerary vestments. With the fire and the reek of sex and my weakness, it could have been some ancient celebration of Astarte. Only lacking is the smell of pig.

Irene's veil is back in place. I wish I could keep the veil on my life, but I am consumed from above and from below, from my own sensuality and the need to justify and explain myself, coming therefore into some kind of existence before I am eaten alive.

O god! you know what the home economics class is, and with what kinds of monsters—loving, tender, helpless monsters—it is populated. Give me the strength to face it, and the winds howling outside!

Her veil is reattached. She turns bright humorous eyes to me. "Helped my cold, though you can't get this pit really warm enough," she said cheerfully, helping me with my pants with an impersonal hard hand. She tied my shoe laces. "One nostril, damn it; that's the assignment. I'll get it after all. I've got to."

Irene was now turned off. Somewhere in her is a switch or rheostat, the increase of which blurs the real world and relegates me to following her fantasies. This time, for her and for me, it ended in a hole and sexual intercourse. Her acme will be reached with someone else. I would have failed the test. Fortunately she was deflected this time with a small bone tossed in her direction.

Now, everything quite normal, we approached the building, blazing with light. I think the girl was by now quite indifferent to me, and I shrank from touching her.

What had appeared to be a simple large modern building was not that at all. There were more wings to the sides and behind what I could see. Besides, it was built on the side of a hill and so had several levels and entrances at different points. I conjectured that at least four or five floors were underground. I tried to fix in my mind the place we hurriedly entered, but the blank glass front and sliding glass doors were so without personality, the carefully potted trees with guide-lines so antiseptic that I couldn't place anything. It might have been a medical center or a supermarket. In the lobby, as a matter of fact, I heard piped music of the neutral variety one hears in hospitals and food stores. I recall being wheeled down a corridor once to the sound of a vague *Vienna Woods*. I remember women in super-markets grazing down the shelves with bovine faces and soft hands under the watchful one-way eyes of supervisors, ready with cattle prods or summonses. Soothing medleys of *Remember Pearl Harbor*, *Annie Get Your Gun*, and *I'm in the Mood for Love* arouse sluggish sentiments of patriotism, sadism, and eroticism, the blend that produces most sales for corn flakes, syrup, and detergent. I philosophize to cadge time. I want to remain in this lobby, where most of us live out our lifetimes, happy enough with potted plants and potted music, happy enough with sterilized remains, corpses of trees and music, both throttled by guide-lines, pasteurized of any nasty virus of genius or pain. I am content to remain on this ground floor, except that it isn't—it's a fourth or fifth floor, but none of us realizes it. There is everything I need on this floor—toilet, commissary, music, other people milling around (not now, just figuratively), probably a library recording other people's odysseys. Enough.

But the elevator indicates arrival. "This is where we begin," my guide said, cheerful as ever. With her kerchief or veil around her shoulders, she blazed from above as vividly as had her fantastic bush below. Her freckles, however, had subsided with the wind.

She pushed me off the elevator three or four floors later. We began a tortuous tracking and backtracking along corridors, through doors, squeezing around tables and chairs stacked in alcoves, climbing stairs to half a floor above and then to another elevator.

"Surely," I protested, 'the girls in the home economics class don't go through all of this when they come to class?"

"They do once," she replied.

All the Monkeys

T ires shrieked time after time; the forty-eight hairpin turns of the Irohazaka Nikko Highway were well advertised and the informed tourist could tick them off for himself. Gary Chalmers' thigh ground against Abby's skinny flank, but the friendly California spinster had at least made his four-day Japan Tourist Bureau guided tour bearable. Abby knew all about Japan from her big, fat guide— the oriental Baedecker. She spent whole evenings with it, while Gary drank slow, tiny glasses of sake in overheated hotel barrooms, decorated in breathless Meiji Restoration Queen Victoria-inspired furniture. Abby had smiled commiseratingly at him across the table, her look implying that she understood the hidden tragedies in Gary's plump, not quite middle-aged American face. Why was he traveling all alone in Japan? She herself was used to traveling alone, every other winter quarter.

They braced for the next curve.

The female tourist guide, or "courier," pounded on the microphone to make sure it was on. "We're passing some rocks where monkeys have lived for centuries," she said.

A bottomless pit of information, Gary thought, like her sisters-in-spirit, with their news of women's underwear, cosmetics, fountain pens, and syringes in department store elevators, and her more elegant compatriots who dispense alcohol in airplanes—and lead prayers from a book as the plane goes down.

What's Sylvia doing this minute, he wondered, feeling flat as he checked his watch and tried to remember whether Japan time was a day ahead or a day behind.

Taking care of her sick sister, but how serious was it that she couldn't make the trip? "Go on," she told him, "I'll stay with Dorothy." To his strenuous protests, she added, "No, I'm not being a martyr; I don't really care to go now. You seem to need a change more than anything else. Go ahead, come back when you want to. If Dorothy gets better I'll come in the spring." So he was packed and sent off. He wasn't sure it was the best thing. Wasn't he a coward to accept Sylvia's generosity? If there was to be a therapeutic separation, shouldn't he initiate it although Dorothy's illness provided a graceful way out?

The girl tapped on the mike. "The monkeys in this area are almost tame, but we're behind schedule, so we won't have time to stop to see them, I'm sorry to say."

In sight was an end of four days of touring; Gary's friend Don Silvers would meet him. Silvers had packed him off into the tour right off the plane. "Best thing," he told Gary, "get an overall view." Gary suspected that he was being treated tenderly, like a wounded veteran.

The guide tapped her microphone. "Not all the monkeys are on the rocks; there are plenty of civilized monkeys in buses like this one."

Gary turned to Abby. "Did you hear that?"

"What?"

He craned his neck to get a look at the guide, but the next razor-back curve threw him against Abby. "Sorry." He couldn't see her expression.

The guide stood at the bus door bowing and helping the tourists off. Her soft voice and exactly repeated phrases seemed calculated to minimize her presence. Passing her, Gary looked at her closely. Out of habit and vague excitement at being alone in a country of much-rumored pliant women he had scrutinized her when the tour started, but disappointed with her business-like, tailored suit uniform, her ready smile and objective attitude, he had quickly stopped looking. For the past four days she had been a recorded message ticking off temples, dates, battles, and "interesting" anecdotes about Japanese history. Now as he looked again he noted little wrinkles at her eyes, and her nostrils were red, as though she had blown her nose instead of, Japanese-style, snuffling. This pleased Gary, as though he had proved his powers of observation by catching her in something she would not like known.

"Very interesting observations you made on the trip down from the lake," he said.

"Thank you." She bowed slightly, but her eyes flickered over his face. "The train leaves in nine minutes."

Abby was right behind him. Gary slung her camera bag and his own over his shoulder. They had compared notes every night on lens readings and filter factors. Abby was a good photographer and made some money with her slides every spring at women's clubs.

"That girl," Abby said as they pushed through the crowded station, "has an interesting face."

"Why?"

"It's not sure yet what it is."

"Did you hear her say that not all the monkeys are on the rocks?"

Abby hadn't noticed. Why was he so impressed, Gary wondered, excited at the thought of her harboring a secret contempt for the tourists beneath her smooth exterior. But if so, it was the same ironic superiority that annoyed him in Sylvia. But Japanese girls were said to be sympathetic and uncritical, a relief from the American woman's unrelenting judgments of a man's performance.

In the icy station were people lined up to buy fruits and candies and wooden trays of rice. Women with babies strapped to their backs stood and jiggled them, vapor trailing from their mouths. Older children and some adults stared at the "gaijin" foreigners on their tour. No matter how many foreigners they saw, they always stared.

With the group settled on the train for the two-hour run to Tokyo, the tourist guide went into the club car, and Gary followed. Around a stereo juke box a group of young Japanese in tight pants clustered, keeping time to the rock and roll beat. The fields outside were a sea of mud in which hunched-over shapeless women worked with young rice plants. There was too much noise.

"How about a cup of coffee?" Gary shouted to the guide. "Isn't it too hot in here? Can I ask them to turn down the heat?"

She looked up and smiled.

"I haven't gotten your name all this time."

"It is Sachiko Mitsui."

"Well, you know mine, Gary Chalmers, it's on enough tickets, receipts, and luggage tags. I enjoyed your comment about the monkeys. Do you like this kind of work? Does it get boring?"

"Well, I do like it. I used to type all day long in an office. This is much better. It's a very good work for me."

"But your English is so good. Couldn't you do something in the government, or get a job overseas with an airline?"

"Yes, but it's very difficult for us to get that kind of work. Many girls wait for years to go to another country."

The waitress came by and she spoke to her. In a moment she brought coffee. As he handed her the cream, Gary touched her fingers, and he felt both sharp excitement and distaste. Her fingertips were smudged with ink.

"Do you do this all year long?"

"No. This is the end of the busy season. Next month will be almost nothing for me to do. I will do typing at my house. In April many tourists will come again. Then I work every day and sometimes I work all month without holiday."

"Where do you live?"

"In Mitaka. It's a suburb of Tokyo, about an hour from the center."

"With your parents?"

"They live in Kyushu. I came to college in Tokyo. I studied Japanese literature, then I stayed."

"So you learned English all by yourself?"

"I don't speak so well. But I want to learn Spanish. Tours of Spanish people come to Japan and almost nobody can be a guide for them. I will have more work if I can learn Spanish, but now I have no time. I studied a little with a book."

"Ojala, entonces habla usted un poco de espanol?" Gary asked.

She laughed and put up her hand to hide her mouth in the Japanese manner, but immediately took it down. "*You* speak very well."

"I spent some time in Mexico and then I traveled in Spain for about a month. Say, could I discuss things with you some other time? May I have your address!"

She nodded and wrote on a piece of paper. Abby came into the car as she handed it over to him. He felt guilty and elated, and also relieved that Abby was there to break up the question and answer period he did not know how to stop.

When Gary left the train Sachiko bowed, but she looked up just in time to catch his eye. They both grinned.

Gary's friend, Donald Silvers, lived in a three room apartment with his Japanese wife Kane and six-month-old baby girl. He taught English at one of the large language schools, where he was a director. Silvers' wife was young and plump, her eyes rarely leaving the child where it played in the crib as she kept refilling the sake cups.

"We'll have to go bar-hopping," Silvers was telling Gary. "The hostess bar scene in Tokyo is one of the main attractions," Silvers said as they finished dinner, a thing of many courses, raw fish and fishy soup and bits of meat and vegetables floating in watery sauce which, Gary noted, took hours to prepare but to him tasted bland and flat.

"Delicious," he said. "Well, why not tonight?"

"Can you handle Connie-chan, honey?" Silvers asked his wife. "Gary and I want to go out on the town tonight."

She didn't seem to be really aware of her husband, Gary thought, a great relief—privacy. What a tedious thing it is in America to share everything with the wife, the friend and buddy. An American husband couldn't say to an American wife, "I'm going to a hostess bar, honey"!

Kane kneeled on the tatami, a straw mat covering a little room that doubled as bedroom, and handed Gary his coat, muffler, and gloves. His shoes were ready, pointed toward the outside door in the entry hall the Silvers shared with their landlord and his family. Kane bowed to both of them in turn. Silvers kissed the baby as she held it out to him.

After the smell of the kerosene heater, the air was crisp. Pointing to a telephone pole on the corner with wooden signs hung on it in different directions, Silvers laughed, "Silvers, Squarci, Psarofaghis, I don't know them but where else could you see something like that?"

They took a taxi to an area next to one of the enormous railroad stations where tiny bars one next to the other filled whole narrow streets. Standing behind glass doors, girls were ready to open them and bow. Every door was a different color, so there were blue girls, green, yellow. Although most were in Western clothes, a few wore flashy kimono and elaborate hairdos.

"Let's work up to the hostess bars by going into some small ones first."

111

They drank Sapporo beer and Silvers reminisced about their friendship at the university years earlier, even though they had not been great friends. Only when Gary told a mutual acquaintance that he was going to Japan, he casually mentioned that Silvers was living with a Japanese girl in Tokyo. When Gary wrote, Silvers had answered so eagerly that when he arrived he was willing to go along with Silvers' amplified memories.

"Kane's a great girl. I never could have done as well in the States. She's a little sloppy right now with all the nursing."

"Her English is very good," Gary said.

"She was a student at my school. The directors weren't very happy when I announced our engagement. They know the teachers sleep around, but marriage is something else. I guess they got used to it."

"You don't have any feelings of, like, regret or any problems trying to communicate?" Gary asked. He visualized sitting on the rush mat floor, eating dinner all his life on a low table, crosslegged, and he knew that Kane carried the baby on her back. He felt ashamed, but somehow that was how he visualized peasants in Mexico and savages in Africa. "I mean, when you're explaining a joke, or how about her family?"

"No problem," Silvers said briskly, filling Gary's glass. "We go down to her family's village—he's the head man of a local fishing fleet—and they treat us like royalty. It's expensive for them, so we don't go except on holidays. Oh, there's probably a little prejudice, but no one shows it. For a girl of her class, it's several steps up."

They drifted into another bar. Silvers was drinking steadily. After a few minutes he crushed his cigarette and tears suddenly rimmed his eyes. "Jesus, Gary!" He threw his arm over Gary's shoulder. "I was sitting in the school library the other day and I remember a girl, you know Sue Anthony—remember we called her Susan B. Anthony?"

Gary recalled a girl who slept around quite generally.

"Well, I never told it to anyone, but I hurt that girl. I met her again a long time after I graduated, and we started going together. Then she got tuberculosis. I told her maybe after she got better we would get married. Well, she got better, but we didn't get married. I left town. Nothing was ever definite. I wrote to her and then I got a chance to come to Japan. That was all, but I think about her, and sometimes it comes back strong."

Gary knew the girl. At least two of his friends had had brief flings with her, a willing, amiable, undemanding girl, not too bright, nice to be with. He couldn't imagine anyone taking her seriously, so hurting her seemed out of the question. What relevance did she have for Silvers now?

"Well," Gary said, "everybody has someone like that in his past."

"But God, I sat in the cold library and remembered her, lying in bed. I told her how I cared for her and promised, and then I took off. She was Catholic. I met her family. She told me they wanted her to marry in the faith, but she thought they'd come around. I remember how helpless she was, lying in bed."

Gary wondered if he had slept with her while she was so helpless, but instead changed the subject. "How about one of those hostess bars?"

Silvers brightened at once. He led the way to a place where electric guitars could be heard even outside. Sylvia once wanted Gary to take her to one of the new discotheques. He never would because of this loud kind of music, but now he could understand its appeal; it filled him with a tense, blocked expectation. Seated at one of the dim tables, they ordered beer, and two girls slipped in next to them. Silvers spoke in Japanese, explaining something about Gary. One of them nodded sympathetically.

"America-jin?" Gary's girl asked.

"Hai," Gary said, carefully tamping his pipe with raw Japanese tobacco. Silvers quickly offered a pack of Peace cigarettes. "Thanks, I'll smoke my pipe tonight. Anyway, I prefer Hope or Golden Bat to Peace."

Gary's girl giggled and put her hand over her mouth. The beer came, the girls poured. Both had ample bosoms, maybe the results of generous injections of paraffin. Breast doctors advertised every day in the English language newspapers, the *Japan Times* and *Asahi Evening News*: "Non-surgical, guaranteed results, no bad after-effects." They were laced into evening gowns. Some hostesses seemed barely in their teens; others were obviously very comfortably in their 40s or older, listening to formally dressed businessmen-types. There was an edge of sweat in the air.

Silvers was more than ever jovial. He winked at Gary and slid his hand along his girl's thigh. She giggled. When Gary looked again, Silvers brought his hand down on the girl's breast and cradled it. The two girls laughed and squirmed, and Silvers laughed, his face flushed and excited.

"She wants to give you her card, Gary," he whispered. "She wants you to come back to see her again. She likes you."

Gary took the card and she squeezed his hand.

When the bill came, Silvers insisted on paying, the girls helped them with their coats and walked with them to the doors, waving when they were in the street. Other couples of men were weaving on the sidewalks, and someone was being sick into a trash can. The only women in sight stood duty at the many-colored doors.

Gary wrote to Sachiko asking if he could take her out. He wrote also to Sylvia, humorously relating his experiences in the hostess bar, with the maiden traveler, and touching upon his conversation with Sachiko. "When do you think you can come?" he wrote. "It's supposed to be blustery and cold for another month, but then there will be plum and cherry blossoms and we can rent a car and tour the country."

In a few days Sachiko wrote back and arranged to meet him at his Western-style hotel. He waited for her in the lobby. She was late, and as he idly watched the revolving door a girl in kimono pushed through, scanned the room and came toward him with quick, little steps. He stood up suddenly, embarrassed at not having recognized her in kimono. He handed her a large bouquet of flowers with the self-conscious thrust of a boy.

"Oh, thank you, Mr. Chalmers. They are too beautiful. Grown in the Izu Peninsula. These are too expensive flowers in Japan in winter."

She appeared to be really excited with the flowers, and Gary was glad to see some animation on her face. She was very elaborately made-up, and he barely recognized her even now. It was odd to see so much powder, eyebrow pencil, but no lipstick.

"Do you prefer a Japanese restaurant or Western one?" she asked.

"Please just call me Gary. Whichever you like, but should we have a drink at the bar before we go?"

If the waiters were appraising them they kept it well hidden. Gary felt like a child with an elaborate toy on his arm. A waiter carefully held out a chair, but Sachiko quickly moved to the next, leaving the offered chair for Gary. Patiently, the waiter followed Sachiko and pulled out another.

"What will you have, Sachiko?"

"What you have," she said.

"Vodka martini," Gary told the waiter. "Two."

She watched how Gary ate his olive and ate hers too.

They went to a Japanese restaurant where Gary removed his shoes, Sachiko her sandals, and stepped into felt slippers. They were ushered into a dining room decorated like an old farmhouse, where a drummer, singer, and samisen player were just finishing a song.

115

"Do you like Japanese or Western music?" Gary asked.

"Oh, I prefer Western music," she answered with distaste.

Two girls did a graceful dance, their kimono fitting more naturally than Sachiko's. The waiter brought a menu in Japanese. Gary took it and smiled, but Sachiko spoke abruptly to the man. Gary noticed several heads turn in their direction.

"What did you say to him?" he asked.

"It was very stupid of him to bring the Japanese menu, wasn't it?" she frowned. Other people were eating on beautifully arranged little plates, but the food that Sachiko ordered was that weird combination of Western food one found displayed in plastic effigy outside many restaurants in Tokyo: A meatball, potato salad, rice and spaghetti, a half-peeled tomato, but Sachiko was pleased and handled her knife and fork with elaborate care.

She said she would like to see a James Bond movie. She told him that a movie company was making a Bond movie in Japan.

"Are you going to try to get a part?"

"Oh, no, they want very beautiful Japanese girls."

She wouldn't hear of his taking her home by taxi. "I have my season pass on the train."

The next day he called Abby. They strolled through an art gallery. He had wanted to discuss Sachiko with her but held back. As they had dinner at her hotel, Abby watched him, and when they had drunk enough Gary told her what a wonderful manager Sylvia was, and how they went everywhere together. But her family loyalties had prevailed and here was Gary in Tokyo, taking a vacation alone for the first time.

It was a great comfort to talk with Abby, who condemned nothing, who was sympathetic and understood the kind of short-hand that Americans can use with one another with perfect mutual understanding.

Later, Gary wrote Sachiko a note, asking if he could take her to Kabuki in a few days.

"I am happy to come," she wrote. "Please be in front of Kabuki-za Saturday at 4:00 p.m. I will bring tickets." Gary called Silvers to ask if he would like to come too and have dinner later at the Palace Hotel.

The theatre resembled a huge pagoda, although it was only ten years old and concrete. Taxis and buses crowded the curbs, and throngs of people pushed at ticket windows. There was much bowing when people met their friends, the crowds behind them parting with no complaint.

Silvers rushed up. "I'll have to get a ticket. Kane couldn't get her sister to stay with the baby, so she'll meet for dinner." He returned frowning. "I hope your girl friend can change my ticket to sit near wherever you are. My Japanese isn't equal to it."

As Silvers spoke, Gary spotted Sachiko coming up from the Higashi Ginza subway. He had hoped that she would be wearing kimono, but she was hobbling on very high heels and even from a distance he could see a bright slash of lipstick. Gary took her arm. She was wearing a very tight, short skirt. "Don Silvers, this is Miss Mitsui." They both bowed. Silvers murmured something in Japanese.

"Thank you," Sachiko answered clearly, "I am fine."

Silvers looked embarrassed.

"Mr. Silvers," she said, "do you have your ticket? The 'Forty-Seven Masterless Samurai' is very popular."

"I got a ticket. Where are you sitting?"

They compared tickets. Gary and Sachiko were on the second balcony; Silvers was on the mezzanine. When the usher took them to the seats Sachiko spoke to him, indicating Silvers. He shook his head, drawing his breath in the hiss Japanese make when they have to refuse, or a problem is too difficult.

"No! You had better bring another chair," she suddenly said loudly. "You're crazy!" A dozen heads turned in amazement. The usher disappeared.

"Hey, hey, look, never mind!" Silvers sputtered. "I'll come up during intermission. Never mind, never mind!"

"They think they don't have to do anything when it isn't a foreigner who asks," she said, sitting.

"Well, it's crowded, like you said."

Gary was interested in the music of flutes and drums. The man playing the part of a court lady swept onto the stage with her attendant maids, every movement stylized and deliberate, delicate and learned. At every famous pose, someone in the audience called the favorite actor's pet name. The first time, Gary jumped; the enthusiast was sitting right at his shoulder.

Sachiko shook her head. "Idiots," she said.

Recalling her kimono, Gary thought she had been very wise to wear Western clothes to a gorgeous traditional performance of Kabuki.

"Do you like it?" he asked.

"No, I don't like it very much. It's too slow for me. And every minute—cut!" She made a motion of putting a knife in her stomach.

"You mean, why don't they just leave the country instead of disembowelling themselves?"

She shook her head. "It wasn't so easy then. It was the whole world for them, their masters."

Gary worried that he had never told her specifically that he was married although he wore a wedding band. She wasn't likely to ask at this point; why should she? The sheen of Sachiko's net stockings on her bare knees when she crossed and uncrossed her legs was very like a knife in his own belly.

On the way out during intermission she kicked the orange peels scattered in the aisle. Silvers was still nervous, but very knowledge-able on Kabuki. Sachiko stood silent, taking no part in his explanation.

The leader of the displaced samurai stood in the mist in front of the dead lord's palace, while the palace slowly receded. An incredible effect, Gary thought, really touched; thinking of events unredeemed by wishing, of failure and loss. He recalled Sylvia in her moments of softness, the tears she used to shed over a minor careless word of his. She usually ignored his lapses now.

Without conversation they collected their coats and stepped into a light, cold rain that doubled on the pavement the neon lights of the Ginza. As they approached the Imperial Palace moat, snow began to fall. Kane was waiting in the tenth floor bar of the hotel.

Sachiko ordered in English: "Vodka martini, please," watching Gary, and he felt a pang of fear in his bowels. As he sat high above the velvety water, he felt weary. Cars with headlights dimmed waited for the signal to change, then glided over the wet pavement as if on tiny stilts.

There was really nothing to say to the other three.

Sachiko had a week's tour; then he would meet her at Tokyo Station, take the train with her to Mitaka and later go to a performance of No.

The sun was brilliant and cold. Gary had on his long underwear, sweaters, and overcoat, feeling lumpish and uneasy. Who was this Sachiko he was meeting and why? It was the kind of day for brisk walks in the country, for being young, but he felt middle-aged and displaced instead. Over the weeks he had discovered the haunts of two distinct classes of Americans: The American Club and the coffeehouses in Shinjuku. At the former, American businessmen and their wives led an insulated existence as closely patterned on the United States as possible, all the time complaining about Tokyo's high prices, the government's inefficiency, the hopelessness of trying to figure out the Japanese. They drank good scotch. In the coffeehouses it was possible to see interracial couples, bearded Japanese with guitars, and passionate listeners to jazz or Beethoven's Ninth. Gary was too well-dressed, not young enough to sit with any of them. There were older men always waiting for their girlish Japanese boyfriends to show up. Introduced by an acquaintance to the Press Club, Gary met American officers' wives, hungry-looking here as at every post, drinking far too much, and when not too loud, ominously silent, nervously contemptuous of Japanese servants and waiters.

Displaced. Frankly, he thought, I just want to be in bed with her. He didn't want to think past that.

Again, as she walked toward him, he almost couldn't recognize her. He always pictured her as something quite different. Today she was wearing make-up around her eyes. She was young, she was healthy, what did she need with him? Didn't it cost her something to come to him? The space she walked to reach him in this station, in the heart of Japan, didn't she know it couldn't be done? That he wasn't changing to meet her, that flowers were only flowers to him?

But she was happy to see him. "Look, Gary, I brought you narcissus," and put it in his overcoat lapel.

"Well," he said awkwardly, "how was the thundering herd?" Somehow, he wanted her to go, be off, let him alone, but instead he hailed a cab.

Outside her apartment building was a dusty playground with some weary-looking climbing toys. They walked three flights of stairs. Producing a key from her bag, she opened the door and bowed him through. She had put travel posters on two walls, Grand Canyon and Niagara Falls, but on another wall was a long Japanese scroll, a bright red heron. A desk covered with papers leaned against one wall, a bookshelf, and the usual low table.

She hurried to turn on the kerosene stove. He heard her strike matches in the kitchen to light the gas ring for tea.

"Please sit down," she said. "There are cushions and a back rest." She spilled a package of flowers. Stooping to pick them up, a fold in her kimono opened.

"Do you wear traditional clothes very much?"

"Oh, no. But I wear them sometimes."

Why today? Why for this particular tour? Gary wondered.

He sipped his tea and tried to arrange his legs comfortably, while Sachiko crouched and carefully arranged the flowers. She had tuned the radio to jazz. Gary wondered how many layers of clothes there were under her kimono. She brought fruit, stooping on his side of the low table to peel an apple for him. He tried to think of topics they could discuss. In cases like this Sylvia always had something to talk about.

He had a long wait, time to imagine Sachiko without kimono, while she bathed and prepared herself for the evening. He soon exhausted his interest in the English and Spanish grammars he found on the bookshelf.

The No theatre was in a part of Tokyo next to the Sumida River, where pleasure boats used to float down to the bay. Houses still overhung the river, now an open sewer encased in concrete. Chanting, masked No players unraveled stories as simple and inevitable as the Greeks'. An imperiled young king, no more than nine years old, sat still as rock while passions and plans for his assassination were discussed above his head. With dignity he hid beneath an over-turned boat while demons in red masks stormed around. A humble fisherman and his wife revealed themselves to be gods who desired to preserve the boy-king's line. At the end each personage paced his deliberate, solemn way down a long, smooth

121

passageway, the door-curtains rose and fell.

Gary and Sachiko stopped in for roasted yaki-tori chicken.

"I think I'll go with Abby to Kyoto," Gary said.

"How long will you stay there? It's too cold now. You can wait for a month and I can show you Kyoto," she said.

"Well, I'm not sure I can wait. I think she may leave Japan soon and I promised her. She's alone, you know, and—"

"Here!" Sachiko snapped open her shiny, plastic purse. "Here is the key to my apartment. I am leaving for four days tour. Same one as your tour. Wait for me at my apartment. Do you want to?"

He took the key, but his heart sank. Here was his adventure! How many times had she done this before? Never mind that, what was his purpose? What part did he play in her life? How long would it take for him to be classed with the "monkeys in the bus"?

"Sachiko, do you really want to give me this?"

She should have looked solemn, but she laughed. "Don't you want it?"

He sighed. "What time will you be there?"

"Sometime after five o'clock."

What if he asked her what she saw in him? There was no time right now. They drank hot, bitter tea with their chicken.

Scattered flakes of snow were in the air when he turned the key four days later. There was the usual stale, faint sewage odor of bad drains, and he heard the thin voices of children playing below. The air was close and cold. He lit matches for the kerosene heater, but the flame wouldn't turn blue. Wisps of cinders settled on his white shirt. He looked at the deep tub in the bathroom. Almost automatically he put in the plug. He sat on the side of the tub waiting for water to rise above the two holes connected to the gas heater that heated the water. Often, he sat on the side of the tub while Sylvia took her bath, telling her the events of his day or listening to what she had done.

More than anything, he would have liked to tell her about his infidelities, which he had begun a year or so after they were married, usually with older women, with whom neither Sylvia nor anyone else would ever have suspected his connection, affairs in comfortable bedrooms and kitchens with women who had been pretty and were now charming. Women, he realized, who would have had nothing to do with him when they were in their real youth. What was wrong with Sachiko?

He didn't hear the door.

"Oh, Gary, that is nice. I am so tired. The monkeys were always either too hot or too cold."

"Like I was on the train?"

"Exactly like you."

He got up from the edge of the tub and his hands hung awkwardly. He felt like a boy of fourteen, but with the paunch of a man of fifty. She came and faced him, he raised his hands and put them around her waist. It was the very first time. She leaned to him, and he felt keenly how resilient her body was, how it rose from the hips and breathed like a pulse. He put his lips on hers and they were cold, astringent.

She was helping him take off his coat. She unknotted his tie and unbuttoned his shirt. Every piece of clothing she folded neatly and put on the floor of the other room. She pushed him onto a little wooden stool. She dropped all her own clothes except her brassiere and pants and began to soap his body. Automatically he observed the play of her veins and muscles, and as her armpit reached his vision, he noted with fascinated distaste her curled luxurious hair wet with exertion. He knew he should be astonished and elated, but it was as though he were watching someone else in his place.

She washed him meticulously and thoroughly, and then rinsed him. Japanese men are used to this treatment, he thought, they can let themselves be handled gracefully. But I feel like a baby, he thought, an old baby. Her face showed nothing but the exertion of covering all of him.

She swept her hand across the surface of the water, turned off the heat, and helped him in and left the room while he steamed. He heard her humming and setting out the futon mattress on the floor.

As he climbed out of the tub and dried, steaming in the cold air of the bathroom, he wondered what to put on. Sachiko hurried in with a man's kimono.

"Can I wash you?" he asked.

She shook her head and pushed him gently into the other room. He supposed she wanted him to get into the bed. The bedding on the floor reminded him of boy scout camp, getting down on the ground and into a sleeping bag, hearing the unfamiliar crack of trees, the sky low and filled with stars, the night filled with exotic, exciting fear.

Kneeling on the floor he was ashamed of his loose belly and awkwardness. It was wrong to get into bed first, but there was no place to sit comfortably, and he couldn't stand while she bathed. Finally, he decided to get into the bed.

The quilt was so heavy that he felt crushed and pinned to the mattress, utterly helpless, but also taken care of, the ultimate in dreams of passive acceptance—a beautiful young girl to minister to him, almost the stereotype seraglio or Arabian Nights harem. Hadn't he hoped for this when he accepted Sylvia's suggestion that he go to Japan by himself? To find himself in bed with a girl whose one thought was for him, not for committees, or shopping, or small dinner parties?

The room was dark and the only sound a thin hiss of kerosene in the heater when Sachiko slipped under the quilt, but Gary thought wryly of the narrowness of the mattress and the broadness of his

124

behind. How ridiculous he was, yet a fresh rush of desire for the still, slim girl flowed through him. He began to kiss her mouth, her eyes, her neck. She responded, kissing and biting, twining her legs in his. She was very strong for all her slimness, twisting under the heavy quilt, surging against him, hungry to touch and caress him. He was soon sweating, not used to such displays of passion. He distrusted it, yet he bitterly complained that Sylvia didn't respond or give back what he gave her. He entered Sachiko almost hoping to drive her back. He was so aroused, so worried, that it was soon over.

Soon, too soon, he fell away from her and lay on his back. She sighed and cradled her head on his arm. Too soon, too precipitate. If he were at home now, he would be caressing Sylvia trying to bring her to the exact temperature they were never able to reach together. But Sachiko made no nervous movement, seemed to feel nothing lacking, however brief it had been.

He dozed, woke up cramped, his arm aching, feeling burdened under the heavy quilt and untidy down below. Again he slept and woke needing the toilet, but the air was so cold that even his nostrils burned.

In the morning, as soon as Sachiko disappeared into the bathroom, Gary crawled from under the quilt and threw on his clothes. She had already turned on the gas ring to boil water for tea, and when she came back from the bathroom, she rolled and slid the bedding into a closet and put tea and a bowl of rice in front of him. She served him so simply that Gary could find nothing to say about the night. "What are your intentions?" he wanted to ask, and "What do you think of me?" But that would be ridiculous.

When he found a seat for her on the train, she glowed so that it seemed nothing in the world could have pleased her so much as being given a seat by Gary, who would have taken it for himself if he had been a traditional Japanese husband. His heart turned to see her eyes half-closed, hands in her lap easy and trustful.

A few nights later he took her to the Silvers' for dinner. The women bowed to each other, but hardly spoke, and neither girl took part in the men's conversation. Gary began to understand the lure of hostess bars—laughter, talk, movement.

Silvers asked Sachiko about her family.

"Before the war I would be a girl in a shop, maybe. But I could go to Tokyo for the University. My father and mother think I had better go back to Kyushu to Kumamoto and marry."

Silvers laughed. "I think you're in the wrong business. You would have made a gorgeous geisha in old Edo," he said, "or anywhere."

Sachiko frowned. "Geisha are beautiful, I am not. They are also useless. They don't know anything. I think they are glad when they become old and ugly and have to marry and live in some little village and make children."

She was not looking in Kane's direction, but Silvers seemed annoyed. Assuming a cheerful interest, he retorted, "Well, you're sort of caught in the middle, aren't you? What *do* you want to do?"

Gary was afraid of the possible answer to this question, but Sachiko's earnestness evaporated; she smiled and murmured in Japanese to Kane, who rose and brought more tea.

In the mornings Gary waited eagerly for Sylvia's letters. Dorothy was recovering. Sylvia was involved with redecorating her apartment to make convalescence more cheerful. There had been a lot of rain, someone was being divorced after nine years. In her letters was a hint of wistfulness—she hoped that he was absorbing Japan, staying well, meeting interesting people. Gary discovered that he needed guilt pangs to feel illicit, since Sachiko was so direct, unashamed, and undemanding.

"What would your parents say if they knew you were sleeping with a married, middle-aged American? What do you intend to do?"

126

he would ask, and she smiled or touched him lightly or busied herself with a flower arrangement. She began to take lessons again and spent hours, while he was at her apartment, arranging flowers. He began to bring books to read, but his shoulders ached and he felt he must get out. He anticipated and dreaded their nights on the futon.

Sachiko might have work to type, and her machine would continue into the night, while Gary sat, feet always cramped, at the low table, trying to read or write a letter.

Once, on a national holiday, she put on her best kimono, taking hours to get it and her hair just right, and as they walked on the quay at Yokohama, Gary felt like someone from a nineteenth century steel engraving, a sailor or diplomat, with a native girl on his arm.

She had received a letter from her parents. Her eyes were red. She held the letter out to Gary as though he could read it. "My mother has heard from one of the neighbors here something about us. She wants to know what I'm going to do."

"I've asked you that. What are you going to do?"

"I'm not going to do anything. Why must I do something?"

Abby called him at his hotel. When they met in her hotel lobby, she was with an elegant young Japanese woman, a teacher at the university where Abby had begun to teach a few days every week. While Abby stepped forward the friend demurely hung back, almost the proper Japanese wife. She poured tea and sat quietly with her hands in her lap. There was something between them that excited him and made him a little ill. How did he feel when he touched Sachiko? Did Sachiko sense his shame and pity his hopeless rush to climax? She never said anything about it.

They spent evenings with other mixed couples. The men declared that they had no desire whatever to return to America. Meeting some of their employers he thought he detected something in their attitude both respectful and a trifle sneering. In Tokyo it was so easy to drift—in and out of bars, exhibits, concerts, or bed, to make of the bath a whole evening's occupation. Gary awaited some call, an insistent sign of departure. The spring and tourist season began to set in so Sachiko was gone much of the time. He wondered if she met men she was attracted to on these trips, but she never asked him how he spent his time in Tokyo. He went to a turkish bath and requested the full, famous treatment from a middy-clad girl. It was like a surgical operation, and when it was over, he felt no more empty than usual, and no more guilty. A Japanese friend explained that such treatment was only a logical extension of massage. No guilt, so no issue.

On one of her free days Sachiko arranged a visit to her old professor's home in Saitama Prefecture, eighty miles north of Tokyo.They transferred to a cold, pre-war train that rocked and clattered. Men spat on the warped floorboards. The fields were gray, and the black freight cars at switching stations reminded him of war movies.

Sachiko's professor met them at a dreary little waiting room adjoining open urinals next to the station. He bowed again and again to Gary after handing him his card, bustled them into a cab that he carefully paid in advance, and led them on a motor scooter to his house. The tatami room had a fine old scroll in the corner shrine, but also a two-foot-tall, glass-boxed Barbie-like doll. The wife bowed and served them lunch.

"She does not speak English," the professor said. "Do you like to watch television?" He snapped it on—color. Sachiko was all murmurs and politeness. He switched it off again. "Shall you like to take a walk around the city?"

"Very much," Gary answered, "thank you."

The town was full of bicycles and people who stared as though Tokyo and America were centuries away. They walked to the town exhibition hall.

"Here are products we make in Hanyu City."

They peered into dusty glass cases full of rubber boots, school uniforms, bolts, rivets, cloth and dye. Gary wondered if Sachiko wanted to illustrate for him what she had escaped, the dreary life of a factory girl like those who craned their necks to get a glimpse of them as they passed, and then giggled and chattered, innocent of any desire to be anywhere else.

Gary felt a rush of warmth for Sachiko. His fear of her passion seemed foolish in the bright sun. She would always be grateful to him and she was quick and intelligent. When the professor wasn't looking, he squeezed her arm.

As they crossed a street, a muddy bitch with swinging dugs slunk out of an alley. Gary turned and she shied into the street and under the wheels of a truck. The truck thundered by in a cloud of dust and Gary cried, "Oh, no! Don't!" and clutched his head, while the dog bounced and rolled. Whimpering and biting at itself, it limped and staggered out of the street into another alley. Sachiko and the professor, who had seen everything, hurried to ask Gary if he was all right, deep concern on their faces. "The dog—" he said, ashamed and angry.

It was hot and smelly on the train. Sachiko appeared to have no inkling of his renewed distaste. He could hear the dog in his sleep for nights.

Walking from the train station to Sachiko's apartment he took an unfamiliar turn one night. He knew if he kept bearing right he would get to the proper street. From a crack in a fence a brilliant light shone. He peered in just as an archer drew back his bow, poised, and released an arrow. His grace and strength was of the same order as that of a Kabuki warrior or the No king. As he passed on he saw a glitter of many eyes at the side of the road, rats or cats creeping over garbage. He felt sick at the thought of the cringing bitch dog and her muddy hanging dugs. A car passed and the eyes became discarded tinsel.

Cherry trees blossoming in the Musashino plain near Mitaka called them out. Sachiko and Gary strolled in a park with thousands of other couples.

"I'm going home, Sachiko," he said. "I'm going to leave in a week. I'm sorry."

She stood under a fragrant, elaborately blossomed tree and one or two petals floated into her hair. She was young and beautiful, he saw, in awe and irritation. She was just too much like a full-color Japanese illustration. She said nothing.

"You're going back?" Silvers said. "Why, when you don't have to? You're crazy. What for? I can get you fifteen jobs if you want to stay in Tokyo."

"It's not that," Gary said.

"What about Sachiko?"

"I don't know."

"Well, she'll get over it. I don't think any Japanese girl really expects it to last. I'm not sure but that Kane thinks that I'll pick up one day and leave her and the kid and take off for the States."

When he called on Abby to say goodbye she met him without her friend. She was even thinner and not quite so bouncy, but seemed settled for an extensive stay. Gary had the feeling of being on a moving belt, waving at people to whom he had inexplicably lost the clue.

The time was set and his tickets were ready. He climbed the stairs to Sachiko's apartment to say goodbye. She didn't answer his knock. "Hello, Sachiko?"

The smell of the last blossoms was in the air. There were no lights on in the apartment. Between horror and elation, he knew Sachiko was in the bathroom. He cursed himself for an old fool, knowing that certain things happen only to muddy dogs and in stories like Madame Butterfly, not to middle-aged Americans and tourist guides.

He almost collided with her as she ran out of the bathroom. He was so relieved that he grabbed and kissed her harder and better than he had ever done before but she pressed herself to his lips until he felt flattened, and his joy melted into irritation for himself and his melodrama.

"Gary, you know what?"

"What?"

"I quit my job, like you said."

"Sachiko, for God's sake, why did you do that?"

"It is what happens in Japan. My father wrote the tourist bureau company, please to transfer me to Osaka, close to my home. I will not go, so I quit."

"But what in the world are you going to do? You don't want to go back to the office."

She took his hands. She was glittering, reckless. "I will study Spanish," she said. "And look!" She dragged him into the main room. "No, wait, close your eyes. Keep them closed."

He heard her run to the light switch and then back to him. She pulled and pushed him until he knew he was in a corner of the big room.

"Now, sit."

He began to crouch, but his bottom hit a cushion. He opened his eyes. He was on a chair, one of the expensive, uncomfortable, wood and imitation leather chairs from the "Western" furniture section of a department store.

Sachiko kneeled on the tatami and laid her head on Gary's knee. Her hair covered his lap. "It's your chair, Gary."

She pressed her chin into his knee until he winced.

"How do you like it?" she asked.

Boris

Miss Chaliapin glanced at her watch all too casually and brightly announced: "That's all the time we have for today. Stop in the other room on your way out for tea and cookies. I'll see you all next week at the same time. *Dosve danya.*" She high-stepped in place like a small expensive lighthouse emitting little flashes of teeth while fielding questions in the manner of a celebrity who expects someone really important any minute. Most of the group of Russian emigres did not try to keep her. It didn't matter anyway—these weekly meetings were but an unstated requirement of continued support, physical and moral. Once, when Boris was coming back in as she left, he saw her expel a big breath and take one in with obvious pleasure when she was out of the room, and Boris knew that to Americans Russians smell bad. Most of them had not learned to dress lightly for Los Angeles weather. What clothes they had were heavy and durable, permeated with years of all-season living. Russians know about deodorants, but did Americans know that they smelled like *nothing,* or else like artificial flowers? The Hermitage, where Russians went to see great paintings of flowers, even *sounded* like a place where one had to wear heavy clothes all year.

Los Angeles was like a compulsory stripping for entrance exams, a humiliating probe in front of contemptuous officials. With layers of clothing, one took comfort that he was not a turtle without shell, but substantial, counting for something.

Because everybody in Los Angeles wore jeans, not just *hooligans,* how could he know when and to whom to be respectful, since even in the Home of the Brave some people were clearly more important than others?

Which made for Boris a feeling he thought he'd never experience: homesickness. Russia, Leningrad White Nights of endless day and no sleep, running around in a shadowless midnight, palaces, parks, fountains prettier than Paris and more stately than Vienna, the Neva with its mighty icebergs larger than the biggest skyscrapers in Los Angeles.

Here, Boris noticed, people laughed a lot out of the corners of their mouths because they were on some substance or wanted you to believe they were. Not real laughter, not belly laughs, like at home. Where it can be dangerous to laugh, there one laughed a lot, with real comrades. Here, even the word *comrade,* a perfectly fine word, was supect.

Americans all knew what Russians were like, and also had very clear ideas of how Russian emigres should act: they must act *Jewish.*

Nobody leaves Russia who hasn't declared himself Jewish, so willy-nilly (a good one—willy-nilly), Boris was Jewish. Boris, who could have passed a Gestapo physical exam without a blush, a Jew. Boris, never once in synagogue (where was it?), a Jew. Not that he liked them any more than most Russians. Actually, he distrusted them, since Jews had once been top officials in Russia, and one distrusted officials.

So he walked into the social hall of the Jewish Federation building, called derisively by some, "The Jewish Kremlin." There was Sonya standing by the samovar. Samovar! What Boris wanted was a cup of hot thick espresso, almost Turkish, with sugar and cream. If he wanted tea he could stay in Leningrad. Sonya was pure Russian, cream and strawberry. Some Cossack had surely done the dirty on one of her ancestors! She was the only good-looking girl in the whole Thursday afternoon Americanization group. Her family was probably rich. Naturally, they pretended to be poor—lifetimes of craftiness served them in a new bureaucracy. Boris knew about the short attention span of do-gooders, and he intended to disappear into the mainstream. He was old enough to be independent, he went to college. He was learning computers.

Boris also knew if only Sonya went to bed with him he would be able to marry her, her family would set him up in business, and what happened after didn't matter. In Russia he wouldn't have been able to get within ten feet of her.

She wore a white linen sheath, which proved she hadn't acclimatized as much as Boris, whose designer blue jeans were pure American and went perfectly with a T-shirt advertising a rock star. He had the clothes already in Russia from a tourist. It took a year's savings, shady deals. He didn't care that getting this costume endangered his family's exit visa. So what? He was no refusenik.

He ambled over and coolly took the cup out of her hand. She turned in astonishment, mainly put on, he thought, and frowned. "Come on," he said in imitation of James Dean, he hoped, "let's go and get some real refreshments."

He kept smiling as she grabbed for her cup and spilled some tea on his hand. His smile turned to grimace. "Ow! you want to cripple me?"

"Boris, go away," she said in Russian.

He raised his eyebrows comically and waggled them, trying out a Groucho Marx imitation. "No, no, speak English. You are in America, we are Americans here. There you say 'nyet' to me, not here. Here you say, 'Sure, Baby, let's split. Later. Let's lay tracks.'"

"My mother picks me up in one half of an hour, Boris, is that correct? I have homework."

"Let's do it together, Sweetheart," Boris said, taking her cup again.

"Just across the street. I get you back in one half of an hour. For sure." He imitated Anwar Sadat. "For sure, for sure, for sure."

And waited for her reaction. She still wore her hair thick and long, Russian-style. Even her legs, in nylons, betrayed her Russianness, because they were still hairy, although with her fair complexion you could hardly tell. Boris stared at her hungrily, as though she were a pastry.

"I get you a fresh strawberry tart, Sonya. How about it?"

She could not resist a fresh pastry. He had seen her eating with the dainty greed even well-brought-up people cannot hide.

An hour later, he walked her back to the front of the building. The Black security guard smiled at them. Security! It was to laugh. Anybody could get in, drop a poison pellet into an air shaft and kill half the building in ten minutes.

Sonya's mother was waiting. She smiled distantly at Boris' prerevolutionary bow. The afternoon was smoggy, hot and damp, but her brow was only slightly shiny, her gloves still brilliant white. Sonya took her mother's arm without a backward glance at Boris and got into a relative's car.

Not much, taking a Sonya in the daytime to a coffee shop. Still, a beginning.

Boris leaped on his bike and pedaled toward the apartment. He wanted a ten-speed, not this clunker, although a car would be better. That was out of the question for now. He wanted to own things, but how? He was far from graduation, let alone making real money. He thought of Sonya with a pang—maybe he really liked her. He did like the way she ate her tart, a little at a time, head dipping to bite like a delicate bird. He thought of her enfolded in *his* wings, protected and proud. But he needed new clothes. These he wore were carefully hung out every night, but he had only one change. His shoes were Russian, and he was ashamed of them—he needed Tretorns or at least Nikes.

Boris passed rows of neat duplexes with evenly cut grass. How did people get them? Accident of birth, he knew, or stolen at little money before inflation. The giant buildings that nudged the little houses on Wilshire were owned by people whose parents had stolen land a generation before. Rockefellers, Carnegies, Kennedys— respected families now, their grubby or shady days obscured by present genteel philanthropy. And rich Jews, who subsidized the Russian and Iranian immigration—how did they get their money? What blood guilt were they paying off? He never had met even one of them. They paid but stayed away. There was so much money laying around—why couldn't he lay his hands on some? He only needed a stake, a beginning. Afterward, anybody could be honest and laid back when he had enough money.

Taunting the driver of a new convertible, Boris rode slowly against the light across an intersection, smiling as the driver leaned on his horn.

The worst thing was that here truly was the land where everything was possible. In Russia, nothing is possible, and that made it all right. When he was uprooted, they broke his mold, they woke him up, but that's all. They gave him room, food, a bicycle, and a ticket to attend community college to learn computers. But these days even computer programmers were laid off and wandering around without jobs. Computer technicians were just like new Americans, homeless, confused, angry. Boris was tired of not being Russian anymore, but also not an American.

Despite the authentic clothes, he knew he did not *look* American any more than the stocky Armenian girls with short skirts who ran in packs, smoked Lucky Strikes, and looked over their shoulders to check on the impression they made. He was aware that young Blacks thinly veiled hostility by ignoring him from their special places on the quad where they congregated with large radios cradled like mechanical new borns, deliberately turning up the volume to annoy instructors and bystanders. Boris did not like to hang out with other Russians under *their* tree.

Unable to sleep, he took the bus to school very early Monday morning. His first class had been programming, but he had been dropped for irregular attendance. He smouldered with resentment against the teacher, a Jew! who turned a deaf ear to his earnest excuses—each time another death in the family.

"If this were the first or second time," Dr. Goldberg told him, "I'd let it go, but you've lost too much classwork. Take it next semester."

"But I need the class to graduate next semester!" Boris had heard from other students this sometimes worked.

Goldberg smiled with irony. "But I see that this is your very first semester, Boris. How do you expect to graduate next semester, I wonder?"

Smirking superior functionary, smug time-server, he didn't know he was obsolete, dead! Boris should have taken the course from an Arab, maybe he'd have gotten some decent human sympathy!

The computer practice room was open, and Boris walked in. A new terminal had just been installed and a quick glance under the table told him that the cable that was meant to secure it had no lock. Boris looked behind him back into the corridor. Nobody. Heart pounding, ears whistling, Boris lifted the machine, amazingly light, turned it sidewise and put it under his arm. He draped his jacket—a Russian carries his jacket even in hot weather—over the machine and strolled out of the building.

Unbelievably careless, Americans. No wonder Russia can so easily get under their defenses to spy. Glancing back at the windows of the computer technology office he felt he was looking into the glasses of a blind person.

He stopped at the first bus stop. No, stupid, not this one, so close to campus, take the next.

The first bus that came by was going to Hollywood. At home how would he justify this impressive new machine? No one would give or lend him such a machine. He would have to sell it! Where? A pawnshop.

He spotted one on Hollywood Boulevard, got off the bus and stood in front of the shuttered and closed store. A sign on the door told him he had two hours to wait for it to open. What were two hours? But not on the street, a cop could become suspicious, so he went into a coffee shop.

Boris sat with a coffee and read a newspaper. Cold War, new provocations, First Soviet Secretary persona non grata—that could be him. He shivered. Shipped back to Russia, without his parents, in disgrace, jailed over there for hooliganism—or would he be praised for tricking Americans?

Boris's first feeling of elation—he even thought briefly of telling Sonya of how clever he had been—quickly faded. Maybe the pawnshop checked serial numbers and registered them with the police. It would be suspicious if he filed them off. He needed a crooked pawnshop or a fence, but how to find one? There wasn't time. Robber barons had no such problems before the era of serial numbers. And only with the Nazis did people carry numbers like machines. He did not like lumping himself together with them. The only thing that sustained him was the thought of Goldberg's face when he found the machine missing.

When he walked into the pawnshop several people waited in a line, shabby downtrodden people, victims of the system. All of them appeared to be carrying automobile tape decks, and to each one the fat man smoking a big cigar in his steel cage shook his head, "no." He looked just like Russian caricatures of American or Jewish capitalist exploiters.

When it was his turn, Boris quickly unwrapped the machine. To his horror, he saw large letters identifying it as belonging to the community college. The man chewed his cigar and looked at him in complete silence. Boris noticed hanging in the rear of the cage the picture of a young man in a skull cap and prayer shawl.

"Wait!" the man commanded as Boris muttered something and made to cover up the machine.

Boris waited with a doomed trapped feeling, waited for the man to summon a policeman from his back room.

"Where did you get this?" the man demanded.

"Someone sold it to me," Boris mumbled, "but I can't use it."

The man tapped his cigar on a heavy ash tray once, twice, three times, as though ringing a bell.

"From Russia, are you?"

Boris ducked his head.

"Aren't you?" the man insisted.

"Yes, I am from Russia, but what business is it—"

"No business of mine, kid, no skin off my back, but look, do yourself a favor, take this back. Understand me? I'm going to turn around, and you weren't ever in here. I got kids too. You're no crook, yet, you don't know anything. People gave you a chance, don't spit on them. Take it back, there's still time. Now get out of here."

The man picked up his cigar, stood, turned his back and stared at the picture of his son in his Bar Mitsvah outfit long enough for Boris to cover the computer and run out of the shop.

Was the man being kind or afraid of being caught with stolen goods?

Now what was Boris going to do with this dead fish that stank in his hands? He felt like crying, but he was too old, and furthermore it would look suspicious on Hollywood Boulevard. The sun was hot and sweat rolled down his neck.

While passing a phone booth he got an idea. He put money in, called the college, and asked for Dr. Goldberg.

"This is Dr. Goldberg."

"This is Boris, Dr. Goldberg. Boris, your former student Boris? Remember me?"

"Yes, I remember you. What can I do for you?"

"It's not what you can do for me, but what I can do for you. Look, did you know you have a thief in your department?

"What's that? What do you mean?"

"Somebody came by it must have been last night or early this morning before I got up and left a computer outside my door. I don't know why they left it with me, but it belongs to the college." Boris waited for Dr. Goldberg to speak. "The name of the college is written on it," he yelled. "I wouldn't take something that wasn't mine, you see? Do you want me to bring it in, or do you want to come for it?"

"I understand," Dr. Goldberg said. "That's very kind of you, Boris. Which do you prefer?"

"I'll bring it in. But look, it's going to look strange, and I wanted you to know what happened. I can be there in a few minutes."

"Do you want something in return for this kindness?"

Sincerity coated Boris's voice. "No, no, not a thing. I only want for you to take it back where it belongs."

"Well, Boris, the least I can do for your honesty is to reinstate you in the class. Would you like that? Would you come to class every time?"

A truck rumbled by and Boris shouted, "I'll come every time, Dr. Goldberg. Yes, sir! I'll come right away."

He leaped out of the phone booth, almost dropping his precious burden, and ran to the bus stop. The tall buildings smiled from every window, streets gleamed as though paved with gold, and every pedestrian smiled. Boris got an instant seat on the bus where all the advertisements promised a great future.

Earthworks

I carry a very healthy respect for coincidence dating from the time I was found by my foster parents, a starveling bundle of rags and bones, on a rock outcropping in a remote area of the southwest desert.

What made them begin shooting pictures as they approached my rock, long before they could have spotted me? Only much later, with fine enhancement of the image, could they even make out the slightly lighter mass that was me as I clung there, for how long I have no idea, as I have no memory whatever of a time before that hot dry afternoon.

They were an eager young couple, both paleontologists, and even more strange, both experts in child psychology; otherwise how would they have known so well to wait patiently until I was ready to climb down from my rock, not to force me before I was ready?

If something unknown was influencing them they denied it, being scientists. Later they told me it must have been the unusual configuration of the rock that attracted them, but that couldn't have been the real reason, it was just another ship rock, not unusual in that desert, although most are not composed of brown aggregate.

Because I had no language, they put me with baby humans and chimpanzees to see what I would pick up from both groups. There were other animals too, mammals and cold-blooded, and rocks of every kind. For a long time I most resembled the rocks. I sat utterly still for hours. Animals moved freely around me. Curiously, even large rocks appeared to move about where I sat for any amount of time. My foster parents took pictures of designs I caused, runways from the look of them. Animals felt comfortable in them to the extent of giving birth to offspring that grew larger and stronger because they were born in them.

Apparently I did not recognize any essential difference between rock and animal; I felt their identity at some deep level, deeper than their common carbon bond, at the level of continuity, the endless play, splash, and return of mineral into vegetable and back again.

I even looked a bit like a rock as a child; where there ought to have been baby fat were bunches of muscles rather like outcroppings themselves, considering my overall brownness. As small as I was and continued to be, would-be bullies made a wide berth around me once they experienced the hardness of my body. I could knock their heads together with ease. Although I was no little superman, perhaps some of the requirements that went into my composition were different than theirs.

The consuming interest in my life, when I learned that I *was* one individual life, was to study how it is that things that don't appear to belong together *come* together, when they need to merge. For example, how did rock become soil become animate life? There are many missing links in our theories.

I studied mainly by sitting, first among my animals and rocks, then in the libraries of the university. My foster parents had the good sense to leave me alone to evolve in my unorthodox way.

Sometime during those years a young woman appeared in the carrel next to mine. After a while I noticed her. Her eyes were on me, her mobile features as swift as mine are slow to change. She "spoke," I answered, I didn't question how she came to be there, or how we came to speak. It was a pleasure to see how she looked at everything with a combination of joy and astonishment. Even if I had been deaf, as she is, I could have followed her meaning by looking into her eyes and at her mouth. Even her hair seemed electric, changing its shape like lightning as she moved her head.

Of course, I learned sign language, even though it wasn't really essential. Someone else might use the words, "stone-deaf" when speaking about her, but I reject the phrase—even stones can hear in their way as well as you or I.

We married, after it was agreed that our marriage would not stop her research into natural and synthetic diets for animals, particularly their mineral requirements.

So our interests dovetailed. When children came they were not led to scientific interests, they took to them the way a coelacanth takes to water. Important elements come together, with patience, though I never know why.

After years of work, saving up, some discoveries regarding nutrition that brought in modest royalties, we were able to buy a rambling huge wreck of a house on ten acres above Pasadena, where we moved in our assortment of children, animals with their stone runs and shelters, and assistants. We planted hundreds of drought-resistant crop plants and bushes with deep roots, and other hundreds of fruit-bearing trees, to be ready for years of wet and those of dryness, both of which are common to this part of the world.

Pasadena is a kind of outcropping of Los Angeles and at the same time its mother lode. The mansion, built by an eccentric among his middle-western neighbors, rides high above the earth on a native-rock foundation that also apparently extends many feet into the earth so as to provide vast storm cellars against the twisters he remembered from his native place. We use these cool stone caves for the countless jars of preserved fruits and vegetables flowing from plants. Because the geological table has bedrock extending to within a few feet of the surface here on the palisades above Pasadena's

Arroyo Seco, the foundation may actually be anchored to it.

From the windows of my study, located on the third floor, I look out on dozens of old pine trees under whose shade only moss grows, along with mounds that witness to the intense activity of numerous gophers. Their mounds are like pockmarks of meteors on the moon or miniature battlements flung up around earthen forts.

Everybody gave me advice when we moved here on how to get rid of these little workers, but I enjoy their work. I feel close to them, I envy their almost symbiotic association with rocks. Gophers are the world's greatest rock-movers, next to earthworms. I love to watch them at work moving a boulder out of their living room or hallway, heaving it over the side, pausing as if to say, "That's a job well done!" And popping back down again for another shove.

Very early in the first light I like to get to my desk while gophers are still at work, which has something to do with atmospheric conditions, the time of year and specific necessities of the season. Their ingenuity and engineering prowess are endless. I feel a connection between where I come from and what they do.

My gophers do a curious thing. They shape their stone walls like a massy stony wedge. Imitating them, I also have built massive stone barriers to the same shape, like the apex of a triangle and facing the mountains.

One morning as I sat down at my desk, I looked out into an atmosphere swimming in vapor, heavier than fog, lighter than rain. I could distinguish the branches of the pine trees, but nothing at all beneath the second story. After some time I could make out a kind of movement that was like a giant brown undulating snake. I made a sudden movement that slopped coffee on my arm and looked away for a moment to swab my arm. When I could look again, I saw that what I had taken as a connected movement *was*—hundreds, perhaps thousands of gophers were at work close to one another, throwing up ever-higher battlements of earth and stone. Sometimes two worked together to heave a boulder larger than both of them on one of the growing mounds.

Because gophers *never* work together, at least above ground, I was intensely excited and ran downstairs spilling my forgotten coffee on every side.

At the front door I hesitated, afraid that I might scare them, but they paid no attention as I approached. I almost thought they *smiled* at me as they continued to work. (Gophers don't smile, not with those sharp curved teeth!) Then I thought, here I am strolling around like a building supervisor not even thinking about what other zoologists in the San Gabriel Valley were finding!

I retreated to the kitchen, where my wife with her usual energy was clearing up breakfast things with the help of one of the assistants. On a work table were rows of gleaming jars newly washed and waiting for the day's canning. I touched her shoulder as she turned to greet me. "Have you noticed our gophers this morning?" I signed.

She smiled, feeling my excitement, enjoying the urchin in me that clings to every phenomenon having to do with life.

"Are they doing something unusual?" she signed.

I took her by the arm and led her to the front door.

She looked a question at me. I saw that whereas the evidence of their work was everywhere apparent, the furry animals themselves were not.

"Looks like they're planning to build a local version of Stonehenge," she remarked. "Anything else you need?"

I scratched my head. "Why did they go away?"

She kissed me and went back to the kitchen. When phenomena don't quickly explain themselves she tends to go back to the familiar that keep reproducing, like dirty dishes, test tubes, feeding bowls, and jars for canning.

Phone calls to other zoologists came to nothing. Apparently the gopher population in the rest of the San Gabriel was up to nothing unusual.

One thing was becoming apparent with the naked eye—the cloud cover, increasing every minute. Again there was no way to tell the ground from sky. There had been no advance notice of a front of such magnitude, but clearly a peerless storm was on the way.

The children straggled in, sent home by headmasters, principals, and administrators of their various schools who also had examined the sky and found it ominous enough to dismiss their charges. The children quickly took their usual stations among our animals, numerous in both species and numbers, feeding, calming, battening down. Our children all have a joyous communion with animals, an intuitive grasp of their habits and needs. Even as infants they were more like cubs as they romped with clawed, fanged, and furry beasts, almost never taking any kind of hurt.

They were engaged now primarily in reassuring the animals who were nervous about the rapidly changing weather.

Too bad so much fruit remained unharvested, but it could be collected from the ground after the storm and salvaged although bruised with my wife's particular formulas, canned, and then added to our very large supply of canned food stored in the voluminous cellar.

Wind stirred the branches of giant pine trees, sweeping them from side to side as though to say, "Yes, yes, yes." The color of one kind of vegetation began to bleed into that of another, and all into the atmosphere, which took on the coloration of an aquarium, with us on the bottom.

In my heightened state of participation, I looked up, half expecting to see gigantic faces peering into the tank to see how the creatures within were taking the changes in the weather.

In fact, the clouds scudding overhead, churning and fuming, *did* look like faces, their contours constantly in motion, giving the heavily laden vapor first the appearance of a frown, then a smile or look of deeply involved conversation.

I wanted to point this out to my wife, but she was engaged in marshaling our forces, conferring with some worried neighbors who were bringing their own animals to us for safekeeping, and who then stood around uncertainly, not ready or willing to go back to their own homes.

The first drops began to fall, a relief after so much tension and waiting. The temperature had not fallen much. It was going to be a tropical storm and the runoff that much greater since none of the moisture would be retained in the form of snow at higher elevations.

Soon gutters were running high, even overflowing below our property where storm drains glutted with debris could not take the water, but merely passed it on.

The gophers did not reappear, leaving their curious towers against—what? The rain? Flood?

I had a flash of, perhaps, memory. Of the time before my adoptive parents found me clinging to that rock in another dry arroyo. I saw myself splayed against my rock, brown thick water swirling around me molten with its cargo of earth. Was there also a dreadful freight of people, screaming or dead, bloated animals, splintered trees? In this century there is no history of such a flood. The last such flood occurred a full century before I was born.

In my memory I see myself crying, numb with exhaustion and fear, clinging to my rock, around which water slices and is flung upward to a great height, leaving me just a little space and air to breathe.

At this point, I greatly desired to view again my parents' films to see if the rock had been shaped like an airfoil that really flung water up and away from me like a streamlined bullet train.

147

No time now, with everything streaming with water. I threw on my poncho to go out and see what was happening in the arroyo. Instantly wet to the skin, I flung off the poncho and everything else.

I peered down into the valley, and could see nothing at first, but then the wind blew away sheets of water and for an instant I could see below. I saw huge boulders and rubble. With a shock I realized that the natural-looking rock formations were remnants of the Rose Bowl. Already the arroyo was more than half-filled with water from side to side—nearly a mile across, an instant Mississippi, gouging the walls of the canyon with uprooted trees, houses, girders.

For the first time I thought about what might happen to our house. How high could the water go?

I turned back.

A changed landscape greeted me. Houses surrounding mine were being undermined and undercut by great sheets of water. Most of them were already off their foundations, battered into splinters by their own weight.

My house rode high above the waves on its stone foundation, aided in its stability by the wedge-shaped rocks we had laboriously placed in imitation of the gophers.

Water gushed around, deflected as by a stone-cutting edge, a stone knife that sliced water on both sides.

As though the house and grounds were a land-based ark.

And here we stay, well into the second month of steady rain, with no idea whether there remains any city below us. We have no communication with anybody except ourselves, our animals, and those neighbors who elected to stay until it was too late to think about leaving. We have plenty of food for humans and animals.

I can't get at the films to check about that rock on which I was found. Was it really similar to the one on which we safely cling? Is it strange that the skills we possess as a family are so relevant to our present circumstances?

From time to time, I continue to look upward for another glimpse of that strange configuration, so like gigantic faces etched in the tumultuous clouds. I find myself addressing the titans, the lords above. I have begun to pray that they stop the flood. It is time. I have thanked them humbly for leading us to Pasadena and for placing me on my first rock.

Even for finding me adoptive parents whose family name provides a clue, a hint, to what I was chosen to do.

And if it is true, that I was chosen for this work of keeping safe a few people and a few species of the vast variety of animals and plant life, perhaps they will some time answer my request.

The Weight Goes On the Downhill Ski

S now tires didn't seem to help much at sundown on the icy Julianer Pass. Sol cursed the automatic steering on the big car. At each slight sickening slide the little girl, perched on her seat in the back, said, "Don't go down the mountain!"

"Have I ever done that?" Sol sang cheerfully. Betsy, from her side, chuckled something to the little girl, then stared grimly into the gray skin that pressed against the windshield.

Vacation time, again. From nothing to nowhere. At least the present self-induced danger kept out other gray haunts that arrived in various touching forms in the flatlands—by messenger, by mail, by accident. Sol coughed into his handkerchief, looked briefly from the road to see, hopefully, if there was another string of red. Just dark phlegm, about the color of the ice tears on the corners of the windshield. Nature and he afflicted with the same catarrh or congestion or infection.

"I was really worried for awhile," Betsy said.

Sol was almost startled. The car was being strafed by the last bits of sunshine, they were in the high valley of the Engadin, no more ice on the road, all downhill into Winter Wonderland—skiing, sledding, ice skating, health, sauberkeit. Sol sighed. Saved again. Thanks be to his healthy peasant forebears. Would the little girl go blind, deaf, arthritic, suicidal, in her time? Now she chirped from her seat: "I want something to drink."

Betsy unlimbered the plastic bottle.

"Will you go out when we're at the hotel?"

"Maybe," Sol said. "Let's just try to get there first."

The somber Swiss, millions of dollars in colorful and fast ski clothes, their one release from lives of steady industry, common sense and peace conferences. How did they avoid suicide, behind closed doors?

Betsy yelled after him, as he hurried over the snow to get out of ear-shot: "Go on, destroy yourself, do it, go finish yourself off."

He clenched his jaws hating her, wanting to kill her, to snatch his little girl from the hateful bitch, run off into the world with her, wander over the face of it, mendicant, poor, saying and savoring sweet insights over candlelight as she grew to pubescence and eventual incest, sweet guilt, and then the knife.

She's right, of course. I wait on news of my contemporaries' defeat, savoring dementia or demise, so that I can feed off them. They stood neatly in a row:

1: Gordon, off to live on a commune, 40, like Sol, suddenly one eye gone, the other in immediate danger of falling perforated like confetti. Gordon, soon to be sitting still in the Northern California sun blind and probably cheerful.

2: Wendy, hopeful unattractive student, two abortions in succession, perforated womb, infection, running sores for life, or did Sol only hope so?

3: Strange Al, hairless monotone, health addict, bringer of books on nutrition, dead via Christmas card of "hardening of the arteries."

4: Del, thrice-married begetter of children, colleague at Sol's college, brittle, superior, sneering, marrier of his students, reader to their ignorance through whose clouds he shone, suicide at 48, bullet through the head.

Betsy saw Sol writing off letters to everyone who knew Del, asking for details, details. And why? And I should have known, been less hard on him, let him get away with more. Sitting at the typewriter, coughing, asthmatic. Del was asthmatic, he wore pink-tinted glasses, an ass. Betsy bitter. "You don't have any feeling for these people. You're trumping it all up. You need something to do."

Vacation from a vacation in the Engadin, where the sun is, where Nietszche, Mann, Hesse all went to hold court and walk and ski. Me too, thought Sol. Them and me, and Betsy and Meredith. Up through ice to sun to the tops of mountains, and down on twin knives.

It was not clear, it was not even emerging, but all the dreams pointed toward it, as he interpreted them. "No," the analyst said. "I don't see it that way. They're just too theatrical, too easily turned into poems and stories, as though they're being manipulated."

"Well, how could I manipulate my own dreams? They are unconscious, aren't they?"

"They're so ironic. As though you're bending over backward to accommodate the drama of it. I don't want to take them seriously."

Forty years waiting for simplicity, for little brother to take the reins in a temporary cease-fire through sickness, drugs, or carelessness of the superior intellectual irony. Then fatigue. Psychosomatic sickness also pointed the way: either simplify or die. Now or ever.

"All your weight on the downhill ski."

I can't, it's not logical. So the downhill-turning ski point wavered in the air and down he went. Faith. It requires faith. I don't have the faith. I have the vocabulary. The doe-eyes of Sol's ski instructor rested comfortingly on him. "That's better. But less upper body, more—this." He demonstrated, retarding his natural grace. Sol couldn't. His head was independent.

"How about going crazy and killing you instead of committing suicide?" Sol enquired of Betsy over morning coffee.

"Well, the chances of your finding a Jungian analyst in an

institution for the criminally insane aren't too good unless it all happens in Switzerland."

"They'd probably extradite me to California."

"They didn't extradite Leary."

"He's well-known. 'Nacht und Nebel,' they'd just ship me out and there wouldn't be a word in the papers. I'd have to kill you first. With a bullet. Give you iron, fast, no more anemia." He thought of knives.

Betsy wasn't smiling. "You'd like to do that, wouldn't you?"

She wanted to talk to him, she believed that she used to talk to him and he would answer. That was belief. Memory. He wanted to believe in memory. *It* didn't play tricks. It was at the service of some other master. His magnum opus would be on memory and it would retrieve for him everything lost in the folds of time and he would be healthy and the sun would come out and no place for madness germs to hide. Meanwhile, madness was preferable to out-and-out suicide. How much of anything is due to a deficiency in iron or thiamine, or if you ate just two pounds of Bircher muesli every morning mixed with yoghurt could you write *Hamlet?*

Flinging off the crushing down cover just before dawn, Sol heard a horse-drawn sled on the snow outside the hotel window. He opened the curtains. Three of them passed in the blue light, under his feet. He looked up at the mountain range etched white against the coming brilliant day, briefly considered dressing and going out. Very cold, very romantic. I could stand outside Nietzsche's house in the dawn. I could go and attack that snide psychiatrist's wife and see what the little fat man would do, with his form-fitting polyethelene boots and form-fitting British professionalism. The trouble is, I know nothing for sure. That man can go on forever, certain he's superior, certain his wife is a creature of his, certain, certain. He won't ever crack, he's too roly-poly, unless I break into his room and rape his wife. But it wouldn't be rape. It wouldn't be anything.

"Do you identify yourself as an alienist wherever you go, like you did to me?" Sol asked Alex.

"No, sometimes I do."

"Do you ever feel that you never get outside your own claque, your own type, ever hear anything disturbing, new?"

"Of course I do all the time. I have my patients."

"Did anybody ever go crackers on you while you were on vacation, just because they knew you were an alienist?"

Alex looked at him, professionally friendly. He avoided the question as Sol knew he would.

"No, never."

Meaning, not now either, I'm having enough trouble with these polyethelene boots, very dear, cutting the ankles. We have been coming here for years, thank you, and we find it very comfortable, although the wine list leaves something to be desired.

"Don't you think that people sometimes travel in order to make contact with people of a social standing superior to their own at home?"

Alex's wife tittered. Something like a real expression appeared on Alex's face. I scored, exulted Sol, and then immediately fell down the glacier. So what? Does that make *me* more? So he comes from the lower Caucasus, harks from muddy torn boots far from synthetics. He comes from the real thing, lives in the patent-plastic and advises patients to "buck up," which is what they need sometimes, not lengthy reductive analysis. Common sense.

Sol abruptly went back to the room. Meredith was there, building a city. "What shall I do next?" Sol asked her.

"With me?" she asked.

He pulled her up off the floor and hugged her and tried to kiss her cheek. She squirmed and made herself into a slippery pole.

"I'm building a city. With me?"

"I want to go into St. Moritz to look for a fox-skin coat," said Betsy. "Do you want to kill me now or later?"

"Both," Sol said. "So I won't take lessons this afternoon. Go ahead."

"No, it's a great opportunity for you to do something real for a change. Go on, I'll stay with Meredith."

"Why don't we go to bed and make love, screw, have intercourse?"

"For want of anything better to do? What do we do with Meredith?"

"Let her screw too."

"Wouldn't you just like to."

"Yes, I'd like to."

"That's why you wanted a girl so much."

"Well, you won't let me screw girls outside the family."

How to turn this traffic jam into a joke. "I'll take her ice-skating, go to town, go ahead. I don't mind."

"No, take your lessons this afternoon."

After all, she did love him, or at least stayed with him years and years, from the end of her 20s now to her middle 40s; that was something. Gordon, writing to a friend: "Tears flowed from an empty eye socket when I got your card." Del's heavy head, entered from which side, temple to temple, or mouth to crown? Meredith's sleeping head, so heavy on his knee, Vivaldi and Pergolesi in the Schloss at Rapperswill, and her eyes perfect horizontals arched by rainbow eyebrows, shaded by delicate almost feeler-like lashes. His heart caught in the strings of the plucked harpsichord—I could be looking at her dead body. I could scream and slash myself. Needing the sacrifice of the little girl to accomplish my dreary extinction?

It all comes of being too idle. Asthma, neurasthenia—never would happen if I had to be a truck driver.

"The downhill ski, all the weight on it. Don't hold back."

The sweet simplicity of the ski instructor, Sol and he on the double-bar lift, the wood solidly behind them, bumping up the hill.

"What do you do in the summer?" Sol asked in German.

"I go on the tramp."

Ski-bum. He knows precisely how to handle would-be homosexual men, wealthy American women. Just look at them, in a helpful way. And they learn. They tip. After the day-long lesson he waited, but Sol did not tip him. Revenge. The young man quietly went away to make his report to the tourist office.

One way to bring, by capillary action, the mud of the lower world up to this insistently bright clean place. Sol fondled himself. In the bath his glasses steamed up. He couldn't read ever any more in the bath, because he needed his glasses to read. Everybody in his family disintegrated young: teeth, eyes, ears. Was it the post-nasal drip medicine that made him feel so distant, so stupid, or incipient schizophrenia? "I don't use those terms loosely," Alex said. "What do you mean by schizophrenia?"

"I mean being numb and beaten in at least two identities," Sol said.

"Is my daddy sick?" Meredith asked, stumbling against the bed in the darkened room.

"He's tired, sweetheart," Betsy said. "Let's go into the dining room."

She looked at him, he knew, acidly. Giving her more to do, copping out.

"I want my daddy."

"Well, you can't have him now. Maybe he'll wake up sometime today."

When they left, Meredith protesting all the way, Sol threw off the covers again, padded into the bathroom to take a Seranex Forte, a

Swiss patent medicine with codeine, not available in the U.S. except by prescription. The Swiss dispense poisons (*Gift*, in German) in precise metal containers with Rosetta Stones included at no extra charge—every label in three languages. The humblest item translates itself. Even the trams issue tickets, validate, run, and stop without the necessity for contact with any living being.

No point in blaming the Swiss for efficiency. That comes of hard work, and what happens in the dark nights of their souls isn't publicized in newspapers.

"My daddy is up. I want something to drink."

As Meredith slid on her double skates over the ice, Sol, holding her, was proud of the little giggling thing beside him. "Will you remember ice-skating at Sils Maria, little girl?" What is your memory-bank like? Will you retain me? Am I there? Will you talk sadly to some acne-laden intellectual in 14 years about your father, who was always in bed, or wheezing, or yelling at your mother? Can't we just play through and leave out this bit?

"Your dreams have Caesars and Oedipus in them, you wouldn't have these dreams except that you see yourself in situations with literary figures."

"What about archetypes?" Sol asked.

The analyst shook her head. "I just don't know. It feels to me that they are too literary. Can't you stop being so conscious about things, let go, let it go awhile? Let Little Brother speak and play?"

"I can't help thinking that every bit of enjoyment is the tip of an iceberg—it costs so much just to get there, and then I can't enjoy it. I may be missing something. Everything has to count, I have to count. I'm always missing out."

"Alex, you're around 40 too, don't you fear the dead-center, the self-satisfaction that comes from surrounding yourself with ciphers like yourself?"

157

He changed the subject hurriedly. He isn't interested, or he knows I'm annoying myself into a breakdown. He doesn't want to be involved or responsible.

"Get up off that bed."

"I'm being an odalisque."

"You're the wrong sex for being an odalisque, you're more like a sphinx-ter." Betsy looked happy over her play. Sol slowly got up. There were amounts of, how should he say? light, by way of putting away the groceries.

Another bright cobalt blue sky day. Today is the day to go crazy. But have I left Betsy enough travelers checks to get me to an institution?

"Daddy, Mary Dee is dead."

"No, is she?"

"Yes. She's gone to sleep in a box."

"You don't go to sleep when you die," Betsy said testily. "Why do you put those ideas in her mind?"

"I said you get sick and the doctor can't fix you and so you go to sleep forever. Can you think of a better explanation?"

I've got Meredith thinking about death too, Sol thought. Worse than fingering her crotch.

Betsy looked worried. Sol thought he could read her mind. She had hoped coming up here would take his mind off his permanent wet cough, the failure of his last two novels, two aborted beginnings, petering out of energy.

He watched his car turn off the road onto the iced-over lake.

Betsy screamed, "It's not thick enough. We'll go under!"

"How do you think ships do it?"

He woke up hot and sticky. Meredith coughed. The horse and sleds came by. He knew without looking that it was dawning another merciless day.

Engadin, what does it mean? The doe-eyed instructor helped him up. The others were standing like Indians on patrol. Screw them, thought Sol, you haven't got a forty-pound brain on your uphill ski. A child of two slalomed by without ski poles at ninety miles an hour and stopped on a dime. Sol pondered smashing him into powder snow. Actually, he thought, I don't resent him, I resent his parents, I especially resent *my* parents. Where were they when they built ski lifts in Bucharest? Why didn't I get lessons in skiing, Greek, and Latin instead of in the clarinet?

He padded painfully toward the hotel, stopped in front of Nietzsche's house. "You went mad, but you had an awful lot published before." Sol felt curiously elated. His whole body ached. He was tired. He was hungry, and he thought he would probably taste the food tonight. Betsy and Meredith were waiting for him at the hotel to hear about his exploits.

Snow is antithetical to life.

No, it isn't, it isn't anything but snow. This is nothing but a house. I am nothing but a man who is here right now, at this time, with a wife and child. The snow crunches beneath my boots with an altogether satisfactory sound. Wait, I am almost being satisfied. "Stay, you moment, you are fair!" and that means losing my soul. Rather lose my life. Turn into a placid bovine of a middle-class middle-aged man.

That girl has a beautiful ass. Wait for me, I want to talk to you. I don't want to talk, I want to take your hand and go into an altogether different dispensation from this one. What's wrong with this one? It has a paunch, asthma, habits, a medicine cabinet. Would Little Brother like to go off with her? She skis like a ballerina in the wind. They tip glasses over fur-tipped after-ski boots. The air buzzes with sex, candles drip and puddle on a glass-topped table. "Yes, yes, I felt that way too, when? Just at that moment? You too?" Heavy heart, lips

159

THE INNER GARDEN

touching, but always the same, the same words. In the beginning was the word and at the end.

Betsy vaguely touched the sliding doors. Two weeks here, a polite note from the management: at least the first week's pension. Sol in bed in the darkened room, slips of paper on the floor beside the bed, "Another bright cobalt blue day. Stay, moment, you are fair."

"Is Daddy mad at you?"

"No, Daddy isn't mad at me."

"Is he mad at me?"

"No."

Pause. "Then is he mad at himself?"

"Maybe, I don't know."

"Then he has to be happy."

Sol was glad he wasn't using the bath. He was paying for the bath, but he wasn't using it. He was wasting money.

"I guess you heard about the suicide of . . ." "Tears flowed from an empty eye socket when I got your card . . ." "What I like about Sol is his need to play the main part in Hamsun's *Hunger* while he drives around Europe in a Mercedes-Benz . . ."

Sol giggled. The Russians were big on the sleeping cure, but he wasn't sure about the temperature. Maybe he should sleep on the ice? Was he driving Betsy crazy? Was she consulting Alex, were they whispering about him?

Despite himself, the ski instructor came into focus. Suddenly, Sol put his weight on the downhill ski.

"Life has to be both black and white and color," the analyst said. "The problem is to retain the spontaneity while coming to consciousness at the same time."

"That sure is a problem," Sol said.

"That's it!" the ski instructor said. The other students beamed. They're not so bad, Sol thought. He loved the instructor. How

160

would he be as a babysitter for Meredith? Would Betsy want to go to bed with him? No, don't complicate the moment. Evaporate the forty pound brain, put it low in the center of gravity, about where his balls would hang if they went plumb down. Take Betsy away from the dividing curtains. It's not right that she should absently finger the fringes. Why do I punish her?

One of the first things to remember is that *she* is not being punished. Why did she marry me, Sol thought with dramatic flourish, if she didn't enjoy the tension? For a moment he was almost pleased. *Almost.* Presque, ziemlich, casi—every thing fits wherever you fit it in. Of course I would remember the word for *almost* (k'mat) in any language I've ever encountered. Almost, a bigger word than love. Almost committed suicide, almost had a best seller, almost made love, almost lived. All and most, most all.

"Are you all right?"

"Almost," Sol murmured.

"I will help you." The sweet-eyed instructor leaned over to help Sol get himself back onto his feet. Sol was pleased at almost losing consciousness, almost having to be taken back to the hotel on a stretcher. Instead, only an extra stiffness in his already stiff neck. "A stiff-necked race," saith God.

"Pardon me?"

"A quote from my Bible, it helps me in moments like this."

"Pardon me?"

"Do you take your patients seriously, or do you know they can really be better if they'd only buck up and try?" Sol asked Alex while he rummaged in the hotel bookshelf. He found a respectable-looking volume and opened it toward the middle. Alex pulled out his cheroot. Sol saw his eyes focus a bit and then skitter self-consciously toward the window. Sol was shredding the page into long narrow strips at first to bug Alex, but then it acquired a fascination of its own. Of course books were sacred, part of the tradition that says: time is sacred, education is sacred, and even strips from books are sacred. So Sol made them as regular as he could.

Alex was red—furious or embarrassed at being related to him, at least guilty by association. But he would ignore Sol's action.

"People are people, they'll always do what they want to do, whatever they call it. I believe they ought to be allowed to do it, even if it is messy."

Had Alex been gotten to the point of telling Sol to bug off, commit suicide if he needed to? Possible, but not easy, to get to the heart of a matter but you've got to violate a man's sense of property or propriety.

Now Alex looked at the growing pile of paper with something like professional calm. Betsy came in, checking. She saw the pile, then looked at Sol's busy hands, at his smiling welcoming mouth. She turned on a string and walked out without speaking.

Alex's mouth turned down but Sol continued smiling, with effort. He got up stiffly, as though in report to a jury. "She won't be surprised," he thought.

He sat on Nietzsche's stone until his rump went numb. "If I were a truly serious man, the coldness of my ass wouldn't make any difference, I would be so concentrated on the gravity of decision-making. Therefore, if my ass troubles me at this juncture, I am not serious enough. The problem is: how do I become serious enough, without further troubling my loved ones, for . . . it?"

Sol's thoughts were increasingly couched in what he called True Confessions (Fiction-Ominous). Betsy stayed away from him as much as she could. She didn't mention going back down the mountain. She seemed numb. Or paralyzed. Possibly he simply didn't hear her. He was an invalid. He went back to the slopes. Despite every intention, Sol grew more skillful. He no longer snowplowed but made fairly neat stem turns, kept the tips of his now-longer skis parallel and did not have to remember to bend forward. It was increasingly difficult for him to fall down. Consequently, the sloe-eyed instructor spoke to him briefly or not at all, only waited to see if he was following.

Sol's brain did not stand aloof. His fantasies turned to avalanches under which he himself was not trapped, but in which he was digging to get someone out.

"I seem to be turning toward images of health." These things he could not discuss with Betsy, who seemed locked into a permanent mask of silent, sullen anger. He could only switch on his vacant idiot smile when he saw her.

"How long has it been?" Five, six days at most, since the icy Julianer Pass ride up here. Then, an avalanche, a "to the valley thrown," of . . . what?

"I've got tickets, Sol, we're packed and the taxi will be here in a minute. You take care of the bill however you can and take care of yourself too. Meredith, give your Daddy a hug and a kiss."

Sol bent automatically before he opened his mouth. "But wait, the ice is breaking, there's a chance of spring as well as avalanche. I've been reading the reports."

"There's no way out. All the passes are closed. You're risking your life and my child's life."

"Will the car fall in the river, Daddy?"

"Your daddy is joking, Meredith." Betsy put her arms on hips, looking through him with hate or contempt or . . .

"I like the ski instructor's eyes more than yours," Sol said.

"I would wish you luck, but he probably has younger maniacs for lovers," Betsy said.

"I'll pay him," Sol said. He saw the car teeter on the edge of the partly frozen river, hesitate, then topple over with that metallic sound of ice ripped open, and then the blue, the opaque green, the silence. And the peace?

"No, don't go. This is all charade."

"I'm sorry, I never had patience for parlor games. My daughter and I are going back to America."

Sol sat down in front of the door.

"Please," Betsy cried, "don't do that. It won't do. I'll miss the taxi and the bus. I have to go, Sol. I'm sorry, but I have to go, I can't stand it anymore."

"Mommy can't stand it anymore, Daddy."

Sol got up slowly. He stood aside. He saw them go through the place where the door was, when it was closed, but a space in the wall when it was opened. Then, he imagined, they went into the corridor and passed the other doors, mostly closed, and then went around an L-shaped bend to the desk. Goodbye, goodbye. This is really cooperation. St. John and The Dark Night of the Soul, alone and in mysterious communion with the hotel room . (. . . .)

Braced for a jolt. Sol picked up the last suitcase, took another look around the room, found one last toy, looked out the window at the ice skating rink. He wasn't a glorious deadly failure on the slopes, after all. He could put his weight on the downhill ski; in fact, after awhile had no real choice in the matter.

He exchanged commonplaces with the manager while he paid the bill.

He couldn't find Alex. "Skiing's a pretty good therapy-tonic, isn't it? I find it that way, I get downhearted too, you know, but skiing always picks me up." Goodbye Alex, you're a wise man.

Pick me up! Meredith, Sol thought, I need to go and pick her up. He walked to the Verkehrsbureau and left an envelope for his instructor.

Now, to go downhill and take up the leaden reins of life, Sol thought, settle into it, all right, almost?

He thought of sitting on Nietzsche's rock again. No, no time. And so the Engadin cures yet another storm-tossed soul.

The car smoothly negotiated the curves down toward Chur and the valley floor. Meredith slept, Betsy dozed.

Hear Anything From Bakersfield?

S am's father Harry sits in front of his high-rise window occasionally looking out at the demolition of an old tile-covered apartment house.

"What do you think they're going to replace it with?" Sam asks, to be saying something.

Harry shakes his head slowly, his lips pointed down. At eighty-three, his head is still topped by a bush of snowy, showy white hair. Sam wants to stroke it, but by unspoken agreement the only touching between the old man and his middle-aged son is a handshake hello and goodbye.

"Too bad you're going to lose that view," Sam says, "you won't be able to see the kids lining up for movies on Wilshire."

Harry doesn't respond. Probably he hasn't noticed theatre or kids. What does he notice?

"It's a big job," he sighs, grimacing, holding up his swollen fingers. Even this he does vaguely.

Sam pushes open a window. The clouds are magnificent, it is a spring day without smog; Santa Catalina Island is clearly visible from the thirteenth-floor window. Everything in Westwood Village is upscale, bright with posters, billboards, the air pulses with youth and other packaged goods. Sam wants to ask his father about Romania, about the uncanny resemblance of his daughter Channa to his mother Esther, dead thirteen years before of multiple cancers. More and more Sam wonders about his mother, as he sees her daily reenacted by Channa, or is it that frustration and impotence smear because their locus is impossible to pinpoint? Channa is stubborn, she doesn't seem to want to learn anything she doesn't already know. She appears to get most of her satisfaction from frustrating others' expectations.

"Would you agree that my mother's main characteristic was stubbornness?" Sam asks.

Slowly, Harry turns his head from the window and looks blankly at his son. Then irritation almost animates his features. "That's the stupidest thing I've ever heard. She's dead, so why don't you leave her alone?"

Sam cringes. What else did he expect? He wants to explain, "I don't mean any harm to her memory, I just want to understand before it's too late to do anything about it. I'm a link, life is too strong a current for me. I'm a fuse in danger of burn-out. If I have to be a burnt-out hulk at your age, I don't want to live so long if I can't change anything, save something, improve. I'm *not* nasty to her memory."

And yet he remembers the pictures he took of his mother, helpless in her bed the day before she died. She couldn't stop him, slap him, or even cry. Grimly, she watched him suck up her image like a blowfly. When she died, she was only a shell, death-light.

Harry has been a small merchant selling what came to hand all his life. Sam also became a vendor of miscellany, a variety-store academic. He could almost grasp several universes, almost he is spread as thin as Donne's "gold to airy thinness beat," almost he feels life and death beat their wings in his breast until he is almost breathless with compassion, which irony turns over: "This is only fear of death."

In the residential hotel residents trudge up and down the halls waiting for breakfast, lunch or dinner. They sit in the lobby among a thicket of sticks at their feet. The dead are spirited away at night, because nobody wants to be completely aware of the nature of his own stay at this place for those in training to die, a terminal of old people stacked waiting for the control tower to beam them down or up, according to religious belief.

Some residents leave their doors ajar. Going by, one sees the few things they salvage from previous lives—a lamp, some law books, a couch. In the dining room, dark and vital recent immigrants serve the feeble white elderly nonfat, noncaloric, nonsodium cuisine.

Not to sneer, this is the *best* that awaits. One of a couple is passed-over by the sudden attacks and comes to Westwood Horizons, where everywhere he or she finds smiles, smiles, as if for a retarded child.

Sam's father does not sit in the lobby, but when he goes down, he ponders the tropical fish. He has a tender name for each of the gaudy specimens, but because his eyes aren't so good, he also has a name for one of the exotic rocks, not minding that it doesn't move.

Harry doesn't watch TV much, because he hasn't got a remote control and it hurts him to get up and down to change channels. He listens to Luciano Pavarotti over and over. His record player does that because it isn't sophisticated.

"Do you hear anything from your friends in Bakersfield?" Sam puts a slight ironic twist on the word "friends" because he doesn't believe his father ever made any friends, only cronies at best, coffee companions at mid-morning and afternoon, mornings when Esther took over the till and afternoons when Sam did, and Harry could go have several sugar-heavy cups of burnt coffee at the Last Chance Cafe (which said First Chance on the other side of the sign), every spoonful of which now hung on the tips of his diabetic fingers.

(O Channa, do you read this years later, after your grandfather is gone, and I am gone, and marvel at the bitterness, the anguish, impotence, the years of terror, rage, lack of understanding hanging to the tips of my fingers? Sam thinks.)

"What friends?" Harry replies, as though knowing Sam's thought, which he surely does, as Sam has fretted him about how few people call him, dreading the same in his turn, because Harry is interested in nothing, thinks about nothing, reads nothing, only sits, sits, in front of the open window fronting the blank scar across the street, so fresh as to resemble a new mastectomy on the torso of the neighborhood.

I envy the successful dead, thinks Sam, members of my generation whose last months in the hospital are made grateful by masses, banks of flowers and cards, visits from cadres of friends and associates, old lovers and students, and the faithful attendance of wife or husband. Dying, one flow after another dammed by obstruction or disintegration, there remains sufficient awareness to need recognition. When all channels dry, morphine opens mysterious others. They die with smiles on their lips, every one of the successful dead, whose number Harry and Sam are not destined to join.

"I don't even know who's alive," Harry adds unexpectedly.

"Well, who is, for sure? Maybe we'll take a ride one Sunday. Do you feel up to it?"

And wonders, what if the old man gets sick or dies during the trip, and Sam's daughter Channa were with them, freaking out?

"Max Polin and Helen. I know they're alive. We can visit them. When do you think we can go?"

This is the most Harry has spoken to Sam for months.

"Next Sunday," Sam decides quickly. "Channa will go too."

It will not be the first time Channa has gone to Bakersfield on pilgrimage, dragged to Sam's growing-up house, part of his desire to show her it was possible to live simply and without major appliances, with only one bathroom, an attempt to orient and plant her in a place and time. She had met Sam's sanctuary, his high school English teacher. He watched their reaction to each other, in an attempt to recapture the fragrance of his own fifteen-year-old self, which he had lost or misplaced. Channa is the anchor he can throw at various depths to secure his present ship. Unlike parents who believe their offspring are roads to the future, Channa was for him a battering ram into the past, more unknown than anything before him.

"Isn't there anybody else but Helen and Max Polin and their brain-damaged Jonathan? They weren't really friends. Always too rich, weren't they?"

"You want to argue or do you want to go to Bakersfield?" Harry says. "Get me my cane. It's lunch time. You want lunch? I'll pay."

He is practically effusive, Harry. Sure, Sam will have lunch, and speak Spanish with the waiter, since that is sure to annoy his father, who will say, "Hombre loco, no?" And the good-looking Hispanic will put his arm on Harry's back and say, "Es muy buen hombre, mi amigo, Harry," and look fondly into his face.

Sam will smile crookedly, envious because the waiter can touch Harry without his shrinking.

Channa agrees to go because she knows that this is the holy mountain for her father, hated homeland and totemic place of never-changing elephants and ancient ice cream parlor, loathed from birth in Mercy Hospital for its heat, insects and rednecks, known for giving birth place to Merle Haggard and Earl Warren, Jr., country music and Supreme Court, cattle, cocaine, Kern County.

Channa would go, she got lots of points for this one.

"One condition," Channa demands, "not your pediatrician. I definitely will not go to that house with her smelly dogs and hands." Channa refers to the born-again explorations of the eighty-year-old hands of Sam's school pediatrician, who fondles Channa's hair and ears with joyous tremble. Sam loves her and likes her praying over him each time. Why not? She is old and competent, unlike his father. What can be wrong with the Holy Ghost in her hands?

"Then sit in the car with the air off," Sam retorts, knowing that she knows he won't make her. And she knows that she will finally, reluctantly, go inside, if only for the cakes and cookies, cocoa and candies that she puts out with her religion.

This too is life. The ancient physician continues to be Sam's pediatrician, although she doesn't bill him. She has told him that she prays for him and his family every night. Sam likes to believe this. He believes her prayers go somewhere, if only to a cosmic vault from which he receives interest from her invested capital. There is for Sam no heaven and no god, but *she* believes in the divine, and Sam receives what she deposits there as surely as Channa will inherit what cash Sam possesses at his death. This is all the religion Sam gets, by reflection, as to look directly in its face is to tempt the fate of all those who look directly at Medusa.

Once, sullen at the doctor's continued ministrations after Sam felt he was too grown up for them, he told a lie about her to someone's parents. He didn't remember any more what the lie was, but it was shocking enough that it got back to her. After examining him, she took his shoulders in both hands and said, "Sammy, I know you didn't mean it, and you are sorry for it, and it did, yes, it did, hurt my feelings. I know you are a good boy, and you will be a good man, and I don't need to forgive you, and God doesn't need to forgive you. But will *you* forgive yourself?"

And this was prophetic, because so far he hasn't.

It is still spring, sometime in the morning, the Polins alerted (Sam wants to write "altered"), when the tape begins to wind on the voyage home, as though to a distant star although in reality only two and one-half hours away from Westwood. Dew still besmears the newly opened belly of the lot across the street from Westwood Horizons. Fresh loam—it must stir uneasy thoughts in the breasts of the old folk, so resembling freshly turned-up graves come to them, practically nuzzling like a frisky brown baby animal.

Nonsense, they think no such thing. Sam does not know what they think, or if they have any thoughts about their mortality. Maybe such thoughts are all used up by the time real old age begins, even as the impotent old man no longer thinks or feels sex in any plangent manner. The worst has happened, it has oxidized, it's gone, nothing more to worry about, the tenant has left without notice.

Almost the valleys and mountains greet them as they traverse them, lupins and wild poppies appear, without charge, working up a blush on the thighs of near hills, mocking all talk of old age. Sure, there are wrinkled mountains, those tipped on their sides, feet in stirrups, undergoing exploratories by road and freeway. They cross the uncertain old road and the brisk impersonal new one. When nature hands us mixed metaphors in blues and greens, bare rock and lush meadow, cloud wisps hugging bone precipices, why not report it?

Sam's father Harry sits stoically in the front seat, buckled in. Does he know what to do anymore? What is there to do? Is there any reason to touch a hand to somebody's person? Does he know when it is OK? Is he afraid? Does he ever care what goes on between the covers of a book, or is that too promiscuous? If one no longer knows what is appropriate, perhaps it is appropriate only to maintain radio silence, emitting as little heat as humanly possible.

Everything here depends on that old man. Does he think of that? No use to try to second-guess him. As well try to get him to comment on the rust of poppies, the pride of lupins.

"Do you remember when the fields of wild flowers were really spectacular?" Sam asks, "after the war, when the fields were still plowed but after cotton wasn't being grown anymore because we didn't need to provide uniforms for our soldiers and the Russians and the British and the Martians? Do you remember?"

Aware of Sam's need, Harry says only, "I don't remember nothing."

Channa stirs herself. "Do you feel proud of your son?"

Harry doesn't even turn around. He knows that one, his son's daughter. "What do you mean, feel proud?"

"I mean, are you proud of your son?"

"Your daddy?"

The landscape flashes by like Wells's Time Machine. Soon they will be back to the woolly mammoth, tusks will pierce the cowl of the one-engined craft Sam tools over the Tehachapi Mountains, which are folded into one another like chocolate-chip cookies. Will an earthquake snatch the road out from under them?

The motor hums, bored.

"Well, I tried," Channa says.

"Thanks," Sam says, "it wasn't very friendly. Look, the hills up there are just like in Fantasia. I expect unicorns and flying horses. Mobil Oil used to fly horses. I wish I had one of their signs."

"How much longer?" Channa asks.

"I used to do that, but I was serious, you're not. You make fun of this whole enterprise. But it's serious business, I'm very serious about this trip. I don't know if your grandfather will ever make another to Bakersfield. I want this trip to be serious. Can you manage that? For him? For me?"

Without meaning to, Sam gets into the cadence of Beethoven's Pastorale Symphony.

Later, they descend the Grapevine, where the road once laced itself back and forth on the instep of the mountain, and where large rigs broke loose and tumbled down into the valley, breaking and losing parts of themselves before the final explosion. Many men lost their lives. Now a ten-mile-long talus slope erases differences between valley floor and mountain.

173

Everything is improved, even the road personalized for their protection, like the paper in restrooms. They are directed to speed up and slow down where there are dips, roadside business. Everything is tamed, but the San Andreas Fault reminds them of nature's dueling scars. Gorman, Lebec, Holland's Summit, Fort Tejon, where people struggled to get over, on one horse or on foot. Sam has many horses anonymous under his hood. Air conditioning encloses them in its cocoon. His father, cane between his legs, apparently is satisfied that he will never drive a car again.

"Do you remember when you fell asleep at the wheel and drove your pickup truck into a tree along here?" Sam asks.

"I don't remember nothing," Harry replies. "Didn't the tire blow out?"

Sam is ashamed. "It was a tire, that was what it was."

Channa jabs him in the back. She smiles slyly in the rearview mirror. He is sorry that he is teaching her bad habits. It is very easy to teach her his bad habits.

The old local road to Bakersfield timidly announces itself at an edge of the giant ribbon of new highway. It has oleanders and giant eucalyptus alongside. It shoots straight at Bakersfield as the freeway pulls in its skirts and heads straight north, no stops.

Eateries, dairies, gas stations, pretentious and ramshackle, hold out their hands as they approach the town.

Why does he animate everything? Nothing makes the aging easier, or that he has got no farther than two and a half hours from Bakersfield in his entire life.

Where Sam's elementary school used to stand there is now an old shabby motel. The family house is still in place, its screen-enclosed porch open again. Sam remembers hiding behind a metal swing couch while his parents desperately tried to figure out a place to send him where he might be forced to learn to curb his mouth.

"You lived in a cute little house," Channa says, only half-joking.

The line of roses Sam's mother cherished is blooming, although vacant lots on both sides are gone. The irrigation ditch where crayfish swarmed is cemented in and wire-fenced.

Nobody wants to get out to walk around; they need a bathroom. Sam drives around looking for the Polin house. Harry has given him the wrong number, so they drive slowly up and down the street. In front of one Sam spots an old man waving. "Who's that, Dad?"

Harry looks. "Stop in front there, that's Jonathan Polin."

Jonathan isn't old, but his gestures are vague, and he is stooped, his face much scarred by an auto accident that left him for months in a coma, victim of the old road. Now he looks after his parents.

"Gosh it's good to see you again, Harry, you look terrific." His mouth slides downhill on one side, and it's as though all his words collect in one corner before spilling out in a bunch. "How old are you, Harry?" Jonathan assumes a TV interviewer's tone.

"Eighty-three, and not getting any younger."

It seems to Sam that he speaks more firmly, his eyes focus.

"And you're Sammy's little girl," Jonathan announces.

Channa puts on a demure face. Sam is glad and grateful.

"You're really beautiful, young lady. But let's not stand here on ceremony, come on inside. The folks are waiting for you."

He opens the door, the smell of sealed rooms rolls out. The furniture in the living room is covered in plastic. Little plastic pathways stitch them to one another. Time stopped about 1945. Jonathan blocks their way, one hand against Sam's chest. "Just one thing I want to mention." He is going to tell them a stunning secret. "Mother isn't what she was, and Dad had an accident a few months ago and so his arm's in a cast, and he can't hear you unless you really shout. Otherwise, they're in great shape, you'll see."

He is a car salesman getting them ready for a really terrific deal if only they recognize it. Jonathan fills all the space in the hallway. He doesn't seem to want to move. They peer around him at Max who sits in a straight chair in the dining room. He looks up; without teeth the face is much simplified from the one Sam remembers from forty years before.

Max Polin made his money during World War II selling scrap at hugely inflated prices, which Sam's father was scared to do. "You fool," his mother hissed when Harry sold something at the frozen price, when he could have sold it for twice, three times that.

Max looks at Sam. "Sammy? Is it really Sammy? And Harry?" He is luminously happy. Sam is surprised at the gush of warmth coming from the huge round face propped like a doll over the chair.

They continue to stand around. "Can we go in the living room and sit down?" Sam asks Jonathan. Max used to threaten him with a small paring knife on his watch chain. "Are you going to be good, or do I have to stick . . . ?" he would smile like a gangster, and Sam was always a little bit worried.

The idea of using the living room is almost too much for Jonathan. "In there? Sure, why not. Dad, let's go into the living room," he shouts into his father's ear.

Sam spots a picture of Jonathan and a woman in a very red dress, lots of makeup and hair piled up on her head. "Your wife?" Sam asks.

"Yeah, we're separated temporarily," Jonathan says, "that's my wife, all right. Sadie."

Nobody moves. They continue to cluster around Max's chair, and he keeps beaming. "Harry, we're old farts now," he yells, "we're not going to make any more money."

"Never mind," Harry says clearly, "if you saw a hundred dollar bill on the floor you'd manage to stoop down to get it."

Sam is amazed and delighted. He looks for Channa, but she is already gone to the living room, where she is looking at pictures on the walls.

Jonathan settles his father in a chair. He fusses around making sure the others sit somewhere, a lion tamer with his ancient cats. "I'll go get Mother."

She is already in the hallway, speaking as she enters, looking and talking only to Jonathan from under a very wide-brimmed straw hat, a trembling ribbon hanging from it. She pushes it away every moment, but it always flutters back.

"Jonathan," she says in a gentle mother's voice to a small boy, "when are you taking me to temple? We're late, darling, we need to be going." She looks around at the room full of people, eyes wide in exaggerated surprise and reproach. "Who are these charming people, Jonathan? Max, why didn't you tell me we were receiving people?"

Jonathan says plaintively, "I told you, Mother, there isn't any today. It was yesterday, Mother."

Max grabs up one of her hands and strokes and holds it, smiling up into her face.

Helen has lived in the back bedroom of this house for over sixty years. Her picture as a young girl was sent to Bakersfield from a village in Romania that was dominated by her father, and that she with her beauty ruled. In Sam's boy's eyes, she was the most enigmatic beautiful woman imaginable. He never saw her except in her darkened room; she was preserving her complexion. Max managed to get her to marry him, but how could she, such perfection, live with Max's crude loud voice, his bragging, the little knife?

Helen was tall and willowy. She wore flowered dresses and high-heeled shoes, her mouth always perfectly outlined in rose lipstick. She wore gloves and hat, always. Only half a dozen times or less was Sam allowed to enter that sacred back room, and he knew it was a

177

royal audience. She told him every time that he was a good boy and a special one and that his life would be unique.

Now Jonathan takes his mother's hand firmly and says, "This is Harry and his son Sammy, and that is his daughter, Channa. Isn't she beautiful? She looks just like Sammy, doesn't she? Do you look like your mother, too, Channa?"

Channa hangs her head. Helen takes her hand. "Who are you, beautiful girl? Are you going to temple with us?"

She drops Channa's hand as though it were a stone, and goes to Max. "You bad man, not dressed yet and we're so late. Put on some nice trousers, Mr. Polin, and get ready, make yourself presentable. Are you going to take us, Jonathan? Please, we must go to temple."

"Mom," Jonathan says loudly, "it's not today. Today is nothing at temple. I told you before."

"Don't you speak to me in that tone, young man. I'm your mother, please remember that, always remember, and we are inexcusably late. Now, please, let there be no more delay."

She sees Channa again, and again takes up her hand. The beautiful linen smile appears. She must tip back her head to see at all under the hat. "Whose beautiful little girl are you?"

"Momma, this is Sammy's little girl. Little Sammy. Remember?"

"Of course I remember, silly boy."

He realizes that she is actually no taller than his mother, under five feet. Sam goes a little dizzy as he tries to keep Helen's impatient fingers in his hand. "Helen, I'm very happy to see you again. Do you remember Hotel St. Regis?"

She drops his hand and a frown travels over her face. "St. Regis. Of course I remember the St. Regis." She does not stamp her foot, she purses her lips in a noncommittal smile. "But do *you* remember the St. Regis, young man?"

Lovely, she remembers how to tease.

She turns to her husband with the real issue: "Are we going to temple or to St. Regis?"

Max grasps her hand it seems to propose marriage or other wild things, he croons as he strokes, "Oh, we're going to the beach and it's sure to be a peach, and we'll two make love in the mo-or-or-ning!"

Helen stands stock still for the entire song. After he is finished, he takes her hand to his lips, kisses it, smiles into her eyes.

Helen puts her glove back on, continues around the room blessing us and asking who is going to take her to the temple, as though this goes on all the time or that it never does.

"Boy," Channa mutters, "this is just like a grade B movie."

"It's life," her father says, "this is life, not a movie. Life is stranger than any movie."

"When we going?" Channa whispers. "Let's get out of here. She's really crazy."

"She's not," Sam replies, "anymore than you are or I am for being in our own movie. She's the most glamorous woman in the world."

The Polins lived in Ocean Park all summer at the St. Regis Hotel, just down the boardwalk from the bandshell, where a live band played on Sunday afternoons. Hotel St. Regis was covered in Italian marble and boasted three elevators. Harry could barely afford a one-room apartment, icebox, and roaches. Still, it was better than the eczema, asthma and dust of Bakersfield. Sam couldn't remember their having been actually up to the Polin's spread, but they met at the band concert and had ice cream afterwards. Helen never went to the beach.

"Can you understand, Channa, that this is what getting old is? She doesn't know what she's doing."

Helen grows more excited, making her rounds faster and faster, blessing the strangers. "May the good lord give you everything you've ever wanted," she chants, "may you reach your place in heaven and have everything beforehand in the world good."

On one of her rounds, Jonathan manages to catch her, she shakes free of him, runs to the door, flings herself into the front yard. "Jonathan," she turns to confront him, "I'm not coming back into the house until you promise to take me to temple." She is a beautiful sight in tiny high-heeled party shoes, her ribbon playing peek-a-boo with her eyes. Sam's daughter looks much older than she does.

She arches herself against the grill of Jonathan's late-model car, her eyes dance. "Now, let's go, I'm your mother, and don't you ever forget it for a minute, buster."

Jonathan turns apologetically to all the people standing in the doorway. "I'll just take her for a ride and she'll be satisfied. Do you have to leave so soon?" He is an aging man whose sole purpose in life is to take care of these old dolls. Will he live with his "separated" Sadie again?

They all shake hands again with Helen, who has a puzzled look between her eyes. She hasn't had time to check out who Sam is, or that little girl, or the terribly old man. "Harry," she finally says, "it is Harry, isn't it?"

Sam's father stands up straight, almost twirls his cane, and says, "You bet your sweet bippy it is, Mrs. Polin."

"You see, Channa," Sam explains on the way, "you see that this is real life?"

"I see that it was a grade B movie," Channa replies, "I don't see anything else."

She also sees Los Angeles at the end of two-and-a-half hours. She knows today. She is confident she will remain around fifteen years old all her days, and Sam will be her daddy and be able to drive her in the car wherever they want or need to go. Time stops at the end of every page for Channa, and it does not start again until she elects to open the book on it again. The freeway is complete and all signs point to appropriate destinations, all voluntary.

Straight Razor

Matthew Clay taught creative writing at night to grown-up students who came for the discipline and criticism. They were often tired and depressed, and Matthew enjoyed the challenge to stimulate, even shock them into writing.

"I heard a story on the radio last week that shocked *me*," Matthew told the class. "A man does a Southern talking-blues description of a murder done with a razor, a straight razor. First, the victim was paralyzed with terror, he couldn't believe this was really happening to him, but there was the blood spurting out of his arm like a Rain Bird. I don't remember them exactly, but the words went something like this:

> And you wonder, uh-huh, why he don't come and finish you off, uh-huh, but it don't matter, he don't want to get himself dirty, uh-huh, he waiting til your blood pressure drop way down, uh-huh, and then he going move in for the kill.

Now take five minutes and remember or imagine a climactic moment."

One of the women wrote describing a rape she foiled by jamming her umbrella in the man's groin. Matthew's scrotum coiled recalling her tight lips and vivid finger jabbing the air. He had trouble even imagining men who lived like that. Safe in his car he sent the windshield wipers after the window like slashing dual straight razors.

181

He had a picture of himself trying to protect himself from the slasher by raising his arms, but then he was like a child presenting himself for his pullover to be taken off, who gets snarled, hot and frustrated, in the sleeves. As helpless as that. "Soft as butter, we spill so-o-o easy, uh-huh." The windshield wipers provided syncopation.

At home, he sat at his desk next to an antique Black Forest clock. Sometimes his blood pounded unpleasantly in his ears in time with the pendulum. At times he thought that his already-high blood pressure was speeding to keep time with the old wooden clock. A medieval courtier stared out of the clock face, eyes going back and forth with the pendulum. Matthew thought he remembered that the courtier held a small curved knife in one hand, but he always forgot to check the clock to be sure.

He got up and focused the lamp light onto the cruel, shifty face, partly obscured by a cowl. There *was* a knife in the hand. He was relieved, not eager to begin living the anxiety artfully woven into a dramatic song that he had merely used to good advantage for a class.

He would like to own a copy, though. Hesitating a moment, he dialed the number of the producer of the radio show. "Hi, John," Matthew began in his hale professorial tone, "I got your number from the station. Could you tell me how I might get hold of that straight razor number you did a few weeks ago?"

There was a hollow silence at the other end. Then, a serious: "I think I'd need to talk to you personally. What did you say your name was?"

Matthew apologized and told him his name.

More hollow silence. Matthew wondered what kind of cave he was speaking from.

"I'm in my studio," he seemed to answer Matthew's question. "When do you want me to come over?" he asked.

Matthew hadn't thought about asking him to come over. "That's nice of you. What about tomorrow afternoon about four?"

Rain continued. The man appeared at the door in a hooded parka with fur lining. He wore very tight levis tucked into high trapper's boots. As he pushed back his hood Matthew saw a very serious young face with pale blue eyes and ashy blond hair. Matthew put out his hand. "Come in," he said, effusively, guiding him in by the shoulder.

Matthew's eight-year-old daughter Julie rushed to the door to see what was there. "Who is it, Daddy?" she demanded, looking at the stranger. She was usually more friendly and less strident with young, good-looking people.

"Someone to talk to me, Honey, go play. We don't want to be disturbed."

The little girl put her hands on her hips and pursed her lips. "You promised to go bike-riding with me."

The young stranger stared at her and said to Matthew, "My little girl—although she's not really mine but my wife's—is a lot more cooperative than that."

Matthew's wife, Paula, looking in just as the young man spoke, intending to say hello and offer him something to drink, heard his comment, frowned, and disappeared without a word.

"Well," Matthew said defensively, pushing the protesting little girl out of the room, "I wouldn't have it any other way. She doesn't take guff from anybody."

John said nothing, not seeming even to imply anything by his silence. For him apparently the subject was closed. Once out of the room, the little girl was erased, canceled, Matthew thought, uneasy, and it was as though for all of his life before meeting John, he too had not existed, and was only now in the world courtesy of John. And John didn't care, that seemed clear enough. He didn't care whether people existed or not.

"Why did you, I mean, how did you find the Straight Razor?" Matthew asked, to break the silence.

John waved away the weak question. "Some people feel that piece is immoral. Some people feel that my own work is immoral. Did you want to ask me to come to your class to talk about the program or do you want me to come to talk about my own work?"

Matthew hadn't really considered either possibility, but he always leaped at opportunities for stimulation. "Well, I don't want to take advantage of your good nature, John, but sure, I'd love to have you come and talk to the class. About how long would you need?"

"How long is the class?"

"Three hours."

"Then three hours," quietly, without a trace of bravado.

"Well, fine, so long as the students can get their things in during that time too. Uh, what is your work?"

"I do environmental art. I had a documentation in a magazine and people thought it was immoral."

Here they were surely on common ground. Matthew didn't hold with censorship of any sort, usually. "What was the work?"

"I dressed up in a monkey suit and went over to three friends' houses in the night, in the middle of the night, rang the doorbell, and when my friends answered, I pulled out a .38 caliber pistol filled with blanks and shot them once, and ran away."

Matthew sat quite still. John lounged at his ease, not appearing to wait for his response.

Matthew sighed, pointed to a squirrel running up a pine tree near the window. "We have just the one squirrel," he said, "I like to watch what he's up to." He took a shaky breath. "Well, I have to agree with your critics, John. I think that what you did was immoral. Somebody who's faced a firing squad or been condemned to death and reprieved, well, they've had a unique experience, probably nothing ever after is the same. Maybe from that experience their life is enriched, but still it's a kind of rape, isn't it? You didn't have their consent to do this violence on them. Did they ever find out it was you?"

"Oh yes, I called them, all three, the same night."

"What did they say to you?"

"They told me, 'we appreciated the experience and we thank you.'"

The squirrel ran down the tree and out onto the street, narrowly dodging a speeding car. "It certainly wasn't the kind of thing you could have gotten permission for ahead of time, was it?" Matthew said. "That would invalidate the experience. Still, what about somebody having a heart attack? Being middle-aged, I think about inconveniences like that."

Matthew tried to keep his tone light, but his heart was pounding as he spoke, remembering the first time he had thought about a heart attack; he was on the stairs with the infant Julie, roughhousing, heart pounding with happy exertion, when the image flashed in his brain—he was film running through a projector, broken—the broken film running through the film gate, image still on the screen, but only a second or two before plain white would fill the screen—blank. That was the way death was, all blood stopped, only the last frames still running, full of action even after life was gone. Literature, especially Japanese, was full of tales of bodies sliced from their heads, faces full of the horrible knowledge of what has happened.

"I think about such things." He wondered if he had said that twice. He certainly wasn't overcome with joy with what John was saying about his "art." "Why not be a little more careful about who you invite to the house," he recalled Paula's remarking recently. Hadn't she poked her head in a little while ago? He suddenly longed to have John out so that he could go to her, rub up against her soft, loving sanity. She didn't hold with avant-garde music or literature.

She usually thought they were poor excuses for sloppy people.

"As I recall, Mr. Clay, you did a play," John said quietly, "in which people were handed slips of paper which noted whether they were to be Jews or Nazis. You didn't ask for their permission, did you?"

"But they came to the performance expecting something of a grab-bag," Matthew retorted. "They weren't threatened with instant death by murder."

John smiled a bit in the deepening twilight.

Matthew bustled up out of his chair to turn on lights. He turned them on all over the room. "Furthermore," Matthew continued sharply, "I think the difference is the difference between vivisection and elective surgery. Art needs to be a sharp knife, but not administered from behind."

Matthew could hear that he was lecturing. "Certainly gets dark fast," he said, conciliatory. "Anyway, this sort of thing makes for a good discussion. I hope you bring it up when you come to class with the Straight Razor—on tape." This was not life, this was art, for the class. It could be contained. The real world was a far more lighted place. In the next room Paula and Julie argued about something familiar and trivial. He was needed to umpire the dispute. "If you'll excuse me, John, I'll go to help with dinner."

John stood, put on his parka and slipped the hood over his head, his eyes like dim coals within the cowl of a medieval monk off on some mission for the Inquisition.

He reached into a pocket and handed Matthew a card. "Here's the name and address of the man who did Razor."

Matthew's postcard was typically hale: "I enjoyed hearing your work and hope you can let me know how to get a copy. I can send you blank cassette or reel or please let me know where I can buy one. Yours truly, Matt Clay." He enclosed his address and telephone number.

*

Paula handed Matthew the phone with a small grimace. John's distant echoey voice said: "My art work was performed with people I know well and love. I wouldn't do something that violent with people I didn't know."

"Yeah, well, you probably had some kinds of criteria we didn't get into. Do you have any feeling that you were maybe unconsciously hostile to the people?" Then, hastily: "But we're just on our way out the door, John, don't try to answer that one now. Did you want to give me a definite date?"

"No," came the quiet voice almost without inflection, "I just wanted to tell you that."

Matthew felt he needed to make some comment, show some positive response to what was obviously a sincere attempt by John to justify the horrifying act. "Your friends, they must have felt reprieved, like Lazarus back from the dead, right? Their lives, how are they different now—did you document that? But since they aren't even the same people anymore, they can't even tell you how they've changed, can they?"

"I didn't get that down," John said. "There may be a good idea in that. I'll think about it. You've given me a lot to think about."

Matthew was wary of irony, but decided to answer with a return compliment. "You've given me a lot to think about too, John, I've led a pretty comfortable and sheltered life for someone who talks about violence as much as I do."

A story read in the creative writing class was about a young man who double-crossed his dope-peddling colleagues by shooting them to death in a narrow hallway in his girlfriend's apartment after which he made love to her, then drove off in a hired getaway car.

Matthew questioned how it was possible for the young man to

appear so neat as to raise no suspicions in his girlfriend's mind about his recent activity.

"Maybe when he shot them he had a butcher's apron on," someone cracked. The writer of the story, a serious young woman, frowned.

Matthew quickly stepped in. "Just be sure he shoots them from an adequate distance, and then afterwards, if he didn't kill them with the first shots, he can move in when there's less blood pressure."

The young woman looked quizzically at Matthew, still scenting ridicule, but finally satisfied that she was being dealt with seriously, she wrote something on the page.

"I guess I'm kind of obsessed with the radio piece I told you about a few weeks ago," Matthew apologized, turning to glance at the slicing rain rattling the windows. "What do people feel or think about when their death is suddenly there right before them? We read and write about violence from our relative safety in this room. You pay good money to write about, or listen to, sudden death. Why? What you're interested in identifying, I believe, is that moment of truth, of consciousness, that comes just before the curtain rings down forever."

Matthew wanted very much to stop this lecture when he noticed at least one pair of eyes glaze over, but instead he went on, with a note of urgency: "In 'Silent Snow, Secret Snow' there is a madman whose perceptions are progressively covered over by the white flakes until there is one unique moment and he's entirely buried in them. Remember Tarzan movies?" He knew they didn't, or weren't listening, but everyone nodded.

"When I was a kid I saw Tarzan on TV every Saturday morning," one student remarked.

"But that's different!" Matthew said, "my generation watched it all happen on a huge screen, we saw the bad guy slip off the tree after a tremendous fight with Tarzan, and fall into quicksand, and get eaten by the quicksand. When his head was already covered there would be one hand clutching at air. The End. Tarzan always tried, too late, to save his enemy, but we never wanted that and it was always too late. Jane looked, shuddered, and buried her head in Tarzan's armpit. 'It's horrible, Tarzan,' and Tarzan always shook his sage leonine head. And the chittering monkey would announce with some antic another beat. Remember?"

What were they supposed to remember? To applaud? *He* didn't remember, not any of this, he made it up as he went along, it was as new to him as it was to them, but a nice thing about teaching was the opportunity to do a spontaneous cadenza to find out what he, Matthew, was up to.

Matthew said, hopefully, not believing it, "Can you get that moment into your pieces? Can you write a short-short demonstrating that flickering moment before oblivion, kind of a Short-Short Happy Life of Francis Macomber?" Everyone looked expectant, some sat with poised pen. Matthew sighed. Because nobody will have read it, he'd have to act out Hemingway's story.

It was sometime after the middle of the night, maybe only minutes after he'd fallen asleep, maybe toward morning. Matthew struggled automatically for the phone. It never occurred to him not to answer.

"Hello, who is it?"

A twangy voice immediately responded with an unfamiliar name. "I was in town and I thought maybe you'd like to put me up because old John isn't to home. I sort of got here without much cash on me and—"

The voice went on. John? Who? That fast, sing-songy voice, where had he heard it before? Dread was building before he formed the picture. His stomach knew who it was before his head. He registered

189

these facts as well as an outside picture of himself at this moment, in this place, talking to the creator of Straight Razor, who was calling him wanting to come over, now, by cab, and what are the directions?

Deciphering Matthew's mumbled polite sounds and incoherent directions, Paula whispered, "Tell him he can't come now, tell him to wait in the depot until morning."

Matthew waved her away, but even while waving he wondered why he wanted her not to tell him this, if he was not like the man forcing his way through a barricade into a disaster all signs warned against. A traffic cop was directing him away from a wash-out, and he knew better. He was a teacher, an official guide himself, he didn't need to be warned. And what of going over the edge? There was a film, a retelling of the Greek myth of Hippolytus. In the film, a contemporary playboy careening in mad abandon over sheer cliff roads in his Maserati, finally going over the edge singing his head off, taking off like a bird, like a bird —

"— Continental ain't no proud bird with no golden tail to *me*, huh-uh, not landing me here six hours late in the middle of night."

"Get the airport limousine, it's a bus really," Matthew said, "to Hollywood. Then take a cab. You'll be here in about two hours."

"Much obliged."

He found the phone cradle and replaced the receiver.

"You're letting somebody you've never met come here to stay?"

"He could have come without calling. He had the address." In Matthew's world addresses were for writing to, and the man of the straight razor lived in that world too, didn't he? He *had* called.

Now, isn't this a very memorable moment, Matthew thought, what before the phone call was lost, unredeemed time, drowned by sleep, maybe not entirely lost because there are dreams—images accompanying the cleansing process wherein lactic acid in the muscles and brain is leached away into the blood's rubbish bins, sorting out from the day's grab-bag what will be stored—or some damned thing.

Any kind of rationalization will do so long as one doesn't have to accuse oneself of playing around or being foolish. In his heart, although he had learned otherwise, Matthew knew that play was for children, that life means work and is serious. Art and life do *not* intersect.

Despite Paula's sleepy protests, he got out of bed, put on his royal blue robe—the heavy one with a crest on the lapel—and went into his study to wait under the Black Forest clock. Soon his blood performed its regular act of getting into step with the eyes of the cruel courtier while Matthew peered into the rain waiting for the lights of the cab to appear.

In his desk Matthew kept a hunting knife, for protection he often said, smiling ironically at his imagined confrontation with an intruder, his lunge at the faceless man, his knife finding its place in that body.

The door bell rang. Matthew started, looked out. No cab, but maybe he hadn't noticed its coming, fallen asleep at the switch. Take the hunting knife with him? He waved an arm, "No," as though to Paula.

"Daddy?" came muffled through the door.

Matthew hesitated. "I'm going downstairs, Sweety. Go back to sleep."

"Can I have a drink of water?"

"In a few minutes, but I have to answer the door now."

"Who's at the door?"

"Somebody. Wait for me or get it yourself. I'll be back up in a minute."

He held up the robe so he wouldn't trip, and turned on the light in the entry hall.

"Daddy, watch out for burglars."

"It's all right, I will, Julie." Was this a moment that announced the end of the game? But, having thought that, it couldn't be. Did the victims facing a firing squad think that way too, a kind of sympathetic magic hoping to forestall the event?

"Hello?" he called through the window beside the door.

"Hi, there," the plangent voice answered. "I just got to go back down to the street to get my other suitcase."

Matthew opened the door and stepped onto the porch. The man was leaving the faint light of the porch, disappearing into the rainy gloom. "Can I help you?" Matthew called.

"Don't bother yourself," he heard the man say.

From behind Matthew came a slight crackle as from someone stepping lightly on dried leaves. As Matthew began to turn, he felt a sensation both hot and cold on his throat at the same instant as he saw the hand and knife flash toward him. As his knees trembled and began to fold he felt the way he had as a child given gas at the dentist's office.

He couldn't look to see who was behind him because the man coming back from the street came back not with a suitcase but with a long straight knife that moved directly from the dark in a moment that lasted a curious length of time until Matthew felt both the moment and the knife home themselves in Matthew's stomach. The blood pressure, Matthew thought, it's already so low, so much blood already out, this other knife isn't going to make much difference.

He dropped to his knees, a little corner of his mind alight: "I just hope Paula and Julie don't come down. I hope Julie got her glass of water and went to sleep. I hope they're both in their beds. I hope it was only me they wanted and they'll go away now. I hope they won't talk." He waited for himself to fall.

The hood went back over the parka and Matthew began to hear

what John was saying. "Let's walk him around, you take that arm, I'll take this one."

When he noticed Matthew looking at him, he asked, "How do you feel coming back from the dead?"

Matthew saw the tape recorder John held in his free hand. He felt his neck—no cut. His stomach—no hole in it either. The men continued to walk him around. Matthew pretended to be deep in shock, in order to keep them busy. What method would he use to kill them? Should he lure them up to the study to get his knife? Would a straight razor be better? Could he keep them occupied, but separate, until he accounted for one and got to the other?

His vision collapsed, he wanted only to cry bitterly, but he would not weep in front of these men. He knew it was useless, pointless, to kill them. They would never die.

Then he wondered how he had ever thought it possible to go back to his wife and child. He was long past them. He would have to go away, take another identity, go to another city, do something else besides teach. Teach what? The very thought of it made him sick.

Why was his heart holding up so well, not even pounding very hard? There was not going to be any heart attack after all?

He shook their hands off his arms. He was Matthew Clay, it was just the middle of a night, and the performance was over. He was relieved, even growing rather proud. He had come through it, and they had taken this incredible risk, planned this art work, just for him, solely for Matthew's education.

He felt a great warmth and fondness for John growing in him. The rain tasted sweet on his lips. He smiled at the serious young man.

"I brought you a present," the Straight Razor man said, "I brought you the tape you wanted. I'm sure glad you like it."

Ecospasm

Sol Harris decided to go down to Venice for the first time since his childhood summers had been spent there, looking for an apotheosis—animal, vegetable, or mineral.

He hoped for animal, a girl, dirty, wild and feral, because, for his ikon, he had adopted the beast in the jungle. When he announced for himself the need at thirty-three for a new start, he knew that had to mean death for the old, as it is well known that it is not possible that the hymen be unruptured nor jugular sutured.

He himself was immaculate. Once, for a college assignment, he delivered himself to a skid-row hotel, armed with roach-killer. Five dollars he offered a whore in new bills from Bank of America, Westwood Branch. She delivered one handshake and a confusion of doors. Virginity intact, he got a B+ in the class.

This was the Venice era of large wall murals like mirrors to the street. People drinking on curbs, skateboards, lots of roller-skaters of an elegant sort who ignored outsiders. Some bodies selling fake portable tape recorders.

Very soon, he saw gamine Nadine (her T-shirt told it) at the head of a skate horde. Nor was she beautiful—skinny, maybe fourteen or thirty, or askew between. Lop-eared, crooked mouth, little moustache severe above, or dirt. She wore torn red leotards with black pads strapped over the knees, as though she planned to skate to work in a cotton field. Her complexion was yellow with brown freckles, hair nappy in parts, long in others, particularly forehead.

194

Sol imagined putting her to bed where she would hold court with elaborate teddy bears in her arms—all bones and elbow—a doughy line of dirt on the inside of her knees, her underwear phony lace separated from the crotch in a stalagmite pattern. And she would skate on his back when it hurt.

Her court was pasty white but appeared black, because of leather jackets and chains.

Worse than death in Venice would be life in it, so Sol commenced stalking Nadine. He rented skates on a blustery day that blew grit in his teeth and concreted his eyebrows. It was winter, when once he found Nadine without most of her congeries, in a very short skirt over the leotard. As she stopped for repair, Sol circumnavigated her. She noticed; she was wary of weirdos.

He stared at her, memorized. "Like, can I buy you an ice cream?" he chattered.

Nadine averted her face to the broken leathern strap unsecuring her left insole.

"I'll take off *my* strap and give it to you. How about that? If you don't want an ice cream cone. What's your name?" he asked with disingenuity.

She twisted her lips as though wringing out a wet dish towel. "Nadine," she slurred. "All right, I'll take it, but don't expect nothing back."

At this point she had lighted in front of a mural, defaced by vandals, picturing a Venus of Botticelli skating on the boardwalk, and Nadine was sure sister and twin to the painting. Sol's heart performed a circus act.

"You are more beautiful even than a seal," he explained, ripping off his rented skate.

She left him kneeling, but in almost the same motion she winged back to him. "Thanks," she said. "A lot."

195

"I'm Sol," he yelled into the teeth of the stinging wind, "and you'll see a lot of me, Nadine."

"Oh yeah," he thought he heard her say.

Sol went home and fashioned a simulacrum of Nadine out of gesso and burnt umber. He programmed an image of her on Apple. He approximated her voice with Moog. He apparitioned her with Scentola. He maquetted her in aluminum and coat hangers. He did not have to write her down in his diary, because enough was enough.

He took his three-D camera with him the next time. He was able to park his van only one block from the beach, with a clear view of the boardwalk from the roof, where he set up his tripod and trained his long lens, anticipating a long wait.

He was not disappointed. Many hours later, with not even one image slivered into his camera, he went home, bruised in spirit, knowing the painfully empty quiver of the saint-watcher.

She haunted his dreams, as planned. When he returned to Venice, her followers found him first and did something to discourage his pursuit. They pulled him over and beat him up and left him in tall rank weeds that were growing fiercely at the sides of the Speedway.

Sol believed his sternum broken. He remembered a ride called Loop-the-loop on the old Venice Pier before the great fire. A boat slid on skids down to a lake where it bounded like a skipping stone, but Sol had stood up and hit his solar plexus on the safety rail. The violent blow paralyzed his breathing for so long that he knew what it was like to stare into the world with his life cut off.

Now what he watched was Nadine, for a second separate from leather jackets, skating away from him, over and over again.

He slept peacefully after that, among dog turd and broken bottles. Soon enough she was there again, her face hanging like a sunflower above him. She held out a paw, grubby, gritty, with terrifyingly short fingers. The sky was orange with discharge. Cars skated around. Naturally, money gone, he could offer her nothing.

It was not the sky, but rather a flash from the camera of Hank, Venice Beach Photographer, famous red lips chewing, hanging over Sol, a chewing grin with tic, like a blood-red moon gone crescent, wanting something, but Sol's soul was already smuggled like a rejected art object into the contemporary museum of Nadine's heart, or he would have offered it to Hank, as a bribe to leave him alone.

Hank chewed and with his foot moved Sol's head off a jagged piece of plastic 7-Up bottle. "What are you doing with me?" whispered Sol, "I'm not famous."

Hank grinned with his entire face like a squeezed tropical fruit.

Sol blinked at the sudden light of the strobe that bounced off a deodorant ad on corrugated plastic, which sucked his self into the blind prism of the camera and onto anonymous film. He became something that has a pretty long shelf life.

He was not angry at Hank, who had his job—to take pictures of everything and everybody in Venice who or that might turn up famous in a day or so. He looked his job, a head nearly shorn of hair, moustache painted on, red shirt and suspenders, black tie, gyrating hands for change of lens or camera back, of tripod or filter.

Now that Hank had found Sol, there came into existence a branch in the road. All Sol had to do now was take his cue from the blitter of strobe where he was and what he was doing when Hank took his pictures, and never decide anything at all, since there were only about half a dozen magazine-allowable scenarios, easy enough to follow, like a simple card game.

And actually, Hank's attentions were not that easy to come by. Maybe Nadine had affected indifference, piquing his curiosity.

Maybe he smelled death under her thin wings, or knew she would fall out of the nest provided by the black-clad bikers-cum-skaters, as she was surely on auto-pilot, but who had programmed it? Did Hank need Sol only to provide a little background music?

Were the thugs Hank's minions and only pretending succor to Nadine? Clearly Hank had lost what foreign smell he carried and was completely insinuated among them. He would push them away when he finished, blind naked, somethings without shell, who had jumped on the grill and roasted like flies.

If Sol could get up he would go warn Nadine and even her thugs. But if she were fascinated by Hank, and being in film more important than life?

Sol sluiced the piece of corrugated plastic at Hank's head, but he merely ducked like an expert frisbee player, shooting the buzzing thing high and out into the dark, where he materialized it once more with a bolt of light from the strobe.

Sol found his keys and limped to his van, slept, illuminated with dream fragments, shying among them to avoid being cut.

In the dawn, Nadine was there already, surrounded by her guards, so impenetrable their thicket as she performed her ablutions in front of the Venus of Venice that he could not really see all of her rosy nakedness, every surface crusted with gems of dew.

Click-whir! Hank was there too, behind the rusted hulk of a studio tank abandoned with the financing of a velodrome film.

Sol strapped on nuptial skates, determined to make this flight with the virgin queen higher than drone had ever done in rarified strata, above these clods, higher than laser.

He sped toward the beloved, and right through her! Bewildered, he could not stop and crashed into a light-standard. When his eyes focused again, they took in Hank's red smile, and he knew that he had been tricked and photographed continually while out of control. He understood a little of holography and appreciated how much trouble Hank had taken to set this travesty.

He nodded to the lensman. "That's one for you, Comrade," he mouthed.

Hank did not scruple to respond. As on-lookers clustered to the scene, he made himself invisible, as photographers can. At the same time there was in progress a contest in wet-sand mermaid-in-a-castle-building sponsored by a local TV outlet offering $5 grand for best one.

And Nadine continued slow heart-stopping ovals, nobody else watching. A message for Sol?

Only he saw her suddenly sink below the ambient crowd. Her harbingers were for once off watching the giant mermaids undulate. Hank was neutralized by a persistent cameraman interviewing him on his weird scene.

She could be crushed. Frail, surely undernourished, perhaps sick.

Sol peered down the long stretch of boardwalk toward the misty towers of Marina del Rey. In the other direction jutted the craggy heights of Santa Monica. This Venice was a kind of Shangri-La; to snatch Nadine from it would be to take her with him to the real world.

He had only the old-fashioned kind of rental skates that screwed onto the shoe. Nadine was of course wearing shoe skates that attached the way wings do to an angel or fins on a mermaid. His heart mistook and shook him. How could he consider interfering with this closed universe whose theophany was fixed, and to whose work he was excrescent?

But he had been legitimized by Hank, who would surely not have taken his picture if he didn't belong in it? And if his picture was truly taken, was he not now permanently in the group that surrounded Nadine? And was it not his job to remove forcibly, by rape if necessary, the "maiden" sick to death and burdened with her suitors of an archaic order?

And, he reassured himself, it was not necessary to be heroic in the old mode—he could be aging, soft, excitable, not muscular, even sweaty.

Sol circled and forced his way in through the press of bodies. Nadine was on one knee down on the cement, blindly digging with her stubby grubby fingers in a crack, the fingernail on her left index finger already worn to a bloody shred.

His heart went to her. She had no idea that the real virgin sand stretched out to the ocean only a few feet from where she toiled.

Nadine's eyes fell on Sol. He searched them for clues, but they were Sphinxlike blank, black, without pupil, as though alone in a dark pyramid.

As he swooped her up, her bones seemed to melt on his arms, as though he carried nothing but old clothes.

Perhaps he had only a very few minutes to get her away. Again, he looked up and down the boardwalk. Just a few people who looked as though they had no part, but how could he be sure? At any moment, one of them, stepping out of molding, might try to prevent the flight. His heart was molten; Nadine was a compressed diamond, her facets blinded him as his flesh was consumed. It was a joy to be so fried, a privilege he never expected, but he knew such violent joy was not long possible to bear. He didn't dare the boardwalk. Minions would spring from the cement. Where then?

There was no time to remove skates, so Sol slid from the boardwalk with his precious burden, she murmuring broken little phrases he strained to catch while he swished across the sands toward the glistering margin.

Behind the hulking backs of the crowd he tenderly put her down and made to cover her up. Little molluscs flew from him in the wet sand. Nadine moved her head from side to side, a new sweet smile playing over her features like coy clouds over the serious sun.

Hank was roaming like a leashed dog trying to pick up their scent, saw them, broke his bonds, and made straight as arrow across the desert, trailed by the horde. Sol threw more sand over the nether parts of the beloved. He fashioned sand pediments to her hair, attached a beard on her chin, tickled her with Dumbo-esque ears.

Then Sol calmly waited for them. Nadine the transformed stared at them. The horde went down on their knees while Hank fumbled his equipment.

Sol was lifted high by the horde. The sun flashed in his eyes a brilliant greeting and then he was plunged head down on the soft wet sand next to Nadine.

Moray Eel

We had just been to a sleazy antique shop, one that would have been called a used furniture store in my childhood, full of discarded things, pieces of others of a purpose unclear, though, to anthropomorphize, they seemed to be trying desperately to assert their clear use and independence even shorn from the rest of themselves, rather like the pincers of a crab that continues to snap and curvet in complete detachment from any other body.

Well, so do we, being the three of us—man, wife Sylvie, and half-grown daughter Shelly, in the beach resort city of Laguna, there for a hard-won month of leisure away from the Bay City, occupying an apartment lovingly decorated by its owner-manager, a hale and bluff older woman of considerable girth and an exaggerated sense of the importance of her dwelling. Fortunately, Shelly was not hard on antiques, did not even notice them for the most part, her attention mostly focused on small furry things that would eat from her hand. I countenance a number of these on the theory that as her heart was assuaged, melted, and reformed by these creatures, she would not succumb to the ravages of pimply and horny young men who prey on feelings of lovelessness in the newly fledged female bosom. My whole view of how to live is by innoculation—give me and those attached to me a little sickness so as to avoid the Great Death. Not exactly a formula for vibrant passion, but like many more oceanic belief systems, such a viewpoint may be positive. At least it prevents me from denying Shelly everything of a potentially dangerous nature. I give in equally to the two antipodes of my family—antiques to wife, pet stores for daughter. I stand on a slippery pole, trying to buy tolerance in advance from Shelly for when I am old and feeble, soliciting approval from Sylvie with patience for her old and disconnected objects, storing up intricate credits like an accountant adding tomatoes, apples and worms, pretending to make sense. An addled sense of humor saves me. Mountains remain unclimbed by me in Tibet, dirty streets unexplored in Kabul, bouquinistes in Paris sell tomes describing in minute detail the reasons for universes, but not to me.

My life takes me only every summer to Laguna, so I felt it only fair to accompany Shelly through a shabby entrance with handlettered sign announcing "Jim's Aquarium and Supplies" on the whitewashed window.

Brilliant sunshine we left behind us rendered obscurity in the shop almost solid. "Jim" sat at an improvised desk in the exact center of the store, which we had to approach as for an audience. Extending around him in rays were tanks of fish, their bubbling air tubes levitating him in the gloom. Jim's appearance was fishlike—a globular head innocent of hair, round thick glasses that made his eyes appear lidless, when I could see them. His little thin arms in short sleeves were placed on the wood in front of him, hands interlaced, as though holding an intricate puzzle.

His mouth was rudimentary too, until he opened it to ask if he could help us. Then it showed teeth all over and a pink almost violet tongue that licked the lips after almost every word. Either a bad case of chap or a nervous habit of his species. He looked European to me, that is, stunted and tortured, his karma having been one of pain and deprivation followed by the accident of being swept by a tide to this place for this moment, our entrance.

I must apologize for this the effect of atheism on germ plasm accustomed for centuries to revealed religion; the devil banished at the front door climbing in at the window leaves a trail of irony and superstition. A derailed soul expresses religion with a rant of destiny. I am one of those who believe they sense the many channels beside radio and TV, like ultraviolet and infrared, that pass through us, even when we don't have equipment to capture them, rays that go unread but not unregistered. If I don't pick up a program, isn't it played in me anyway? and stored? What have I picked up from this man before now? Did we have an appointment?

"We're just looking, thank you," I said, glancing toward the front of the store as though up to the surface where the sidewalk and my car with Sylvie in it sparkled through shards of light cast into the deepwater murk of the store. We were in another world, because I willed it.

We came to a tank of eels. Among them was the creature called Moray, with the head and face of a half-formed human. It is particularly horrible because some terrible curse has turned a human being into a snaky sea monster. I stood drawn to it helplessly as it swayed like a cobra, its serrated mouth grinning some terrible private joke.

"Are you interested in an eel, Sir?" Jim asked, floating to his feet. I cringed back, but he didn't approach, only lounged against a tank with hundreds of goldfish swimming like bright confetti.

"Not right now. They are beautiful, in their way. Do many people buy them?"

"We sell many," he murmured, dipping a net into the solid mass of goldfish, scooping out three or four, and, moving so smoothly he was almost swimming across space to the eel, dumped them in.

In a flash, the gaping eel spun itself out, sucked in one of the goldfish and in almost the same instant, spat out the still-moving tail. The others darted in panic here and there, but in a moment they were all consumed.

I stood rooted. No time had passed, but everything in the world was changed—as you like it, I signaled myself. My skin was loose around my body, tight about my skull. My eyes felt throttled by unseen hands. I looked at Shelly, who had put on a standard expression of disgust, nothing special, no more than when she sees me eating a piece of steak (she is vegetarian). The man's face was expressionless, and because I was now accustomed to the gloom, I saw that it was unlined, rather like a retarded adult's.

Was this regular feeding time? He had positioned himself between my daughter and me. I wanted to push him out of the way. A need to protect her from obscure danger suffused my mind like a blush. He expressed no triumph for the shock he had given me, maybe also my daughter, who had her own reasons to disguise raw reaction, something closed off in her head at this time of her life to prevent me from removing her from a primary reaction to stimuli—she had been in my hands long enough and needed to counter life for herself. I didn't want to let go, but she treated me at times, maybe now, like a too-heavy coat that sweltered on her out of season.

I *wanted* her to feel that she had been in some way raped by the man's swift taking of life and death into his own hands, a ridiculous enough thought, since surely people bought Morays precisely in order to see them eat other living creatures. What he had done was nothing personal, having nothing to do with Shelly. He was saying in his subtle survivor's way only that I had no power to keep her from being eaten in her own time. Even though I was nominally the customer, he was lord and master of this place; I could buy from him, but this act was merely a form of eating from his hand, an admission of his superiority, his *priority*. Finally, I was helpless and powerless against instant acid dissolution in some mouth I could not begin to imagine.

205

I walked out, dazed. As though my eyes were in the sides of my head, I could see tanks on both sides, but not the door in front of me. Fumbling for my dark glasses, I flinched from the blazing light that struck pain into the back of my skull, my eyes acting like a magnifying glass that almost incinerated my brain.

Not really. But that is the image. I did have a headache, I noted with satisfaction. I was alive. I got into the car as Shelly pushed through the door of the store.

"You could have told me you were going," she accused, justly, I thought, if I were really so afraid of some nefarious motive on the man's part.

"What's the matter?" Sylvie asked, aware of drama.

"Buckle your seat belts," Shelly commanded.

"What did you think of his feeding those fish to the eel while we were there?" I asked.

"Pretty horrible," she replied with disinterest.

"Did you feel used and abused?"

"What for? My science teacher's snake ate a mouse in front of the class. I didn't leave even though it was pretty gross. Some of the kids did."

"Why did he do it right in front of us?" I insisted, putting the car in gear while waiting for a chance to enter traffic.

The sun was setting into a nice smoggy sunset, bringing to life the tin roofs on trailers across the highway, everybody heading to a trendy restaurant or bar, or an assignation on the beach with weenies.

"Just what happened in there?" Sylvie asked.

"Oh, the man fed goldfish to an eel," Shelly said, "no big deal."

"Your father seems to want to make a big deal of it. How come?"

I had to slow down for two almost naked women who were darting across the highway against the light. They carried a picnic basket between them and snorkeling equipment in a net.

"That man in the store wanted to shock us," I said.

"Oh, Daddy, he wanted to sell us a Moray eel."

"Would you want a Moray eel?" I asked evenly, watching the young women in the rear-view mirror. They barely made it to the other side alive, squealing and swinging their burdens. I pursed my lips.

"You wouldn't get it for me even if I did. They require a salt-water tank anyway," Shelly said primly, full of knowledge.

"He was probably from Europe, concentration camp survivor. Or a guard. More likely a guard," I said.

"Why not the commandant, an escaped war criminal of our own, right here in Laguna?" Sylvie said.

I stopped in front of the apartment. Someone had as usual blocked off the garage and taken the only space. Now I would have to drive around and around until I could find a space to park and call the police who might come to ticket the offending car. I needed to find a birthday present for Shelly. We had a big party planned for her "sweet sixteen." The gift wasn't going to be an eel with a human face and an appetite for goldfish or even the father of a nubile adolescent.

"Why don't you people go on down to the beach. I won't park now. Just call the cops and get them over here."

Sylvie unhooked her belt. "Why bother?"

"Principle of the thing," I said. "See you in an hour."

I really wanted to go to garage sales to be alone to brood over the man of the aquarium shop. Laguna has some really good book bargains. People get rid of their newish books faster here than elsewhere, as though good books and the beach are mutually exclusive, like toy magnet dogs that repel each other. People in Laguna tend to read at the beach books rather like beach balls, thick almost cubic paperbacks with one-word titles. Hard-bound ones bought before beaching go out in sales, and then make their way around town throughout the course of the year, counters as though in a kind of stock exchange like Dutch bulbs in the seventeenth century.

I liked shopping with nearly naked people, voyeurism that carries no penalty. When Sylvie is with me she always catches me out staring. One-way mirrored glasses is no answer, because I need reading glasses to see titles.

I found three books at the very first sales, but as I was paying, I thought I saw Jim walking by on the street. He glanced my way and walked on. Did he smile? If he had opened that shark's mouth I'm sure I would have recognized him. But how could he have closed his store, changed into a bathing suit so swiftly? I watched him recede, his spring-like body not moving much inside the bathing suit. Another thing about nakedness is how everybody's behind is as different as their faces, with individual expressions.

I would have to buy Shelly a new book. These others were for me, an accidental summer's library, books I would never read otherwise, last year's best sellers, a Dutch book on Prussian militarism, another on color separation in lithography.

A day or so went by before I could get back to the store again, alone. I was disappointed to see a very young man at the desk. "Where's Jim?" I asked.

"He'll be back soon. He's out scubaing," the boy said, scratching at a pimple. "Anything I can do for you?"

"No thanks." I noticed other equipment—javelins, tridents, gutting knives, poles with electric shock apparatus, wet suits. He uses his own things, I thought. Likes to kill on his own. Not enough by proxy. Didn't get enough of it in the war. Clever to disguise murder as legal underwater mayhem. If I could only catch him out in the act of spearing or shocking a Garibaldi, one of those outsized goldfish protected by law, it would be—what? Good, very good.

"Has he owned this place long?" I asked.

"Yeah," the boy said, too casually, "a long time."

I walked over to the Moray. I wondered if the boy also fed it; he didn't really seem interested in anything but his magazine, even though I felt his eyes on me all the time. I went out, disappointed.

As I walked down the beach to join my family, I looked up the beach at the bodies lying with legs stretched out to sea and sky, some open, some closed. I wondered if sex organs were as varied as bottoms. The frisbee throwers played as though they imagined themselves Greek discus athletes, oblivious to naked bodies but not to a talent scout who might spot them.

I sat down to put on my mask and fins.

"Aren't the waves a bit rough for that?" Sylvie remarked.

"Don't worry, I'll be back soon." I spat into my mask and walked backwards into the water. Under the water's edge I could see the bottom halves of people thrashing around in the waves, spasmodic. In the calmer deep water I kept watch for two-dimensional-looking Garibaldi that stayed close to rocks and kelp. I saw a diver with air-tank and wet suit. Immediately I knew it was Jim, because he held a trident. He *was* stalking forbidden fish. I had no weapon with me, of course, only my hands, and I couldn't go deep. Jim darted around a submerged rock and I flapped as quickly as I could to follow him, not noticing how close I was to the rock. A wave dashed me against the mollusc-studded part sticking out of the water. Receding, the wave raked me painfully across its surface. My blood spread out in filaments.

I had to give up and head back to shore, skin burning from the long shallow cuts.

"What happened to you?" Shelly exclaimed.

"A little rough out there," I muttered, "it's nothing. I'll just go back to wash out the sand."

At night we watched TV programs about exotic animals, fish, sharks, all eating one another, the food pyramid, and we were on top because we took the pictures, but then we are eaten too, leaving behind a child or so. Within two generations everybody becomes a generic, even the famous. Our birthday present for Shelly, sold at someone's anonymous garage sale to someone who might read these faded words: "For our beloved Shelly on her sixteenth birthday. May this day mean as much to her while she reads this book as she has meant to her parents through all the wonderful years of her life. Love, Mommy and Daddy." Generic as Garibaldi idling away their lives below the surf in Laguna, as the houses that stand through good and bad owners and renters. Murder provides a certain persistence, a slightly deeper cut into the world. Jim was content to kill anonymously. That proved he was spiritually more advanced than I, and being European he had had more chance to suffer and make to suffer than I, American and protected all my life. Damn geography!

Shelly's birthday dawned. I wanted to get up very early to tap out something about it, but overslept, and it was late to go to my favorite restaurant to use my clacking little Hermes. We had to prepare for people invited down for Shelly's dinner party at the chosen restaurant, one beautifully situated above a cove with a good view of ocean and boulders. I had reserved tables overlooking the lawn and the slope down to the sea. We would sit down exactly at five, when the sun began its descent behind Santa Catalina. At that hour the early-bird dinner is in effect.

The main idea was to get through the day in a festive harmonic mood without dissonance, and hold the minor key, please. I enjoyed watching Shelly and Sylvie fuss over her birthday dress. Shelly's almost-best friend Stevie was already in place, from the night before; as a special treat she had been allowed to take a bus all the way from Fresno, arriving flushed and disheveled—no air-conditioning on the bus, of course. We had discussed sending her air fare.

The girls didn't appear to have much to say to one another. They both lay legs stark straight out, dark glasses on, taking the sun, covered with oil on every exposed inch.

By early afternoon, despite warnings, both were uncomfortably sunburned, particularly Stevie. I worried that she wouldn't be able to go to dinner and the evening would be ruined for Shelly, but she was able to get into her dress. We were all in our window seats drinking house wine when Jim appeared outside in his wet suit and trident, going down to dirty this cove too.

I gave Sylvie a look that said: "That's him, I didn't make it all up."

He held his mask like a begging bowl. As he went by, he glanced into the restaurant, showed his teeth, and waved his trident, relishing his role as master of life and death in the sea, while we sat land-locked in the restaurant.

I felt slapped. Also a bit frightened, because I was altogether too *really* angry, not theatrically, melodramatically *safely* angry.

Sylvie threw me a worried look, which lightened my mood. If she believed in my drama, the need to live it grew less important, I could let anger drain through holes in her seawall, and then blame her at the same time for aborting any events in my life larger than her spaces.

Or did Jim wave only to my daughter, with whom he already had illicit contact through the feeding of goldfish to the Moray? Did he deliberately trail himself before me, like bait, daring me to cross tridents with him? The idea was nonsense, but still, suppose he believed me to be Jewish, and he, concentration camp guard, harbored a desire to get just one more?

Sylvie was looking at Jim as though he were an astronaut or at least Jacques Cousteau.

"That's him, Jim, the man from the aquarium shop," I nudged

Shelly.

"Yeah? Thanks, Daddy."

Was she uninterested or merely careful? I widened my perception to include the entire restaurant, the whole of Laguna, I became a wide-angle lens in this time of my daughter's sixteenth birthday, never to be repeated, soon to be generic, and flashed on the time, years before, when the three of us were vacationing on the island of Crete, in a rented air-conditioned car, traveling along a beach not unlike this one. On Crete between road and ocean are fields of wheat. A blinkered ox dragged a weighted plank over the grain. I wanted to take a picture of this process, so I left Shelly and Sylvie in the car with the engine running and ran down to where the work was going on. I passed some old men sitting in shade nearby, drinking. They beckoned to me and I went over to them and made gestures that I wanted to take their pictures as well as a picture of the ox at work. They gave me to understand that it would be all right, but first I must take a drink of ouzo with them. I hunkered down, but suddenly there was high-pitched whine and growl and a dog lunged at me. I fell over backward, providing the men with a laugh, and then I saw that the dog, a bitch, was in labor and frightened by my appearance. She was tied up and had already given birth to two or three tiny blind crawling things. While I sat and drank, she had two more. I thanked the men, took my pictures, and left, struggling up the slope to the car.

The point is, the car and the two people in it were the same as I had left minutes before, but I had traveled widely in time since I left them. Everything was changed while nothing had happened, just as for the Chinese man who dreamed of being a butterfly. And now, when I looked at my daughter, I saw a bitch giving birth to the future that left her spent and helpless.

A few days after the party, I thought I saw Shelly at the end of the beach walking with Jim. I hurried over, but it was two strangers. Another time I looked up from my book and saw a young woman swinging down the beach alone and followed her with my eyes. Sylvie was also looking at her, and with a jolt I realized that the young woman was Shelly.

"She's having a really good time this year, isn't she?" I managed to recover.

"She seems to be," Sylvie said, "are you?"

"Pretty good."

"Do you need something epic to happen?"

I didn't reply.

"What are you working up?"

"I'm writing something. It wouldn't interest you."

"I'm interested in you."

"No sarcasm meant, but thank you."

Sylvie turned back to her book.

"Where's our daughter going?"

"It's a surprise. Can you keep a secret?" Sylvie turned to me.

"Of course. What surprise? Where is she?"

"She's got a job. She wants to earn money so she can buy her own clothes for fall without asking for money or permission."

"What kind of job? Where is it?"

"That's the secret. If I told you it wouldn't be a secret, and she would know I told you."

"Why?"

"If she asks, I'd have to tell her the truth. Don't push me."

I knew without being told where her job was, I knew in my bones. My blood froze. I waited for it to boil.

Without a word I walked down to the water and dived through a wave, and then another. I saw a man and woman with spears stalking a Garibaldi. I rushed back to shore and put on mask and fins and

213

dived again into the waves. I couldn't be sure it was Shelly and Jim, but I furiously paddled down and down to their level, lungs protesting, ears pounding. As I approached them, I moved too rapidly and the mask slipped from my face and filled with water, forcing me to gulp. I gagged and pushed my way upward, sick and panicked.

The next thing I knew someone was punching me in the stomach. I vomited, my head was splitting, the sun burned my brain, I saw a blurry bunch of faces, and someone was crying.

Of course, I had almost drowned. Who was crying? I focused. It was a small boy, nobody I knew. I squinted down the beach. There were Sylvie and Shelly, but so far away they hadn't even noticed the drama, didn't see that I almost drowned—a real event, gone unrecorded for them.

"Who rescued me?" I murmured.

"Some man brought you out. I guess he left," the muscular lifeguard said. "Anonymous hero," he laughed. "You OK now?" He obviously wanted to get back to his adoring retinue at the stand.

"Yeah, I guess so," I said, still nauseated. I staggered back to our place on the beach and lay down on my stomach.

My heart continued to pound. I got up again, muttering that I needed to go home, I would see them later.

"I'll walk with you, Daddy. I need to go into town anyway."

"Where are you going?"

"Oh, just into town for a few hours. Why?"

"Just wondered is all."

Lying on the couch, I waited just long enough for her to get to the store and settle in and then I dressed and drove directly there.

I parked right in front and walked straight in. The carbuncular young man was sitting at the desk with his magazine.

"Where's Jim?"

He looked up with what I thought was a sly grin that twisted around his erupted face.

"He's not here right now."

At that point I noticed the open door leading to a flight of stairs. So he had his living quarters here, and he's up there with Shelly.

"Is he up there?" I asked evenly, hoping for some unaware response.

"Up there? That's the storeroom. He's not there."

"You mind if I take a look for myself?" I was already on my way for the door.

"Hey, that's off-limits to customers," he yelled after me as I leaped up the stairs. He would not be able to catch me in time if I kept the advantage of surprise.

The room above the store was empty, but another door led out to the light. I rushed through it and out onto a roof. I looked all around, but saw nobody. I peered over the side of the roof just as the young man got to me and grabbed hold of my arms and twisted them behind me. I smelled oniony breath, he tightened his painful hold as I caught a glimpse of three people walking on the sidewalk just as they were turning the corner, talking easily and with animation, enjoying each other, even their backs seeming to converse in the sun and light and clear atmosphere of Laguna.

Holocaust Envy

F rom the first moment Sylvia came into Jeremy's office something told him she was different from other long-term tem-
poraries who filtered through year after year. The others, male or
female, had an eagerness that bordered on fawning. All of them were
very interested in, almost obsessed with, Jeremy's wall, where
pictures and newspaper articles covering twenty-odd years were
posted to a thickness of some inches in places, so that his wall
resembled a relief map of some eccentric country. Of course, so did
he.

Sylvia smiled, and Jeremy imagined a Disney-horse version of a
Houyhnhnm, long face, gentle eyes, soft black hair that curled in to
protect a chin that seemed strong enough to endure anything, even
sharing an office with him.

"So you teach basic math to new immigrants?" Jeremy asked,
swiveling back in his chair, safe in his corner. "Do you like it?"

"Oh yes, I prefer it. They're grateful, smart and challenging."

"I guess new immigrants of any time aren't spoiled. It's that I like
to teach psych theory, not just basic behavior."

"I don't just," Sylvia smiled, "I get in other things."

"Special handling?"

Sylvia's smile faded, her face seemed to go even longer, she pursed
her lips. Jeremy wondered what on earth he had done.

"Why did you say that? It's all right," she added hastily, "but did
somebody tell you about me? Of course!" She raised her eyebrows

comically, "you're an old hand here. The division chair probably showed you my resume. You know all about me, right?"

"All about you? I don't know the first thing about you, Sylvia, except that I like you already and I'm really delighted to have you in my office. That is, that we share an office. What does 'special handling' mean to you?" But as he asked, he flushed, realizing what she was talking about, reacting to. A Survivor! Special handling could mean only one thing—in night and fog, *nacht und nebel*, the Final Solution.

Instantly he fantasized several conversations with her, all the conversations he had always wanted to have with a Survivor. Who had he known? One person with a tattooed number ran an ice cream shop, always giving short shrift, treating his laborers badly, underpaying. He was very fat, and his numbers ran like a hiccup across his lower arm.

"But you, you're—well—too young, aren't you? I mean," he stammered, while she smiled wryly, "how old are you, anyway?"

Sylvia swiveled her chair to face him directly. "I don't give speeches, I don't appear before groups. I don't like to talk about it, because," and she paused and raised her chin and pursed her lips, for the comic dramatic quality, and stopped.

"Yes, go on, I'm listening," Jeremy said, looking at her with awe.

"Because," and she leaned toward him, "because," she whispered, "I don't remember any of it," and she laughed.

"Well, what about therapy, hypnosis?" said Jeremy, troubled. "But maybe you don't want to remember."

"I wish I already knew you better," Sylvia said.

"I understand that, I feel the same way," Jeremy replied seriously.

"No," she said, taking his hand, "no, not what you think, it's because I would like to take to myself the freedom to call you an idiot."

217

"Why idiot? I admit I'm obsessed, it didn't happen to me, but it could have, we haven't been able to balance the fluid in the two beakers, or even discover the real nature of the connection—there's an imbalance, but why idiot?"

"I don't remember, but not because I'm a hysteric, but because I was too young. My brother remembers for me, and he wasn't even there! Ah, does he talk, but me, what do I have to remember, a little girl with her mother."

What would she have to remember! The *aktion* that netted them, rousting them out of house or apartment or bunker or from behind a false bookcase. The hasty wrapping of a squalling infant, toddler, or little girl, awake with a jerk, pulled into the dead cold of light flashed from invincible walking forts, great gray walls of men. Wet, hungry, a smell of rank terror emanating from Mama instead of the milky perspiration of an overheated European flat, grating noises instead of soft lullaby that always used to lead the way to sleep, and each night another syllable emerging from smoky obscurity to stand with others that began to make language into sense and the beginning of the formed world.

Jeremy sat numb as images played and as usual had no conception of how long he had stayed in his dream.

"Come on," Jeremy urged, "It's my job and pleasure to show you around school. I've been here forever," he added with a grin, "so showing you everything will reacquaint me with it too."

He slammed the office door, dodged three students who were peering at the door cards, and steered Sylvia like a steamer in shallow water through shoals to open sea.

"There used to be lots of Jewish students, many of them SDS members—that was Students for a Democratic Society—the most radical of all the groups on campus at that time. They broke out these windows in 1969 in order to bring peace to Vietnam." He pointed to dirty water-streaked windows above the stairwell. "The same day a disturbed student of mine decided to challenge my wife for me."

Sylvia turned, curious.

"My wife and I have been divorced for years, so I don't mind telling you about it. Well, stones and bricks came crashing through this window here, as she was charging up the stairs—"

"Who was?"

"My wife. The girl was already up there. Oh, I won't go into lurid details. Nothing happened. Nothing ever happens. I never showed the slightest interest in her, even if she was also a Survivor. Maybe I inspire lust and trust in equal portions. So watch out, OK? The most dangerous thing in the middle class urban male's jungle. Infidelity. In lieu of reality."

"There are also real problems to be found in America."

They walked out into the sun.

Jeremy squinted. "Let's go to the library first, I'll introduce you to the current librarian. The former and lovely one died a few years back of fast-moving cancer. Doctors convinced her she was being hysterical. They don't believe middle-aged women, especially Jewish ones, when they complain. Since most of the doctors are Jewish, they've got this grudge against people who have begun to resemble their mothers."

Sylvia stopped. "Do you really believe all that you say?"

Jeremy grinned. "Are you beginning to look like your own mother? Still, it could be true, couldn't it? Anyway, she's dead, and maybe if someone had caught it sooner . . . ?"

At the library steps an assortment of races, ages, and dispositions of people lounging, some twitching with inward devils only they could see, some deep in what looked like depression. Several waved at Jeremy or tried to speak to him, but he waved all of them away.

"Got my new colleague here," he yelled, "have to show her around. Come to the office later."

He leaned toward Sylvia and said confidentially, "They love me. I run the encounter groups and I get all the weird ones. The *real* reason for the groups is so that crazies, who used to be in halfway houses, have somewhere to go."

"Don't you have any respect for any of them?" Sylvia asked.

Jeremy stopped smiling. "Oh-oh, I've succeeded in convincing you that I'm cynical. I'm not, really, it's just that, whenever I sense that the possibility of the ideal is receding, is fading in me, that I'm getting too comfortable with the life I lead, and I say, with Faust, 'Stay o moment, thou art fair,' I have to sneer at it, I have to go into contempt mode, or else I'm afraid that I'll die on the vine, like all the other petty functionaries here. In Russia, Poland, Czechoslovakia, they have to watch out for what they say all the time. I can do anything I please and people just smile. You had to do anything *they* pleased, just to survive."

"You're starting to bring all that stuff up again. Please don't."

"Really," Jeremy urged, "it's OK for you to be here, for you to take this place seriously, because you've paid the price of admission. Not me, I just play around. Old homo ludens, that's me. Oh, I give at the office, of course, people in class like me, I'm OK, but there's something lacking somewhere. Maybe you can help me find out what?"

Sylvia shook her head slowly all during Jeremy's speech, and at the end of it, she was shaking it violently. "No!" she said. "Leave me out of it."

A vividly painted Black woman strolled by, tight pants outlining each buttock, her high red-heeled shoes ticking and tacking on the linoleum. With her was a dumpy middle-European woman carrying a large portable radio.

"They all come to the magnet, the most powerful nation on earth, but we're on our way out just like all the other powerhouses before us. Pretty soon people won't be able to blame us for what's happening in the world."

"Not yet, Jeremy, I hope, not yet, I only just got here myself. I need to worry about day-to-day things, like assignments, reading papers, taking care of my family."

"Sukey and Val? Sure. I understand." He peered around the reference section. "There's only one librarian left, the rest are clerks. The bosses downtown don't think we need professionals anymore. They're right, of course, all that's left here is the must, the debris, you and me. And we don't matter. Why don't we matter?" he asked, mock ferocious. "Because it isn't a matter of life or death."

"Why don't you go to Israel where it is a matter of life or death?" Sylvia asked.

"Because I don't allow myself to cross the road," Jeremy answered.

A little woman in her sixties with heavy drooping features, a haversack, and a thick sweater, despite the heat, waved at Jeremy vigorously and made to cut across the reading room to reach him, but he took Sylvia's arm and resolutely turned away.

"Who is that you're avoiding?" Sylvia asked.

"Another survivor, an old one, tearful, very sweet woman, very grateful for all I've done for her, et cetera."

"Why aren't you as interested in *her* story?" Sylvia asked, the wry crooked smile on her face, as though she had found him out.

"She's not intact. It's the difference between finding tiny pieces of amphorae and the whole vessel. You are infinitely more interesting. I don't identify with her."

"In other words, I'm more sexy."

"In many other words, yes. Men have to be that way. Everything, including sympathy and anguish, is associated with our members. You ever see sport clothes with the label: 'Members Only'? Well, that's us men. Everything must be prurient, even pornographic, or we lose the duplicity of vision that makes us men. Without it we become women."

"And so women cannot be interested in pornography?"

"No," he smiled at her firmly, "you cannot, or you're perverse. Men are by nature perverse. Without our members half up and saluting we lose interest. We've got to be never more relaxed than parade rest, at all times ready to mount any strange steed."

"You're talking complete drivel, Jeremy, do you know that. To hear yourself do what passes for thinking."

Jeremy was silent while they walked back onto the quad. Finally he said, "Are you worried that your husband might be just the same? I don't say that there isn't more to the best of us. But for most of us, we are our genitals, our genitals are us, predicate nominative—I mean genitals are we—copulative verbs, whatever you like, but up there and down here, it's an identity, a wash, a complete sameness."

"If you are nothing but an ambulatory organ, where is friendship? What's the payoff for me?"

Jeremy kicked at a clod of grass and squinted at the leaden sky. Three miles away vague outlines of downtown Los Angeles that he hoped to see quaver and then fall, soundlessly, giving him the opportunity to compose himself before the inevitable shock wave hit him. "I don't know what the payoff is either, but it must be something, because I don't believe that I've given you the entire package. There certainly is something else I want from you, but what is it?" He sighed. "Let's get back."

They walked silently, and then Jeremy turned again to Sylvia and stopped. "Am I weird? I *hope* everything isn't interchangeable, my modular organ, your modular organ, but I have to say it, because it would be arrogant to claim otherwise. I only wish for the ideal, like Hardy wishing that oxen might kneel before the new Lord, even though he knows it won't happen, can't and never did happen."

"If you didn't dwell on it, you could live a much better life. You roll around in it like a crazy dog. If you are nothing but appetite and attack you can't be a good father and husband or even a good teacher."

"I am neither what I say nor what I think," Jeremy announced. "And maybe if I annoy the Lord sufficiently, She will descend to brush my head with lilac vegetal. Meanwhile, let's go learn the boat people!"

Sylvia took Jeremy's arm while they walked up the dark stairs, an economy measure of the college. "At least you aren't a bore. When you whine you know you're enjoying it and don't expect me to take you seriously. I'm still pleased I share an office with you, Jeremy, believe me."

"I believe you, but I am sorry that you don't take my keening seriously. I'll take yours seriously if you take mine, and I'll let you see mine if you let me see yours."

A student whirled around at that. Jeremy and Sylvia chortled.

He felt good but also irritated, as though he had scratched a bite too hard. He wondered how much of the truth he had told, and how much was the same old posing made over as dramatic and Byronic. A part of the pose was to deride the pose itself. Was he trying to seduce the woman after all? No, no! That rather bovine calm face, with its eyes that should be bloodshot, they were shaped so much like a hound dog's. Seduce her, yes, but only to force her back to her past, to share her memories, not sex. But then why all that organ music? Only to reassure her he wasn't going to sniff around her real secrets, her secret places where she hid the real treasures. What he wanted, he realized suddenly, was more, far more, more like in a movie, *Invasion of the Body Snatchers,* with him as the alien from another planet. He wanted to *be* her. But that was to die, wasn't it? Sex only modulated the module—getting off the ground for five minutes didn't constitute flying!

He walked into his office, pleased, as though he had snatched some reality from a sky so replete with heavy metals one had to push through it like an icebreaker in the Arctic. Sylvia would toddle into the concentration camp universe and he would be by her side, no, *inside.* To do that he would have to take her back, she would have to go there, by an incredible act of will. But why should she go willingly? She would not, she had to run to the market for cornflakes. But he could not kidnap her or hold her otherwise captive, he had no stomach to be a terrorist, or the sick leave for it. How *had* the two of them survived, mother and child?

He would smoke her out somehow, but she was canny, she might try to kill him if she suspected for a moment what he planned to do. Plan? He *had* no plan, yet. But a plan was developing, growing, like a tumor grows. Hidden away, like a Christmas present nobody finds, discovered by accident in the middle of August.

Dear Jeremy:

That day was the first time I knew you had it so bad, and even then I knew it could come to no good. Little did I imagine you would go so far. I knew JDLniks and AZAs as well as Val's serious Zionists, Labor and Religious. It wasn't as though we were brought up with a vacuum around us.

Val and I talked endlessly about our experiences before we decided to go ahead and get married despite his handicaps, his age, and the other family he lost. Not to the Holocaust, you panting puppy! Another kind of fire, a real one, an apartment

224

that went up, and he couldn't save them because of his being crippled with arthritis, in a wheelchair, one hand permanently closed. We love each other, and he is very able with that one hand and good arm to crush me to death in a bear hug if he isn't careful of his strength. I'm through with that other stuff! It isn't good for me to talk about it. I told you that.

And you call yourself a psychologist! Supposed to help plow and replant the past, not go back to it to repoison the ground even more!

In some anxiety,
Sylvia

DREAM
Terrible place, barbed wire, wet and dirty people cluster in front of a hotel. I have no sense of immediate danger, walk up a massive stairway to a central core where the landlady holds forth. I see she holds my 1977 and 1976 calendars next to her breast in a plastic bag, but they are puffy and moldy. I reach for them joyfully, I have missed them. "I have been saving them for you," she says reproachfully. I don't know why, since she doesn't like me. A roving band of cutthroats offers her some stolen silkscreened tapestries, taken from Jews who have been deported. I have forgotten which room I live in, and others are covered with ants and cobweb. The landlady suggests that I write a letter to myself. Behind each dark door is the sound of sexual activity.

The first time Jeremy spent time with Val he was very nervous. Waiting for him to finish an income tax return in the converted bedroom that was now his office, Jeremy wandered the living room. The only furniture consisted of a wicker couch, a too-low coffee table with strange crude inlays, an imitation Persian rug and an oil painting that reminded Jeremy of a Japanese bamboo grove, lashed by rain and wind, bent but eternal.

He went into the bathroom, hoping to find a clue to their personalities, but only ordinary things were in the medicine chest, a hemorrhoid medicine, something for constipation. Nothing to read there about Sylvia and Val, nothing foreign. About the house, either. They might both have been born in Bakersfield.

Val rolled out, carefully missing scattered toys, barrel chest leading. "Coffee?" he said in his booming voice.

Jeremy nodded and followed his host into the kitchen.

"Now, what do you want to talk to me about?" Val asked.

"Like someone stung repeatedly by bees I've become not less but more sensitive, more allergic, to the way things are done on this planet. I've—"

"Why didn't you consult your therapist?" Sylvia snapped, "don't bug me with it."

"Your husband understands," Jeremy sighed. "I told him how I view the Holocaust, like a stain that was an animal on the freeway, rolled over until nothing is left. I want to reconstruct the living, breathing creature. I can barely stand to be in the same world with the memory. I need to go back into it, like you have to allow yourself to fall in a dream until you come out the other side. Otherwise, you'll never get over it. You did that, you came out the other side."

"We are not the same person," she explained carefully, "and you cannot put yourself in my skin. I haven't any answers to furnish you. But I do have papers to grade." Her usually twinkling eyes were black and somber with a hint of alarm, as though an armed guard had heard something beyond the gates.

Jeremy pulled on his dead pipe, grabbed it from his teeth in a gesture that seemed to pit teeth and hand in mortal combat. He managed to wrest the thing from his mouth, stared into the bowl, at the gray mass of cinders, and tapped it into a flower pot.

"That's cloisonné, one of the few things I still have from Warsaw," Sylvia said with irritation.

He continued to tap on the edge like a blind man trying to find the way.

They stared at each other. A child's cry drifted in from the bedroom.

"Sukey. I don't want to be rude, Jeremy, but I have my work to do, and Val will be out any minute and he'll be ravenous. He gets particularly hungry when he has to sort out the financial affairs of a femme fatale."

Jeremy hung on the jamb of the door. "Goodbye, and say goodbye to Val for me. Tell him I hope I wasn't too taxing." He wanted to hold her forearm to his mouth to suck up the essence of her number, but she would only complain, "Babies were not assigned numbers!"

A girl Jeremy knew slightly belonged to a Zionist youth group, and to be near her, he went with her to a meeting where a movie was to be shown. It was *Night and Fog,* he was thirteen and the year was 1955. Intoxicated as he was with the idea of being somewhere in the dark with a girl, it took some time before he became aware of the quiet steady voice of the French narrator or the images on the screen. Nazis were herding people his age out of a house, beating them . Their hands were up in the air. He saw them put into cattle cars. He saw faces behind wire, Nazis with police dogs. He loved dogs, particularly large dogs, and his heart rose as usual to see them on the screen. But here they were guarding Jewish prisoners. How could he participate in this scene? Where was he, with the dogs or with the children? He could not bear to be the child ripped out of a parent's arms, but that left only the jackbooted soldier who smiled and smoked a cigarette while holding lightly the lead of that beautiful smiling animal at his feet.

The girl was annoyed that Jeremy was paying no attention to her, but he was gone, forever rapt into night and fog, lost in Holocaust, in the first of thousands of images, books, pictures, articles, exhibitions, in the need to always compare his dates with the dates of the Warsaw Ghetto, with every anniversary of the Holocaust.

When lights went on, the girl, maybe sensing that she was with a different person, said, "My uncle was in a camp. He's always telling us he doesn't want to talk about it."

"Does he have his number tattooed on his arm?" Jeremy asked, feeling his own and finding it strangely smooth.

"He had it removed, but you can see it sometimes anyway."

Now a woman stood at a lectern; big and high-cheekboned with faded blonde hair and blue eyes, she looked like the German women guards who were herded out of the barracks by American soldiers, defiant or fearful. Jeremy noticed that her big breasts rested on the lectern and jiggled like big puddles every time she said a word. Her words were like rocks thrown into them, fanning out until they reached a far shore. She flung back her sleeve to show her number. She said, "I was hidden for two years by Gentiles before I was discovered and taken to a camp. Before that I was taken for a Christian. That was why they could keep me."

Jeremy learned a truth he had only suspected before, the value of not looking Jewish.

Most of the other children were respectful but bored. They had all been herded through this before. The woman on the podium yanked her great breasts off the stand and sang a song. It was the "Ha Tikvah," Israel's national anthem. The children came to their feet. Someone tried to muffle a belch, others tittered, some shushed, and then it was over. Jeremy retained no memory of whatever happened to the girl.

DREAM
Only 625 people left in the world. A council chamber with small trainlike wagon going around and around. Stone chambers. Black boys wheeling a huge machine, sweating. Blank-faced women demonstrating the death chamber in the window of a store, made for those guilty of the crime of being Jewish. They live throughout history. A crimson fingernail comes toward me scratching its way through a thick door. I plead, very carefully, for my life.

Was it better for Sylvia as a source that she be retained at the college or cut loose? Knowing how hungry Jeremy was for everything about her past, she withheld from him even items she would pass casually to a stranger on the street or someone with whom she would share a lunch counter. "Yes, I was in one of those camps, really, I'm not joking," having to convince the other she wasn't just cashing in on a trend, the in thing to be a survivor, over hamburger and coke. "My mother and me."

Between one game of volleyball and another, fifteen boxcars full of people decamped, whipped down the ramp and into lines to the "delousing" chamber, and from there to the ovens. Between one game and a third, the bodies were separated from their death embrace with iron hooks and thrown four at a time into the furnaces. Before the set was over, people who had screamed and shoved and lived were part of the earth.

Was the attraction murder? Can't we get enough of how people die? Do we dwell always in the house of death, dwell *on* it? "Now and at the moment of our death, amen." And: "Now I lay me down to sleep, I pray my soul the lord to keep, and if I die before I wake ..." No, I've got it wrong again.

DREAM

I am approaching something both dangerous and inevitable, exciting, that roils and boils like a chemical cloud. Entrance there is to tempt instant death, as the cloud is both radioactive and intensely hot. It is an oven that encompasses the entire world. Halfway there, I am snapped back to my starting place, like a phonograph record caught in a groove. Each time I am lurched I understand more that I will never be allowed to enter the cloud, never to experience its intimate details, enter its mysteries, never be one of a small company of elect who enter there and emerge to take their place on either side of the path, where they watch me with ironic not unfriendly eyes, making no effort to aid or hinder. "Why don't you demand something of me?" I cry, inside myself, as I cannot make my throat work. In the dream, I awake, neck sore and stiff, fingers painful and twisted, as though they had tried to grasp something too slippery and too heavy to hold.

Dear Sylvia,

Because it is essential that you understand my reasons for hounding you, because I know how much like harassment it must feel, I also want to announce that I will not stop, whatever the cost may be to myself, or, unfortunately, to you.

The whole thing becomes more imperative since I spoke to your mother. Yes, I got her number, don't ask how, just appreciate the depth of my commitment. And she agreed that memory was important, that remembering the Holocaust was important, that *her* memories are important, and that because it is so rare a thing that mother and daughter emerged (relatively) unscathed from the fires, their story/stories need to be told.

But the more I ask you, please, just jog your memory or put

down for the record a reason/apologia/rationalization, every time I ask, you put me off with a joke or a smile. And every other day another piece of Holocaust kitsch comes out, money-making nonsense that denigrates the memories, the ashes, of the Six Million. That's why.

Your silence is criminal, and because no one else has come forward to hold you accountable, I have appointed myself that task. I will prosecute it, to the fullest limits of my power, so help me god, and I will go anywhere, and do anything, to accomplish this task, this pledge, this duty.

Sternly,

Jeremy

Dear Sylvia,

I have come upon some evidence that I think may be of interest, may shed some light on how and why you survived. According to your mother, all residents of Ravensbruck were dignified with better treatment because they had visas for other countries or carried British passports. I checked and all such people held there were either dead or transported to said countries or to Auschwitz *long before* you two got there.

This leaves interesting possibilities. One of them is that you and she were never there, and her story about being a survivor is trumped up. Alternatively, you and she were there indeed enjoying special privileges, but not on account of your visas, but because you were not prisoners at all. Are you beginning to get a glimmer on the direction of all this? Does it seem that I am about to accuse your mother of being a plant, a stooge? Maybe, just maybe, it was even worse, and she was not a Jew at all, but a German pretending to be one so as to ferret out information from real Jews that would ultimately condemn them to death.

"Not my mother!" you exclaim. "Go peddle your filth somewhere else, I'm sorry I ever considered you a friend. How could you, etc., after what she suffered, etc." Still, you don't get along with her, you told me she didn't even mention Holocaust until nearly thirty years after, long enough, it seems to me, for everybody involved who could expose her to be dead or discreetly over the hill. Why, I may ask, did she wait so long? And where is your father? Did you ever know him? No, you did not, he is decently buried somewhere. One suggestion: a good Aryan cemetery somewhere in Germany. Did you ever check? Ask? And your brother, or rather half-brother, what does he say? Does he know something you don't, as evidenced by the fact that he spends half his time in mental hospitals?

If you have something to say to all this—and I would rather we be collaborators than adversaries—please respond post haste. Life has a definite end, you know, and how long for any of us is beyond speculation. Shall I call and ask your mother about this? Her heart condition? What about the condition of those shot through the heart? It cannot have escaped your attention that the Nazi Artukovic was returned to Yugoslavia for trial though senile and dribbling. Who cares how much he drips from both ends, he must pay to educate those who remain . . .

What memories you must have stored somewhere in that child's brain! Hypnotism, perhaps, could bring them forth. We must try. How about it? Val would not have to know. We can both keep a secret. In any event, decide soon, as my hand itches for the phone to Chicago.

Impatiently and Finitely,
Jeremy

P.S.

Do you know how they revive people who've had heart attacks? With an electric fibrillating machine attached to the heart which shocks the whole body with a sudden infusion of, I think, voltage. Did you see *E.T.?* You don't stand to lose a thing. After all, if it happened, it happened, and I can't take that away from you. If it didn't, you are free of the encumbrance of survivordom, and you can live as the offspring of a Quisling who lied to save your lives and perhaps forgot what was inconvenient to remember. And I will do everything to try to comfort you and your family after this great shock.

Revivally,
Jeremy

Val and Sylvia lay back after strenuous lovemaking. They had learned almost immediately after meeting how difficult it would be to avoid hurting each other, his massive upper body with its one good arm above easily broken legs. They managed, there was Sukey to show for it. Pain, however, reminded them of the world and how it bit.

Sylvia frowned at a new crack that mocked the fresh paint in their new house. She wondered how much of the total cost the crack would set them back, and was annoyed with worrying about it, when there was so much for which to be thankful. Then she was even more annoyed, because that seemed almost a paraphrase of something Jeremy had said the day before: "I'm grateful for having been born here, not being a ten-year-old in occupied Europe. Do you feel grateful for what you've got now? I suppose you don't, since the world hasn't given you anything except grudgingly. Don't you feel angry at the U.S. for not having at least bombed the trains, the tracks to the camps?"

"Val, are you asleep?"

"No, I'm looking at that crack."

"Oh, the crack. I'll have the painter come back and sand it closed again. Val."

"Yes?" That deep melodious voice of his, how sexy and mysterious she had thought it when she wasn't irritated at the ringing it caused in her ears. A car went by Dopplering rock and roll through the sleeping neighborhood.

"Val, Jeremy is really getting to me."

"I thought you said you could handle him."

"I could, until he called my mother."

"Your mother! When did he call your mother?"

"Last night. I can't have him bugging my mother. She called to complain, and I got stuffed with the same fury as when I was a little girl. She doesn't deserve it anymore. Neither do I. Jeremy says it's because everything she's told me is a lie. Can you believe that?"

"Believe your mother's lies. Yes, without any trouble at all."

Sylvia giggled and snuggled against his armpit, inhaling the honest mammal smell. "I like it when you don't take my problems seriously. Am I neurotic because every little sniffle when I was a baby my mother swooped down on like an eagle—"

"The American national carrion bird."

"Right. She took me so seriously. I never knew I was waiting for the one man who could laugh at me."

"Laugh with me."

"At me. Don't give me American pablum."

"There is *only* American pablum."

"The point is, dearest, Jeremy is an American, as American as they come, but he would give anything to have my past. In fact, he wants to steal it from me."

"Steal it? How can he steal your past from you?"

234

"Maybe not steal, alter it, work his way inside it."

"Like the egg of an occult species laid inside the body of another, that hatching, feeds on its host?"

"You put things so well, dear man, so experienced is your race in doing just that."

He turned suddenly in the way familiar to walruses, all upper body, the rest weightless, and fumbled for his glasses. In the light from the street his hornrims picked up the glow, but she could not see his eyes. She felt his hand on her breast.

"Val, I don't know if it's because he's chasing me around in it so much, or if my mother really did lie to me, but I'm not sure anymore that I *was* really in the camp." She sighed, a quaver like a sob came out. "There are a number of things that don't add up."

"Look here," Val said to Jeremy. Curious how his voice resonated through every inch of the living room. Lacking much mobility, he compelled attention with his almost operatic delivery, and his one good hand, while the other gripped itself and tried to hide.

"Let's try to get this straight between us. I know you're an honest person, but you're also becoming quite a dangerous one as well."

"How is that possible?" Jeremy exclaimed. "I don't mean you any harm."

"Not me, old man. Personally, I like you."

A wave of love for Val went through him. Val was another piece of the fallout from the Catastrophe, or even a mutant, a new species, part of the new race.

"It's Sylvia I'm worried about," Val continued.

A quivering excitement filled Jeremy. Trembling, his fingers examined a book on a shelf. With his back to Val, he asked, "What's going on with Sylvia? I haven't even asked her anything lately. She told me to stop, and I have."

"Jeremy, what you've done is to convince Sylvia that she never was in a camp with her mother. She half believes her mother is a pathological liar, or worse."

"Well, could that be such a bad thing? If that table can be wiped clean, she can have her own life to live."

Val smiled. "Right, like in a soap opera. That's just what I'm concerned about, Jeremy, the soap opera going on in your mind, trying in its feverish way to remake the world. You weren't there, and it's quite all right that you weren't, but don't you see, it's not fair. What you're doing to Sylvia."

Jeremy felt resentment beginning to burn. He saw the general drift. Val would try to convince him to stop his probe. It remained only to see what he would offer. It would be something Jeremy wanted, irresistible. But resist it he would! He hurried to slam shut the bulkheads in his mind, he scurried about battening down the hatches, securing all quarters while sounding the alarms. Now it would come.

Val spooned powder into cups, poured boiling water over it. The coffee curled, crumbled, and sank beneath the steaming onslaught, turned over and floated on the surface as scum, like people. Then he opened a drawer and took out a spoon and homogenized the mess. Now it was bland brown, proper, all rebellion quashed.

". . . And if you take sugar, there's some on the table," Val said.

Val sipped and gestured with his chin toward the driveway. "She's home. I have just this one minute. Listen, please. The point is, you really do have a great deal of power. No, listen, please! I'm not oiling you up. It's true."

Jeremy's eyes filled. He shook his head violently. He would not be seduced!

"You have the power to cancel her childhood, and if you do that, you may only succeed in canceling Sylvia, the friend you wish no harm to, and her child, who depends on her, as well as her mother, whatever she may or may not be, or was." He wheeled himself closer to Jeremy. "And me, my friend. I need her too, perhaps most of all."

His voice was so charged it filled every molecule of the room and tortured Jeremy's ears. "Honesty, her own life to live. Perhaps there is no such thing? Just what she has, that's what she has to work with. What do you actually know about her? Her ability, her strength, her charm? Are you sure she has always been like that? That she will be able to go on if everything she knows has been a lie? The truth, the truth, pardon me, my friend, but Americans believe truth to be a unitary concept, one thing, indivisible, like liberty and justice for all. But one man's truth is another's death sentence. Please," he whispered as the key rattled in the door, "think it over. We're in here," he boomed.

Dear Jeremy,

I hear you want to be cremated—Val told me. Is that because so many of us were burnt? Do you believe you will become at one with them after death? Have you any idea how burns hurt? Burning is more painful than anything. I believe I have a memory of burning, but it may only be that it was hot and there was nothing to drink. I dream about parching on a desert, burning by degrees, pun intended. You are making me dream nightmares, but I don't know who they really belong to, the others or me. I believe my mother wanted to spare me these nightmares and that is why she never spoke about such things before recently. As though if a door is once opened, like in a horse race, you have to run like hell. Now she is running, and I have to run, her foal, alongside her. You and your color TV, watching nature programs! Must I watch a wildebeest baby, dropped on the veldt, struggle to get up and run within twenty minutes of birth? Do I have to see that baby, wet with birth and looking behind to see what's gaining? I don't need that. Please stop burning, burning next to me. Sukey needs me at normal temperature. If you weren't so rich you wouldn't use your leisure time to rend me.

Admonishingly,

Sylvia

"I'm not suggesting, merely asking," Jeremy said.

"You're not, you son of a bitch, you're accusing. And what for? What on earth for? This is a woman who for reasons that are clear enough would want to put all that behind her. No, I'm falling into your sick trap. If, if, if a huge if, she had been what you infer—"

"The truth, the truth is what we're after, isn't it? And the truth is, how could a girl of eighteen with a little child survive, and have her child survive, in that hell? I've read maybe hundreds of books on the camps and I have not seen one story, not one, in which a prisoner comes through with a small child. Check me out on it."

"How am I to do that?" she hissed through closed teeth. "How, without reading through all that filth," she said pointing a shaking finger at one of the piles of books that always littered Jeremy's desk.

Jeremy looked down. He put both hands on the pile and turned to Sylvia. "You're right, this has gone far enough." He looked up to squint at a flickering fluorescent. "Let's not go into it anymore. Your mother and brother are your only remaining relatives and they're precious to you."

"Not true! Val and Sukey are my relatives. I am not responsible for my mother, or how she survived the Holocaust. I am also not interested in why or what."

"Neither am I, neither am I," Jeremy said. "We stop right here. Or

238

else I really am a son of a bitch."

"I apologize, Jeremy. I didn't mean that."

Jeremy was gone for the day. Sylvia ran her fingers over tired eyes. So many papers to correct, so many comments to put on the papers to soften the blow of circled errors so they would not give up. She looked at the stack of books on Jeremy's desk. All new ones, all on Holocaust. His hobbyhorse. We all look like our totem animal. Val was a bear, Sukey was a cute little ferret, Sylvia was a horse, and her mother? Sylvia stopped smiling in the empty office. She saw in her mind the high shiny black boots, flared riding trousers, a riding crop twitched on the side of a boot, manicured long fingers best suited to playing one of the higher Köchel numbers of Mozart, but she refused to go above the waist. She had to move back from the tight shot of the lower body and take it all in. The fingers belonged to her mother, the apartment was Chicago. The boots disappeared below her view, the riding crop became a metronome, tick-tick, back and forth like a cobra mesmerized by "Eine Kleine Nachtmusik," or "Verklärte Nacht," and little Sylvia sitting in a corner listening and watching her beautiful mother, her still-long blonde hair unleashed to crash like a waterfall to the Lorelei of her waist, and then to hang even farther down below the piano stool, brother banished from the room because he wouldn't be still, beating with his light fists against the parlor door, certain tears wetting his shirt.

Then her mother turned to Sylvia and smiled and held out her arms from which abundant material fell like sagging ice. In the silence the sobbing of the little boy outside made its own counterpoint to which the mother paid no attention, but as Sylvia moved slowly toward her mother, her brother's tears forced her to stop.

"I told you to come here," her mother said in a soft honeyed voice, "come to your mother."

Sylvia pointed at the door with her chin, hoping her mother would not take this as disobedience. Instead, the arms came down and one perfect finger pointed to the door. "Then go comfort your brother and stay out of here," and she turned back to the piano and began again the perfect music.

That woman *could* have been a *blockaltester* or chief *kapo* at Ravensbruck. She could have sent women to death without looking twice, even as she allowed her little son to sit weeping, his passport to her snatched away.

She had been herself so young, and already with a five-year-old on her hip, so beautiful, and with how old a child? That was another confusion. Her beauty was why she was allowed to live, only her beauty! One of Jeremy's accursed books brooded about a woman, yes, she was fifteen, innocent, soft, a blur of adolescence, who, because she was chosen to be assistant, turned into an efficient murder machine within weeks. When questioned how she could perform the terrible things required of her, she replied: "You probably know that I put my own mother in the car that took her to the gas. You should understand that there remains for me nothing so terrible that I could not do it. The world is a terrible place. This is how I take revenge on it."

Not fifteen, but eighteen! She shook her head stubbornly side to side and felt little bones crack in her neck. Her temples throbbed. She got up and opened the window wider, although all that accomplished was to let in more smog. Gas. She went to the phone. "Val? Listen, don't laugh. No, I know you won't laugh. Listen, laugh, that's what I need. One question: is there any real possibility that my mother was . . . was not . . . a prisoner, but one of those monsters who . . . ? You're laughing? Is that what you're doing? You're not. I was afraid you wouldn't be. No, I'm finishing up here. Yes, I'll be home soon. Yes, I am going crazy. I'm going to quit this job and start selling vacuum cleaners door-to-door. Right. I am putting on my coat. I'm throwing papers under the desk. Goodbye, my love."

She did not put on her coat. She walked slowly to Jeremy's desk and picked up one after another of the books. It was Friday, why hadn't he taken his new haul home with him to devour greedily over the weekend as other men played golf or watched football? He had, of course, left them as bait to snare her. But the books were true, they weren't bait. All that had happened.

She slowly settled on Jeremy's chair.

"I apologize for this intrusion, but I am a colleague of your daughter's."

The woman looked him up and down through a heavy security chain holding the door to the jamb. He could see an eye and black clothing.

"Yes?"

"May I come in?"

"For what purpose?"

"I've come all the way to Chicago to speak with you. A matter of some importance to you and to her, I think."

The door closed. After a moment, an eternity, the door opened wide. A woman in a long black dress stood there. She had a still presence about her, a face strikingly handsome, regular, large, accented eyes. She was dressed as for a visitor.

"Pardon me if you were expecting other guests. I won't keep you very long," Jeremy said.

"Come in. It is true I was expecting someone. I have been expecting you."

"How? Ah, Sylvia has spoken to you about my questions? Warned you?"

"Not warned. Take a seat there. Will you have tea or coffee? I make good Viennese coffee."

"With *Schlag?*"

"No, Cremora, much healthier."

"I understand cream substitutes are carcinogenic," Jeremy said, taking the offered chair. He looked around. He had expected heavy European furniture, a dark much becurtained room. But this was light, full of Danish modern of the 1950s. No pictures, not even one of the grandchild, no paintings, no dead relatives on the walls, nothing to say that the inhabitant here came from anywhere else.

"You have made a good adjustment, I see."

"Adjustment? It is almost half a century, Mr. Jeremy, time for more than one adjustment."

"Just Jeremy, please. You never remarried?"

"Married. Yes, I married. I did not need to remarry. I was not married to Sylvia's father."

"She never mentioned that."

"Do you mind if I smoke?"

As Jeremy nodded she fitted a long cigarette to a silver holder. He leaped up and held his lighter for her. She took his hand to steady the flame and puffed deeply.

"She does not know it. Now you have a secret. Take it and go home."

"Not so fast . . ."

She sighed. "So you want another? I give you two. Well?"

"No deals," Jeremy said.

"Then we stop at one. Do you take sugar?"

"I seem to have gone through this once with Val. It takes more than coffee to satisfy me."

"Too bad. Coffee is the one thing we craved even more than food in the camp. Coffee was a good thing to organize."

242

"I thought cigarettes were the main trading commodity."

She looked at him through a haze of smoke that solidified in the afternoon sunlight. Weston, Jeremy thought, took pictures of such women, and Stieglitz. Either she wore a very good bra or was remarkably preserved. She would be, say, about sixty-three. Young, actually.

"Not only."

"What did you offer in exchange for your life and your daughter's?"

She was sitting very straight in her chair, legs open beneath her heavy skirt. "You want me to say, 'my body,' don't you? All right, my body. That's two secrets."

"Is that what you're offering now?"

"You did not pay so much and spend so much time to come and take an old lady."

"In a way it would be an even greater rape than in the camp."

"Sylvia did not tell you her greatest shame was how much a tramp her mother was while she grew up? Affairs I had, the way I used her as a screen to keep it from the man she thought was her father?"

"Sylvia tells me nothing, nothing! I know nothing about her, nothing." He had the curious and exciting idea that she had poisoned his coffee. It tasted strange. He thought it burned going down. He looked around to memorize the room for the long trip he might be starting.

She stubbed out her cigarette in a vase the twin of Sylvia's.

"Actually," she said, "you are right that the years in the camp were the best of them. My other child does not forgive not having been able to share them, just like you."

"Is he currently incarcerated?"

"Incarcerated, like burnt up?"

"Like imprisoned, not incinerated. You're very witty, like Sylvia.

She takes after you, also like Wonderwoman, she catches bullets on her wrist shields."

"She told me something. She said you had the mind of a comic book, all simple primary colors, and not quite in register. She said you were not really crazy, only crazed, cracked, that you cannot stand the heat of your own imagination. She said you sit in your cold kiln and try to make heat from nothing."

"She said all that? You mean I'm like King David, in his old age? Is that me? Impotent, raging, destructive, like an old bull beset by wolves?"

"If you say so." She moved her legs and the heavy material shifted, as though for another take, another photographic plate. Jeremy felt that he was inside a symphony by Sibelius, all silences, unsure even when it ended.

She got up, the stuff of her dress fell down in perfect folds, went to a window and opened it. The curtains puffed around her shoulders. She stood with her back to him. "Wouldn't you be pleased if I stepped out of this window now? What a drama!"

"No," he said and stood, a little dizzy. He stepped to her side and looked out. The light had thickened and buildings across the way blurred, a light rain was falling. From this apartment it was impossible to hear the rain. It came from somewhere and went nowhere. The woman's face was wet.

"Are you crying?"

"It is only rain. I don't cry anymore. Val tells me you are not really a bad man, merely one who is very incomplete. What you call the truth is like gas that fills a balloon for awhile."

"Very pretty."

She walked from the window and opened a door at the end of the room and turned to him. "Come here, Jeremy."

He hesitated, then stepped in her direction. He felt his feet hit the floor, one after the other. Finally, he was at her side. He looked into the room. It was dark. He could make out a canopied bed and a dark form. After a moment he heard a rustle, he saw a movement. A face, all black eyes and hair, and a foot, tied to a post. Tears were streaming down the face.

Sylvia's mother pushed him out and closed the door. "You see, he cries for me, I don't need to do it for myself. That is secret number three."

"But why . . . ?"

"Always why, why, why. It is the thing in itself. In a day or so he will be fine again. And when it is again not so fine, he comes to me, holds out the cord, and I tie it, and he stays here, he cries and cries, and then it is over again. Why? He cries for the millions. Instead of like you, you do not cry for the millions, you try to kill them all over again. Is that better? Is that the truth? Do you love our Sylvia? And so try to kill her? And her cripple too? Do you want to go back in and comfort Sylvia's brother? I give you permission. Go."

She took Jeremy's hand, he snatched it away. She hurt him, she was very strong.

"No, I don't think so, not right now. Now," she said briskly, "it is time for you to take me out to dinner, an expensive one, I think. I do not need to change clothes. Do you want to freshen up? There is a well-equipped bathroom just over there. Maybe you want to check the medicine chest? Yes, I have one of *your* secrets. You will find poison well labeled, if you wish it. I will not stop you, but I prefer you take me out to dine. I rarely go out. Do you know Chicago? It is a complete universe. The Camellia House is very nice. I like it very much, don't you?"

"It's fine," Jeremy muttered. "Now you have told me everything, I just don't get it, right?"

"I will tell you just one more thing. The difference between Sylvia and her brother is very little, very little. Val knows this, and I think Sylvia knows it too. She does not therefore ask what I did, with whom, and when. She has it in a little box, and you are busy prying open the lid. You want to let in light, but it is not light you let in to Pandora's box, but devils that fly out. May they land on your back, the crippled devils with cloven hooves, crying and screaming. She has seen these poor devils in camp, but she does not remember, except to try to nurse them, just as she nurtures her dear husband, the angel."

"Of course! She married him because he is like the sick dying men in the camp. Why didn't I think of that?"

"Perhaps that is the fourth secret, Jeremy, and the very last one. Now, shall we go?"

"Yes, let's go now. Do you want me to close the window?"

"That window remains open. You will keep the other ones shut?"

Dear Sylvia,

Greetings from the Big Windy. Surprise? Or not. I warned you. I told you. This is the *big* adventure for me, a leap into the unknown.

Your mother told me several secrets. I was *very* impressed with her. She played some *very* heavy mind trips on me. I am more than ever convinced that there was some special reason for your survival, due to very "special handling" on the part of your mother. Others died so that you could survive, possibly.

She warned darkly of consequences to your "internal economy" if you allowed entrance to it of "secrets" now in my possession as well as long since in hers. She made mention of Pandora's box and yours. She even made oblique references to hers. Remarkable woman! But I'm not surprised. I'm staying at Bentham House, a dreary wrongly named hostelry, where you can reach me.

Your Pilgrim,
Jeremy

"Jeremy, is that you?"

"Val? Is that *you?*"

"Have you talked to Sylvia?"

"Sylvia? No. Why? Where is she? What's going on?"

"She hasn't contacted you? She left early this morning before I woke up. I read your letter, Jeremy. Listen to me. I want you to go to Sylvia's mother's apartment. She must be there. I want you to get her to take a plane right back here. I want you to fly with her. Let me know when you'll arrive and I'll be at the airport."

Jeremy dialed the number. Sylvia's mother's phone rang and rang. Jeremy took a cab. He looked up and counted floors. Curtains bloomed in the window they had stood in. He took the elevator up. He knocked on the door. It was unlocked.

The scene was familiar, he wondered from where. Then he remembered, Michelangelo's *Pieta*. Sylvia sat stroking her mother's brow. Her mother's skin was greenish. From the next room came low regular howls.

"What happened? Have you called a doctor?" He rushed to the phone.

"Is she alive?" he asked the paramedic, who was busy with a mask and turning dials on an oxygen machine. He and another paramedic did the fibrillation thing Jeremy had seen only in the movie *E.T.* The slender woman arched like a cat. Did that mean she was alive? He was afraid to ask, afraid nobody would answer.

They took her away. "What hospital will she be in?" Jeremy yelled down the corridor.

Sylvia was in the dark bedroom with her brother, sitting on the bed, her legs tucked beneath her, stroking his long hair.

They seemed to have shrunk to mere skeletons. The bed was like the dirt of the camp as they looked into a future in which only some would live.

"Sylvia," Jeremy called, "can you hear me?"

"I hear you," she said. "What do you want?"

"Nothing. I certainly didn't want *this*. What can I do?"

Sylvia put her brother's head down. He moaned. She got off the bed and walked into the living room. Jeremy followed her. She sat down in her mother's chair and spread her legs as she smoothed her skirt.

"I will have to stay here now," she said. "And you will have to stay with me."

"What about Val and Sukey?" Jeremy said, his voice rising, "and what about my job, my students?"

"They don't matter now."

Jeremy stumbled backward to the door.

"You can't leave us, Jeremy, you can't."

"I'm calling Val. He'll come. He'll know what to do."

"Val can't do anything now. You have to stay here with me."

"Me? Why me? She's your mother. I'm sorry this happened, but it's not my fault she took the poison."

He ran out of the apartment. Without waiting for the elevator, he took the stairs, round and round, to the lobby. His spring vacation would soon be over, he had to get back to his office, chair and desk, his corner deep in images, his books, his library of the Holocaust.

He looked longingly for a moment out into the sunshine. Then he turned his back on it, and started back up the stairs.